MORE PRAISE FOR EVELYN ROGERS!

SECOND OPINION

"This plot sizzles with originality. Poignant tenderness skillfully peppered with passionate sensuality assures readers of fabulous entertainment."

—Rendezvous

GOLDEN MAN

"A sexy sensual story you won't ever forget. When it comes to finding a perfect hero, this book has it all. Fantastic! Five Bells!"

—Bell, Book and Candle

CROWN OF GLORY

"*Crown of Glory* sizzles with history: rowdy Indian fights, anti-slavery issues, the pioneering days of the beef industry, all peppered with the Spanish flavor of Texas."

—Calico Trails

LONE STAR

"Ms. Rogers gives us such vivid descriptions that you feel the pulse of the times. She has gifted her readers with a sensitive, refreshing romance spiced with great characters and a powerful love story skillfully plotted."

—Rendezvous

LONGHORN

"Evelyn Rogers has crafted an exciting, emotional romance that is sure to please. The characters are portrayed in such a realistic and touching manner that you will fall in love with them."

—Bookbug

MATING SEASON

"I don't know who you are, but you and your horse are not welcome at the Lazy Q."

"Tell that to Dark Champion here."

"I'm speaking to the one who's supposed to control him."

"Not after he got a whiff of your mare. We must have been close to two miles away." From halfway across the corral she could see the gleam in his eyes. "Nothing like the call of flesh to flesh."

"Horse flesh."

"What else?" he asked, all innocence.

"You're enjoying this, aren't you?"

"More than you know."

"Do you get a vicarious thrill when your beast here performs?"

"The beast, as you call him, wasn't supposed to—" He shook his head. "Never mind. You should be the one who was thrilled, catching the action up close the way you did."

Juliana's cheeks flushed. "I beg your pardon!"

He had the decency to shake his head. "Sorry. That wasn't gentlemanly of me."

"Whoever you are, I doubt you've ever been regarded as a gentleman."

His eyes narrowed. "You really don't know who I am, do you?"

DARK OF THE MOON

EVELYN ROGERS

LEISURE BOOKS NEW YORK CITY

A LEISURE BOOK®

September 2003

Published by

Dorchester Publishing Co., Inc.
200 Madison Avenue
New York, NY 10016

ISBN 0-8439-5214-8

The name "Leisure Books" and the stylized "L" with design are trademarks of Dorchester Publishing Co., Inc.

Printed in the United States of America.

Visit us on the web at www.dorchesterpub.com.

This book is dedicated to the three fantastic authors who preceded me in this series: Elaine Barbieri, Constance O'Banyon, and Bobbi Smith.

With special thanks to our mutual agent, Evan Marshall, and our mutual editor, Alicia Condon, for their dedication and support in the conception and completion of the series. Evan and Alicia are the best in the business.

DARK OF THE
MOON

Chapter One

Newmarket, England

"Dark Champion is a killer."

The trainer's words rang harshly on the warm summer air.

"There's no one to deny it," he added. "Not after yesterday's race."

Matt studied the stallion cropping grass in the middle of the field. Was the man right? Maybe. Maybe not. He didn't have an opinion yet.

Besides, did it truly matter? If Dark Champion was a killer, he ought to feel at home on the Half-Moon.

And where in the devil did that thought come from? He'd better bury it fast. He had enough problems in the present without dragging up the past. First he had to negotiate a price for the horse that he could afford, from an English countess, of all people. In Texas he didn't get much practice dealing with countesses.

If he managed to strike a deal, there was still the little problem of getting the horse back to the ranch. He'd do it, but as of yet he didn't know how. Both tasks, the buying and the moving, could prove formidable. But so could he.

In the meantime, he had the trainer to deal with. Past middle age, small and wiry, the Englishman, who'd given his name as Jerry, had long been employed by the widowed countess, and by her husband before her, and his father before him. A jockey in his youth, Jerry knew horses. At the moment he didn't look too happy about the one in the field.

"After what happened," he said, "there's not a jockey worthy of the name that'll ride Champion. Bloody shame it is. I've raised that horse since the day he slipped from his mother's belly. He came out kicking, and he's been kicking ever since."

And winning, Matt could have put in, at least the races which he decided to finish.

He kept a practiced eye on the stallion, fighting the excitement building in him, needing to keep his judgment keen. The longer he looked, the harder the fighting became. He couldn't remember feeling liked this, not even in his drinking days.

He was sober now, drunk only on what he

saw. The scene before him was like a painting, the sky a cloudless blue, the meadow brilliant green, but nothing could match the beauty of the horse, a black-as-midnight descendant of the famous Arabian Eclipse. He had the short body of most thoroughbreds, a shiny coat and gracefully arched neck, but his real beauty rested in his legs. Long and strong, they were a work of art.

Dark Champion didn't look like a killer, not until he lifted his head and stared at Matt, as if willing his potential buyer to see the devil in his eyes. Matt saw it, all right. He'd be a fool to forget that for all his breeding and beauty, the stallion was an outlaw.

Yesterday's race lingered in Matt's mind—the smoothness of the turns and stretches, the roar of the crowd, the smell of victory in the air, all going smoothly and as predicted until a quarter furlong from the finish line. With the jockey laying the whip hard on Dark Champion's flanks, the front-running horse had pulled up short and reared. In an instant a collective gasp replaced the roar.

Matt could still hear the feral neigh as the stallion's hooves pawed the air, hear the heavy thud as he fell hard against the turf, catching his rider's leg beneath his thousand pounds. And then the sound no rider could ever forget, the snap of bone. It echoed across the viewing stand like a gunshot.

"How's the jockey?" he asked the trainer.

"It was a clean break, but the lad's done with racing for this year. At least he escaped with his life. Last year on the same course Champion's rider fell and broke his neck. He would've won the race by two lengths, like yesterday's chap, if the horse hadn't started in with his antics."

Jerry wasn't revealing anything Matt did not already know. Months ago, back in Texas, he'd heard about the accident, from a gambler who'd been to Newmarket. Right away he'd started thinking, then planning; Dark Champion had gotten in his blood from half a world away. A horse as fine as the gambler said—he'd passed around a copy of the *Racing Calendar* to back up his words—just might be what the Half-Moon needed.

The idea was crazy, but Matt couldn't get it out of his mind. He even liked the distance between Texas and England, and the time it would take to cover it. Time away from the ranch. He had good reason for wanting to leave. His father's prison sentence was almost up. Jack Hunter would be coming home.

If Champion proved unavailable, Matt had told himself, there would be other horses to consider. Some of the finest horseflesh in the world came from this small island.

He was the only one at the ranch who thought he just might be doing the right thing, and that included the wranglers. Like the stallion, he was a bit of an outlaw himself. And a dreamer, though that was a side of him he kept to himself. He'd never been smart—his older brothers had been quick enough to point that out—but he'd been lucky, finding jobs when he needed them, winning races when he gambled more than he could afford.

And he had a way with temperamental stallions. Here in Newmarket, the center of horse racing in England, he was gambling that luck and skill wouldn't desert him when he needed them most.

"I hate to disappoint you, lad," the trainer went on, "but you'd best think carefully about buying Dark Champion. He's a winner, true, but not often enough. And he's shown little inclination at stud. We've tried to breed him, Her Ladyship thinking that was where he would earn his keep. He's yet to produce an heir." He shook his head in disgust. "You've an honest look about you, and I'd be remiss in not telling you the truth. Buying Dark Champion would be good money spent in a bad way."

Not if the horse came cheap enough, Matt thought. Anyway, he wasn't about to start worrying now. He'd been watching the stallion for a week, only today revealing his presence, deciding for sure that if he bought any English horse, it would have to be this one. It was something he'd known when he read that racing report back in Texas.

Even the business about Dark Champion's failure at stud didn't bother him much. He wanted the stallion to race and win.

So what if the purchase proved a mistake? He could handle it. Already he carried the burden of the worst mistake a man could make.

"I appreciate the advice," he said to the trainer, "but it seems to me, with all the problems you've got, this countess of yours would be wanting to get rid of Dark Champion fast."

The trainer shrugged. "Just wanting to be fair, just wanting to be fair."

Matt knew a lie when he heard it. The man couldn't bear to part with the horse, the one whose birth he had witnessed. The truth was as clear as the sky.

Jerry rubbed his ruddy chin and cast a sideways glance at Matt. "There's little purpose served in telling Her Ladyship what's been passing between us."

"Agreed," Matt said, and meant it. "I'd like to ride him," he added. "But I need to do the saddling myself."

The trainer frowned. "Now, Mr. Hunter, think again. You're taking on a task few would choose. There's times our horse there can get a mite particular about who gets near."

"I'll take my chances."

The trainer looked at him long and hard. "Don't say I didn't warn you."

Jerry took only a minute to get the necessary tackle from the stable, handing everything over before heading out to the middle of the field, his heavy shoes leaving a path in the damp grass alongside Matt's boots.

The two men halted a half dozen yards from the stallion. Head high, the horse stared at them, dark eyes wary, most of his attention leveled on the stranger he was trying his best to intimidate. Matt had seen the trick in horses before this one.

"I'll take it from here," he said.

Jerry grunted and backed away. Matt didn't move until the trainer had returned to his post outside the fence. His palms itched with familiar anticipation. Taking a deep breath, he closed his eyes for a moment, forgetting he was in an English field approaching an English horse that visited violence on those foolish enough to ride him—especially, Matt suspected, those with a heavy hand on the whip.

He carried no such weapon. For him it was just man and horse, the horse needing to be in control, but not quite so much as the man. He smiled, relaxed, the tension flowing from him like sweat through his pores, leaving him cool and calm. This was what he was born to do, this meeting of man and animal, this contest of wills. Hands loose at his sides, he took a step forward and in a soft, rolling voice far more common to the Texas hills than to an English countryside, began to speak in a language the horse would understand.

Looking every inch a countess, Lady Charlotte Kingbridge, widow of the late Earl of Kingbridge, descended from the carriage. Resting her hand for the briefest possible moment on the gloved fingers of her coachman, she stepped free onto the drive in front of the fabled Kingbridge stables.

As always, she was dressed in the height of fashion, the crushed raspberry bodice of her traveling dress fitted to her full bosom and small waist, the hobbled skirt accenting her rounded hips. She had forsworn a cloak, unwilling to spoil the picture she presented. Elbow-length suede gloves, black pointed boots, and a feathered black bonnet atop her equally black hair completed the ensemble.

An avaricious glint lit her brown eyes. She had heard of a potential buyer for the bothersome and far too expensive racehorse she'd unwisely kept in her stable. Her husband would never have made such a foolish mistake, especially when the stupid animal proved practically impotent. Notorious for his tightfisted ways, the earl had guarded every tuppence as if it were part of the Crown treasury. It was why he had accumulated so much wealth.

Not a day went by that Charlotte did not give thanks for that accumulation. She also gave thanks for the hunting accident that precipitated his demise three years past. Childless, without family other than his bereaved widow, he had bequeathed all his worldly possessions to her.

If only she had been as wise as he in spending her inheritance. Loathsome creditors, she thought with a shudder. The details of life were indeed quite bothersome.

But enough of worry. She was here to solve a problem, not to brood. Brooding brought on frowns, and from them came wrinkles. And all for naught.

No sooner had the carriage pulled away than she heard the pounding of hooves on the track close by. One of the trainers, a rather irritating little man who should have been dismissed long ago, hurried toward her, muttering something about Dark Champion, something about Texas, something about a surprising sight.

She paid him little mind. Her attention was riveted on the sleek black stallion rounding the near turn and, more directly, on the man holding the reins. Far too tall, far too broad-shouldered for a jockey, he was dressed like no rider she had ever seen, all flesh-toned leather except for the black shirt beneath a fringed waistcoat.

Bent low, his long body extended over the horse's neck, long black hair matching the flowing mane, he seemed at one with the beast, as if he were part beast himself. A thrill fluttered in her stomach. Whoever he was, he excited her in a way no man had in a long time.

Without realizing she was doing so, she moved close to the edge of the track. An admirer of flesh, both manly and equine, Lady Kingbridge licked her lips as the horse thundered past. The rider took him once again on the complete circuit, then reined to a halt not three feet from where she stood, the lathered animal bobbing his head and snorting, sending droplets of moisture onto her person.

She held her ground and watched the man slide from the saddle with the same effortless grace exhibited in the ride. Like the horse, he was bathed in sweat, dampness forming a sheen on his strong brown neck and handsome face.

And handsome he was, not by any prettified English standards, but in a more rugged way, with prominent cheekbones and straight full nose, thick brows over hazel eyes, lips firm and uncompromising. His skin was sleek and tanned, the slant of wrinkles around his eyes evidence of a life in the sun.

He was even taller than he had appeared while riding, and his shoulders broader, his hips leaner. Hadn't her servant said something about

Texas? The earl had invested in land there and talked about the two of them visiting his investment. She had discouraged him—a mistake, she now saw, if the stranger was an example of the men to be found in such a wilderness.

The stranger gave no sign he was equally impressed by her. Wiping a sleeve across his forehead, he looked beyond her as if she did not exist. She pictured the ripple of muscle beneath his shirt. And she felt the edge of anger at his slight.

"He'll do," the Texan said to the trainer, who had taken his rightful place several paces behind his lady.

The trainer cleared his throat, but it was Charlotte who spoke.

"He'll do?" she asked in an imperious tone. "Are you speaking of Dark Champion?"

Slowly, the penetrating eyes of the man turned to her.

"You must be Lady Kingbridge."

He spoke in a cool, laconic way, still refusing to be impressed. But she saw his quick perusal of her. Though he gave no overt sign, she hadn't a doubt that he approved of what he saw. What man wouldn't?

It was time to put him in his place. A dozen lowering comments occurred to her, but he spoke before she could select the one most cutting.

11

"The name's Hunter. Matt Hunter. I heard you had a horse for sale."

How direct, how to the point. It was the countess's habit to assess men by the way they would conduct themselves in bed. This one would not be slavishly devoted to foreplay.

But his voice, deep and rolling, would make up for it. The charm of his accent prickled her skin, as if he had physically touched her.

"You're from Texas, I understand," she said, raising her carefully plucked eyebrows. "That's someplace in the colonies, isn't it? Rather a crude sort of country, I've heard."

He didn't rise to the bait. "The horse."

She smiled and almost fluttered her lashes, then decided that might be a bit much. "I'm not certain I wish to part with my beloved stallion."

"The killer, you mean."

The smile died. "The champion."

"When he chooses. Which is something he hasn't been doing lately."

He had done his background work. Despite the unorthodoxy of his dress, he was no bumpkin.

She could be as blunt as he. "Very well," she said, "I might be persuaded to sell." She named an exorbitant price.

He did not blink. "Winning isn't the only thing he's been avoiding."

"I beg your pardon?"

"Mares, Lady Kingbridge," he said with a glint in his eye. "I speak of mares."

She glanced over her shoulder at the trainer.

"Don't look at him," the Texan said. "All of Newmarket knows of his inadequacy as a breeder."

It seemed a rather fancy turn of phrase coming from such a man. No, he was definitely no bumpkin.

Neither of them spoke as the trainer took the stallion by the reins and headed for the stables. Passing close by, Dark Champion flicked his tail, stirring the feather on Charlotte's hat. She looked after him in distaste, then turned her attention to the stranger, aware they were very much alone.

"It's true that as of yet we don't have many little Champions loping about. But the horse is not quite four years old. And," she said, her voice thickening, "if you look at him closely enough, you'll see he is equipped to do what is necessary."

Slowly her eyes trailed down the tight leather trousers covering the Texan's lean hips and long legs. By the time she had worked her way back to his lips, he was the one who was smiling.

"Looks don't tell the complete story," he said. "Take me, for instance."

She caught her breath.

"You're thinking I'd be fine at stud service."

Her heart pounded, and the flutter in her stomach took a downward path.

"The truth is," he continued, "I haven't had a woman in so long, if one threw herself into my bed I wouldn't know what to do with her. In all honesty, I'm not ready to be re-taught."

By her, he meant. Charlotte fumed. She didn't dally with men often, certainly not so openly, but when she did she was never rebuffed.

And the cad wasn't through.

"Let's look at what's important here."

He paused to take off his riding gloves and tuck them under his belt. His hands were hard, strong and brown, like everything else about him visible to the eye.

"You've got a horse that's far more trouble than he's worth. Already you've had to pay money to one jockey's family, and you're now burdened with another's medical bills. Or so I assume, you being the honorable lady countesses are cracked up to be. And for what? So that you can stroll around the racetrack showing off that fine body of yours? My advice to you is get another horse."

"See here, Mr. Hunter, how dare you—"

But he wasn't through.

"No one need know what you got for the stallion." He offered a sum less than half the amount she had thrown at him. "The trainer heard your first offer. Let him and everyone else think you

14

got what you wanted. I'm paying cash. You're the only one who'll know how much. And you'll be rid of a problem that I'm guessing is more of an embarrassment than anything else."

Charlotte looked at the horse, the sky, the stable, at last settling her ebony eyes on the Texan. Matt Hunter was smart. He wanted no part of her lust—his lone bit of foolishness—but he understood her greed. She struggled inwardly with the two emotions. The bill from her dressmaker had arrived not an hour ago. Her struggle was brief. Greed won.

She extended her hand. He took it, and they shook. She didn't release him right away.

"Do you really think I have a fine body?"

"Yes, ma'am, I do."

Her heart fluttered, and she felt rather like a schoolgirl again. The man did have a nice grin. Without shame she studied the fit of his curious leather trousers. Hardly Savile Row, she thought, but they were perfect for him.

"What a pity," she said with a sigh, "you don't want a lesson in *amour*. After all, life is so very, very short."

He stiffened. She doubted she'd offended him, but something she'd said reminded him of unpleasantness.

"I'll return with the money," he said. "I'll want a bill of sale, of course. Back at the ranch they'll be wanting to know I didn't steal your killer horse."

A week later Matt set sail for home, satisfied with his purchase and the travel arrangements he'd worked out. Within the hold of the clipper ship, Dark Champion shifted restlessly, moving side to side in the narrow space that served as temporary quarters for him and his new owner. Matt did the same on deck. With the deep, dark waves rolling past and the air fresh and cool, he was unwilling to go down to the moldy blanket that would serve as his bed.

He ought to be feeling fine. After months away, he was going home. But home brought memories, ugly ones mixed with the good. No matter how he tried, he couldn't get away from them. Here he was, looking at the glint of moonlight on the water, a beautiful sight for anyone. But he saw the light in a woman's eyes. One woman, Elizabeth Quincy Hunter, his mother, the one who had struggled hardest to reform her wayward son.

The glint was gone now, the eyes closed. A bullet to the heart had closed them ten years ago. And had sent his drunken father, convicted as her killer, to prison, leaving a grieving family, before long a warring family, struggling to save the ranch from crushing debts.

Brent, the oldest, the dictator, and Quince, the

middle son and Beth's favorite, had fought the hardest. Quince was gone now, choosing to face tribes of renegade Apaches out in the western territories rather than his own kin.

Matt had escaped Brent's heavy hand a different way, by gathering mustangs in West Texas, wrangling on wealthier spreads, returning briefly to the Half-Moon to deliver horses and the cash he'd been able to save.

Except for his racing money. That was his. He accepted his gambling losses and he kept his winnings. Eventually they became enough for him to be where he was right now.

Little good came during those years—except for Abby, the youngest Hunter, the most vulnerable, though she put on a show of being tough. He'd passed a little of his money on to his baby sister so she could buy herself some clothes and the gewgaws women seemed to like. It was hard to think of her as a woman. Abby would always be a baby sister to him.

For himself, he lived about as frugally as a man could. Lady Charlotte Kingbridge might think he had paid a paltry sum for her magnificent stallion, but, outside of a stash of traveling money, it was every cent he possessed.

If his luck continued and Dark Champion came through as he suspected he would, the money would be returned tenfold.

And wouldn't that surprise Brent? Quince,

too, if he ever returned. Matt Hunter pulling off something as bold as this. Next thing they knew, dear old Dad, the convict, would be leading the church choir.

Matt was old enough now to see their side. In his youth he'd been a hell-raiser, drinking and whoring, arguing with his mother when she tried to reform him, barely civil to his father even when he dragged him out of jail.

And he'd done worse. Far worse. But that was his problem to deal with, his secret and no one else's.

Since the tragedy, not once had he been inside the ranch house, the scene of the murder, the place where he was born. On his brief visits, he slept in the bunkhouse, or out in the open. No one in the family had ever commented on it. But they must have noticed.

Like Brent, he gave up drinking, although big brother had never hit the bottle too hard. He wasn't sure about Quince. And Abby—well, she had kept on being Abby, riding and roping as well as any man, refusing to admit to the woman in her. How she spent the money he gave her he wasn't sure. He hadn't asked. A gift was a gift. She didn't owe him an explanation.

He guessed that the journey back to Texas, by ship and rail and then overland, would take another two months at least. Jack would be there, released from jail. Matt didn't want to think about the man who had sired him. And he didn't, except sometimes in the middle of the night when he couldn't sleep. Jack—Brent and Quince called him Pa and Abby had always used Papa, but Matt could think of him only by his given name—had ridden him hard for as long as he could remember, finding fault with just about everything he did.

He'd gotten over that a long time ago. But he couldn't erase it from his mind.

The deck rolled beneath him, and sea spray hit his face. Leaning against the rail, he forced his thoughts from the Half-Moon to Lady King-bridge, and to the lie he had told her. It was true he hadn't had a woman in a long time. But if he did, he would most certainly know what to do. There were some things a man did not forget.

He hoped Dark Champion, the disappointing stud, would act in kind.

Chapter Two

Matt saw the bastard as soon as the buckboard entered the main street of Diablo. A hypocrite and a liar, a banker and deacon of the church, Edmund Montgomery gave a bad name to both money and religion.

Standing in front of the bank, oblivious to the people passing by him, Montgomery waved him down.

Butt sore, Matt shifted on the hard seat. Once he got to the Half-Moon, he would stand for a week. In the meantime, he'd deal with another pain in the same part of his anatomy. With the horse trailer rattling behind the wagon, he reined his team of mules to a halt at the side of the deeply rutted street and stared down at the man who had tried to bring the Hunter ranch to ruin.

Even on the dingy wooden walkway, the banker presented a dignified appearance, tall and stately in his dark suit and paisley vest, lean and tightly muscled despite his age, his blond hair barely streaked with gray.

But looks could be deceiving. Matt was not impressed.

Montgomery glanced curiously at the trailer, but gave his smile to Matt.

"Is that you, Matt Hunter?" he asked. "I do believe it is. Seems all our chickens are coming home to roost." He chuckled. "You were no more than a rawboned youngster last time you were in town. I hardly recognized you."

"I recognized you." Flatly said.

Uncertainty darkened Montgomery's pale eyes. But the smile stayed in place.

"As well you should. I've been a friend to your father, and your mother, may she rest in peace, since long before you were born."

A bad subject to bring up. The man wasn't as smart as he tried to appear.

"You wanted something?" Matt asked.

Like maybe apologizing for the threat to foreclose on the Half-Moon mortgage the week Jack Hunter went to jail. The years should have blurred the memory, but there were some things a Hunter did not forget.

Maybe the banker didn't know Matt knew. Maybe he thought the youngest Hunter brother, the wild one, hadn't cared.

He cared, all right. He just didn't let it show.

"You'd best mind your manners," Montgomery said. With a crowd gathering around him, he kept his voice low.

It was advice Matt had heard before, advice he usually ignored, but the banker gave him no chance to respond. Nodding toward the back of the wagon, he said, "You wouldn't be pulling a racehorse in that contraption, would you?"

As if he understood the question, Dark Champion whinnied and moved restlessly in the narrow confines of his wooden trailer.

Matt shrugged, letting the horse speak for him.

Montgomery shook his head. "So you really made it to England and back. The betting money around Diablo went against your return."

Matt glanced at the dozen men and women stirring around behind the banker, some trying to look like they weren't listening in, the more honest ones staring at him and the trailer outright. A few he recognized, but no one he cared to acknowledge. He shifted on the seat, thinking he should have kept riding on through town.

Montgomery's eyes narrowed. "Mind if I take a peek inside? Those slats don't allow much of a view."

"Yep," Matt said, adding, lest the banker misunderstand, "I mind."

"Now, now, son, I mean no harm."

"Then look at his tail. It's hanging out the rear. But I ought to warn you, he tends to kick. When he's not dropping horseshit on whoever's nearby."

Someone in the crowd snickered.

"That's considerate of you to warn me," Montgomery said through gritted teeth.

Matt half heard him. The long journey was weighing on him—the ocean sailing, the cross-country train ride, the switch to buckboard at the San Antonio depot. And he hadn't lied. Dark Champion did tend to kick, and to anoint anyone who got too close. He might not be much good at stud service, but he could sling his droppings in a way that raised admiration in those onlookers standing out of range.

"If you've got anything to say, Montgomery, then say it. I've still got a few hours to ride."

Montgomery looked as if he were about to speak, but he fell silent for a moment. Matt could see the rage in his eyes. But the banker was a cool one. He got the rage under control.

"I've got lots to say, Matt, but I'll wait until you're more in a mood to listen. Things have changed at the Half-Moon. You'll have to find them out for yourself."

With a sharp nod, he pushed his way through the gathering of townspeople and entered the bank. A lion returning to his den, Matt thought, then changed the comparison. A snake slithering back to his pit.

Turning his attention to the muddy, rutted

street, he slapped the reins and left the onlookers without so much as a nod. There wasn't anyone in the town he felt particularly friendly toward. After the shooting, folks hadn't treated the Hunters well, as if the sins of the father were visited upon his offspring.

Matt had deserved their scorn, more than they knew. But not his brothers. And not Abby.

Only one person had been truly kind to her. Iona Montgomery. If he saw her, he would give her a far warmer greeting than he'd shown her husband.

He made the journey through town as fast as the mule team would allow, ignoring the passing riders and carriages. After England, with its streetlights and tree-lined parks, everything looked drab and poor. Even the new hotel had a thrown-together look to it, not like the centuries-old buildings he'd seen in London.

But Diablo was home, or as close to it as he was likely to get. If it weren't for the people in it, he would have felt nostalgic about his return.

It wasn't until he was out on the road that he felt really good about where he was. Even this close to town, the landscape had a wild look to it, with sharp drops and rocky soil, distant hills, clusters of oak and mesquite and the thick, dark shrubbery of juniper growing close to the road.

A half mile out of town, the road lost some of its sharp dips and curves. When the wagon topped a rise, he could get a view of the rolling, broken country that was in his blood. He took a deep breath. The smell of open air was a fine perfume. He was trying to concentrate on the land and the sky and the air, trying not to speculate about the changes he might find at the end of the journey, changes Montgomery had darkly hinted at, when he heard a high, loud neigh from the horse trailer. It was like nothing he'd heard from Dark Champion before.

By the time he had reined to a halt and jumped to the ground, the trailer was rocking from side to side and the neigh was close to a scream. Slashing hooves kept him at a distance, but he needn't have worried about freeing the stallion. Dark Champion managed that on his own, kicking out the slats and, eyes wild, bounding onto the roadway. With the rope that had secured him trailing on the uneven ground, he took off cross-country.

Yelling every obscenity he'd ever heard, Matt cut loose the remains of the trailer from the back of the buckboard, then scrambled onto the seat and took off in pursuit. The weary mules did their best to set a fast pace, but he might as well have been on foot. By the time he got really under way, the racehorse was already out of sight beyond a ridge.

* * *

A crushing sense of guilt overcame Juliana. It hit her hard and fast, like a fist squeezing her heart. Dizzy, unable to breathe, she abandoned her unpacking and hurried to the bedroom window. Resting her forehead against the sash, she waited for the attack to pass. These things usually did, after a minute or two.

This one was no exception. Slowly her ragged gasps eased and she returned to sanity. But not total comfort. An ache lingered in her breast, a sense of loss and hurt she doubted would ever go away.

"Mama," she whispered, but of course there was no response. Months past Mama had died, without her only child at her bedside.

"Damn you, Edmund Montgomery," she cried, wanting to place blame on her stepfather. But it was a shared blame. She should have been aware of her mother's health. Others must have known about Iona Montgomery's illness. They could have let her know. Even in faraway Saratoga, Juliana was not unreachable.

But she'd been kept in ignorance. Until the letters—the first informing her of her mother's death and then weeks later, the second one, the strange communication that had brought on the attacks.

Juliana had been more than grieved. She'd been devastated, and she'd had to leave, to get away from the cocoon of her wealthy widowhood, and the solicitude of her late husband's family. Over their objections, she'd returned to Texas. With her back to the musty upstairs bedroom, she breathed in the fresh air and studied the land that was part of her inheritance. Small by Texas standards, half the size of the neighboring ranch where she'd been born, the Lazy Q had been bought by Harlan on a whim. But after their marriage, they had never lived on it.

For her, the reason had a name: Edmund Montgomery. Her widowed mother's ill-chosen second husband had made her eager to leave the state. Almost a decade later, her memory of him, and a heartbreaking letter, had impelled her return.

Sighing, she stared down at the fenced corral that lay behind the ranch house. Like the rest of the Lazy Q, it showed signs of neglect—too many weeds, too little grass, stretches of barren, hard-packed dirt. But the grass was enough to satisfy the lone horse in its confines, the beloved blood bay mare she had brought with her from the East. Most of her husband's possessions she had been able to sell to her in-laws, including some prime racing stock, but not Pepper. The mare was her pet, her only family, in a way taking the place of the child she'd never had.

Suddenly Pepper's head raised. Even from a distance, Juliana could see the laid-back ears and flared nostrils of the mare. From beyond the corral came the wild neigh of a second horse. In a high whinny Pepper answered the call.

Juliana had been around horses all her life. She knew what was going on. It was impossible. Yet the whinny rang in her ears.

She ran from the room, racing swiftly down the stairs and through the empty house. She burst through the kitchen door into the backyard in time to see a magnificent black stallion soar effortlessly over the corral fence.

"No!" she screamed. Lifting her skirts, she darted toward the enclosure. Pepper was too young, too small. The stallion, lathered with sweat, was a monster.

He was also a beauty, but if she'd had a gun, she would have shot him.

Stepping on a middle board of the fence, she bounded over the top, then grabbed at the ground for rocks, dirt, anything to throw, knowing as she did so that her efforts would be futile. But she could not stop. Something primal was burning within her, a ferocious desire to protect what was hers.

She hurled her feeble weapons at the horse, thrusting herself dangerously close to his massive, heaving bulk, aiming for his eyes, but he veered around too quickly for her. The rocks bounced unnoticed off his rippling hide, and the dirt did little but stick to the sweat.

"Pepper!" she cried, but the mare was too busy

whinnying, rolling her head and stepping sideways, tail shamelessly lifted, to pay her mistress any mind.

The stallion snorted, teeth bared, and shifted his hind quarters about as he pranced toward his destination.

Juliana circled the pair, giving them as narrow a berth as she dared, screaming, flapping her skirt, her heart pounding so loud in her ears, she could scarcely hear the noises of the lustful horses. Pepper ignored her. The stallion, irritated, lashed out with a vicious hoof, coming close to her head. She stumbled backward and sat hard on the ground.

"Kick him!" she cried out, but to her own ears the order was half spirited. A well-placed hoof in the stallion's distended penis would disable him, even render him permanently impotent, but the mare showed no inclination to discourage him.

Instead, more than a ton of horseflesh, male and female, pranced and flexed muscles, keening in a language anyone, rancher or not, would understand. The ground beneath her trembled from their zeal.

With the air full of neighs and snorts and whinnies, dirt from the long-neglected corral stirred into choking gray clouds, she watched in horror as the stallion mounted her precious virginal Pepper, landing against her spread haunches with a force that should have collapsed her.

But the mare held strong, as eager as he, eyes equally wild. With his powerful forelegs hanging limply against the mare's flanks, he rutted, again and again, a thousand times, his massive body shuddering in the throes of lust.

Juliana watched in horror. She could not look away.

Suddenly, shockingly, he stopped the rutting and collapsed backward, spent, his head low, a groan replacing the high-pitched whinnies of moments past. And then came silence, as deafening as the wild lust sounds, the air heavy with the scent of horse and sex.

Turning his backside to Pepper, the stallion walked desultorily to the fence and stopped, his attention focused on the rolling land beyond the corral, no thought given to the mare, not so much as a bob of the head in her direction.

In a way, he reminded Juliana of her late husband, with one exception. Harlan Rains had never shown so much fervor when he mounted his wife. But he had shown nonchalance in the aftermath.

It was a stupid thought. She had no idea where it came from. With a sigh, she pulled herself to her feet, brushing the loosened hair from her face, smudging a cheek in the process. Her once-fine silk dress, a shade of amber that Harlan had said brought out the color of her eyes, was soiled beyond repair. In bounding over the fence, she had caught the hem on a loose nail. The tear could not be mended.

The damage was of little note; she had a wardrobe full of similar dresses. And what use did she have for such finery in the life she was determined to live?

She shook off a fleeting self-pity, an emotion far less welcome than the burden of guilt that had brought her back to Texas. When she walked over to Pepper, the mare had the grace to bow her head low, not in the nonchalant weariness of the stallion, but as if in contrition. Or was her mistress visiting upon her pet a wished-for regret?

She fingered the mare's dark mane, grateful that the stallion hadn't bitten her neck, as was often the case at the moment of ejaculation. Indeed, Pepper looked remarkably unchanged; there was not even a smear of blood where she had been penetrated for the first time. A quick glance as Juliana walked to the mare had revealed the flesh swollen and red, but from friction, not broken skin.

"He really did it."

Startled, Juliana looked beyond the mare to the man standing at the outside edge of the corral. Tall and lean, yet projecting a sense of powerful muscle, his collar-length black hair unkempt, his face bristled, he presented a picture of male determination rather like that of the stallion.

Not that he was equally beautiful. But he almost was.

What if he bounded over the fence? A tingle not totally akin to fear whispered through her. If she had a gun . . . well, she didn't know exactly what she would do, but, isolated as she was, she would feel more secure.

His words registered.

"If you're speaking of the stallion, he most definitely assaulted my mare."

His thick-lashed eyes flicked to the mare. "By invitation."

"Pepper couldn't be in season. She's too young, barely past two. Besides, it's already fall, much too late in the year for breeding."

"Not in Texas. And she looks ripe enough."

He might have been speaking of the horse, but his eyes were on her. Easing out of his leather jacket, he laid it over the top of the fence and rested his booted foot on the bottom rail. He was wearing a black shirt and dark trousers; they fit him like a glove.

Juliana's stomach knotted. Her trigger finger wasn't the only part of her that itched.

She kept a sigh to herself. What was done was done. Her task now was to deal with the consequences as best she could.

Which meant showing no sign of weakness. If Harlan Rains had taught her anything, it was that. Not that he'd given her much opportunity to exhibit strength. But he was no longer around.

"If there's a foal, it's mine," she said.

"For the usual stud fee, of course," he threw back as coolly as she.

"You're crazy."

His expression remained mild, noncommittal, and she caught the hint of a twitch in his lips.

"I've been called worse," he said.

He was not a man easy to insult. She would have to try harder.

"I don't know who you are, but you and your horse are not welcome at the Lazy Q."

"Tell that to Dark Champion here."

"I'm speaking to the one who's supposed to control him."

"Not after he got a whiff of your mare. We must have been close to two miles away." From halfway across the corral she could see the gleam in his eye. "Nothing like the call of flesh to flesh."

"Horseflesh."

"What else?" he asked, all innocence. "By the way, he was wearing a rope. Have you seen it? No matter. I'll add it to your bill."

"You really are crazy."

"Then there's the trailer he kicked to hell and gone. And the wear and tear on the mules and wagon. After your mare perfumed the air, I had to take off after him cross-country. Broke a wheel, too, and exhausted the mules. They're at the front of the house, in case you're thinking I dropped out of the sky. I've some supplies in the wagon, and a valise. I'm hoping they'll be safe enough unattended. It'll take me a while to get them off your land."

"You're enjoying this, aren't you?"

"More than you know."

"Do you get a vicarious thrill when your beast here performs?"

"The beast, as you call him, wasn't supposed to . . ." He shook his head. "Never mind. You should be the one who was thrilled, catching the action up close the way you did."

Juliana's cheeks flushed. "I beg your pardon!"

He had the decency to shake his head. "Sorry. That wasn't gentlemanly of me."

"Whoever you are, I doubt you've ever been regarded as a gentleman."

His eyes narrowed. "You don't know who I am, do you?"

Difficult though it was—he had a maddening habit of studying her as if he could see through any pretense—she studied him in much the same way. He was as lean and muscled and rough-edged as she had first thought, but another quality lurked behind the hazel eyes and sharply honed face, a hint of danger similar to heat, as if anyone who got too close to him would get burned.

Which was no problem for her. If she ever saw him again, she would remember to keep her distance.

"No, I don't know you. Should I?"

With consummate grace he leapt over the fence and started walking toward her. Instinctively she took a backward step. The horses drifted deeper into the corral, as if determined to remain separate from the humans as well as each other.

He stopped an arm's length away. "It's been a long time, Juliana."

Her name was soft on his lips, almost lilting. She swallowed and continued to study him. Something about the set of his mouth stole her attention. A name occurred. Impossible, but it wouldn't go away.

She closed her eyes and pictured a lanky youth, mostly gangling arms and legs, hair longer than he was wearing it now, peach fuzz on a rounder face where now dark bristles grew. There was a hardness around his eyes she did not remember, and fine lines that testified to the passing of ten years.

"Matt Hunter," she said, almost whispering. The wild Hunter boy, only a year older than she, the drinker and carouser at far too young an age.

"You filled out," she added in what had to be the understatement of the year.

His gaze drifted down the length of her, from the loosened fair hair to her dust-covered shoes, lingering at places on her soiled gown she would rather he not notice.

"So did you," he said.

The dry autumn air crackled between them.

"I was sixteen the last time I saw you. It was . . ." she began, then broke off.

"It was at my mother's funeral," he said, finishing for her.

Dangerous ground, far too delicate for her to tread. At least he had been at the service. Her absence at her own mother's burial was part of her crushing guilt.

"You were the wild one, weren't you? If anyone had asked, I would have predicted an early death for you. That, or prison."

"Prison was my father's fate."

She smoothed back her hair. "I'm sorry," she said, genuinely contrite. "I'm not handling this very well."

"No one does."

He wasn't making the conversation any easier for her. But why should he? He was a Hunter. For years, from half a continent away, she had believed them her friends and, more importantly, the friends of her mother.

She had reason to think differently now.

Why was she even trying to carry on a civilized exchange? It was as if Matt Hunter had willed it, from the moment he said her name. He was manipulating her, as easily as his stallion had manipulated her mare.

A small voice reminded her that Pepper had been a willing participant. It only showed the trouble a female could get into when cooperating with a male.

She thrust a hand into the pocket of her gown and felt the letter, the last communication she had received from her mother, the last words, as far as Juliana knew, Iona Montgomery had written before she died.

The feel of the wrinkled paper against her fingertips reminded her of why she was here. Back straight, she hurried to the corral gate and opened it. Much to her relief, when she whistled, Pepper trotted to her side.

"Please leave," she said to Matt. "I'm sorry about the broken wheel, but you used to be good at getting yourself out of difficult situations. I don't imagine that has changed."

Without waiting for a reply, she hurried toward the barn, stopping halfway across the weed-choked yard. She could feel his eyes on her back. Something she did not entirely understand made her turn.

"Care for the mules as you see fit. The water

trough's full and there's hay in the barn. Take what you need."

He nodded, but she wasn't done.

"Until you can get the wheel repaired, I will, of course, have to charge rent for the space your wagon is occupying, if, as you said, it's on my land."

He registered no surprise. "How much?"

"I want to be fair. The stud fee and cost of the rope should even things out. And, as I said, I keep the foal."

She waited for an argument.

Instead he eyed her carefully, as if trying to figure her out. "I heard your husband died. How long ago?"

The question startled her. She answered without thinking. "Close to two years."

"An older man, right?"

By thirty years, she could have told him, but the detail was no one's business but her own.

"No new fiancé?" he asked. "No one waiting to take his place?"

"I hardly see how that has anything to do with anything," she said, puzzled.

"Just trying to understand why you're so prickly."

Her puzzlement did not last long. Matt Hunter assumed that abstinence was the cause of her attitude, making her prickly, as he put it. Did he really think she missed the arms of a man?

He was crazy. And he couldn't be more wrong.
How long have you been without a woman?

She almost put the question to him. But this very day he'd probably stopped by the saloon in Diablo. He could even have spent last night in one of the upstairs rooms. On her ride through town yesterday, she'd noticed the Lone Star open and doing a lively business.

Staring at him, imagining a repressed smirk on his ruggedly handsome face, she didn't pretend to innocence.

"You were insufferable as a young man, Matt Hunter. You haven't changed."

Without waiting for a reply, she hurried into the barn, Pepper following, once again subdued and obedient.

Inside the darkened interior, a figure moved from the shadows. She stifled a gasp, recognizing the hired hand arranged by Sam Larkin, Diablo's lone attorney, after she had written him concerning her return.

It took a minute to remember his name.

"Kane," she said, using the only identity he had given her. "I thought you were out on the range."

"I just got here. You were busy. I figured you didn't want me to interfere. You'll find, Miz Rains, I know my place."

He sounded docile enough, a lowly work hand trying to do his job. But he had a dark, grizzled look about him that didn't go with the voice.

When Larkin had brought him out late yesterday, he'd assured her that Kane would do what was needed at the Lazy Q. Besides, he'd said, the man was the best he could come up with on short notice. She needed to reserve judgment.

She could not be so generous with Matt Hunter. Once a scoundrel, always a scoundrel, she reminded herself. It was a truth she had bitterly learned for herself.

Chapter Three

Matt was surprised he had recognized Juliana the moment he saw her, but her presence cleared up one mystery—Montgomery's comment about chickens coming home to roost. From the looks of the Lazy Q, she hadn't returned to Texas much earlier than he.

In the years before her marriage, Miss Juliana Sullivan hadn't come into Diablo often. When she did, she'd been the proper young miss, much too fastidious for the likes of Matt.

Today she hadn't been so proper, watching Dark Champion mount her mare, her dress dirty and torn, hair coming down, her face smudged.

He hadn't arrived in time to watch her watch. But she had. Indignant though she had been, she hadn't bothered to deny it.

He smiled. He liked her smudged, and the indignation colored her cheeks.

41

What the hell was he doing, thinking of her when he had only one more hill to cross before arriving home?

He caught himself. The Half-Moon Ranch was no more a real home to him than the town had been.

He put the woman out of his mind. Edmund Montgomery's stepdaughter was a complication he didn't need right now.

Changes awaited him. Montgomery had said so, and he didn't doubt it. But the basic situation was still the same, for him and for his father. Death, guilt, recriminations, a hunger for revenge—the memories hung on, like a stench that kept a man from drawing a clean breath.

Jack Hunter would be lurking somewhere around the ranch. Unless he was at the saloon in Diablo. Matt doubted that his father had reformed much during his decade behind bars.

Unconsciously Matt sat straighter in the saddle. He must make a strange sight, riding one of the most magnificent stallions ever seen in these parts, one hand on the reins, the other holding a rope tied to a pair of exhausted mules trailing behind him.

He had started out with the rope tied to the saddle, the mules closer to Dark Champion's haunches, but the thoroughbred had lifted his tail in protest. The last thing Matt needed was to ride in with a pair of dung-covered mules in tow.

Hence the lengthened, hand-held rope.

Turning off the main road, he began the last segment of his long journey, riding into the late-afternoon sun on the winding ranch-house trail. In a field to his left, he recognized a couple of the Half-Moon's ranch hands on their mounts, the foreman Buck Taggart and Curly. They stared at him without waving. It was not an encouraging sign.

He didn't give the low-lying white-frame house itself much attention until he was upon it. It sat in the middle of a vast green valley, looking better than he remembered—warmer somehow, more inviting—though he doubted that was because he had missed the place.

It took a moment to realize the cause. A bed of bright flowering chrysanthemums stretched the width of the house, providing a welcoming boundary for the front porch. His mother had kept flowers blooming in just the same place, but these were the first he'd seen on the ranch since the shooting.

Stomach tight, he looked at them longer than was smart. There was much to see—the old rocker at the corner of the porch, right where his mother had always kept it, and the herb garden that was, like the flowers, once again well tended. A picket fence, shining white, surrounded the garden. In the space between the fence and the barn a half dozen chickens pecked in the dirt.

He took a sniff and smelled rosemary, the herb of remembrance. On this day devoted to getting things taken care of, remembering was not on his list of chores. Yet he seemed to be doing a lot of it everywhere he went. Most of the memories were unpleasant; the good times had been few and hard to recall.

He was about to dismount when the front door opened and his brother Brent walked out. Matt remained in the saddle, holding still. Not so Dark Champion, who stepped about restlessly, head bobbing, eyes dark and wide.

Dropping the rope connected to the mules, Matt tightened his grip on the reins as the two brothers stared at one another. Unlike the house, Brent did not look welcoming. He looked surprised, but the reaction did not last long. Tall, dark and lean like all the Hunter men, Brent watched his brother with the cool detachment that had marked their relationship for as long as Matt could remember.

Brent broke the silence. "You came back."

"I said I would," Matt said, keeping his voice steady though anger burned in him. His word apparently didn't mean much. It was another fact of life at the Half-Moon that had not and would not change.

"You always were quick to take offense."

44

"I was always given cause."

Brent shrugged, not bothering to argue, then stepped off the porch and made a wide circle around horse and rider, showing respect for the unknown temperament of the thoroughbred. Matt did not warn him about Dark Champion's habit of spraying his droppings. Brent wouldn't have believed him anyway.

"He's a beauty."

"That he is."

"How could you afford him?" Brent, practical as ever, was not a man for evading a touchy point.

"He came cheap." And then, because he, too, did not want to evade a point, Matt added, "He caused a jockey's death last year. The day before I bought him, he seriously injured another. Her Ladyship was glad enough to get rid of him."

"A woman owner."

He could read his brother's mind. Brent never had much to do with the fair sex, but he seemed to think his little brother rutted every night. Matt never bothered to tell him he was wrong.

"A countess, as a matter of fact. A young widow."

"Attractive?"

"She thought so." And then, because he liked riling his stiff-backed older brother: "So did I."

"You negotiated successfully."

"You might call it that."

Once again the two brothers studied one another. This time Matt spoke first. "He'll win races."

"He'll have to."

"What are you talking about?"

"We've got money trouble again." Needlessly, he added, "Pa."

"And the bastard banker."

"He loaned him money to buy land."

"We didn't need land. We needed stock."

"We've got that, too. A couple of dozen mares he picked up at triple the price he should have paid. And a horse. A racing thoroughbred. He thinks he's got one that will solve all our problems."

Matt could hear what his brother was thinking, what he didn't bother to say out loud. *Kind of like you.*

But Dark Champion hadn't cost the ranch a single greenback. And he would win races, if whoever rode him could hang on until the finish line.

As for breeding, a test was already under way, in the belly of a deflowered mare back at the Lazy Q.

Matt slid from the saddle, for the first time in months standing on Half-Moon land, keeping a tight grip on the reins as he slipped them over the stallion's head. The dirt felt ordinary enough under his feet, not cursed or heavy with the blood of old wounds. But the blood was there, though it couldn't be smelled or seen. And the curse of trouble lay in every clod and every blade of grass.

Damned if he wasn't turning philosophical. It must come with getting close to thirty.

His gaze shifted from the house to the distant fields, to the corral, then settled once again on his brother.

"It took ten years of hard work to pay off the first debt."

"With the way Pa's adding up debts," Brent said, his face tight, his voice tighter, "it looks like it'll take another ten for the second."

Matt muttered a few Texas curse words and one or two he'd picked up abroad.

"I saw Montgomery in town when I was riding through. He said there were changes at the ranch. I should have guessed what they were."

Brent started to speak, then fell silent.

"What is it?" Matt asked.

"I'll tell you at supper."

"I'll chow down with the men, the way I used to."

"Tonight you might want to come inside."

Matt started to protest, then took a more careful look at his brother, noticing a new grimness around the mouth, and fine lines etched at the corners of his eyes. Whatever problems were thrown at him, Brent had always seemed like a man sure he could handle them. He didn't look so sure now.

Changes. Matt got the feeling that a new mortgage was not the only news he was going to hear.

"I'd better get Dark Champion watered and brushed down," he said. "Can the men see to the mules? Oh, by the way, I've got a wagon with a broken wheel over at the Lazy Q. We'll need to bring it back here. And there might be the remains of a horse trailer on the road about a mile out of town. That's ours, too."

"You care to explain?"

"Later. I'm thinking we both have some talking to do."

He was halfway to the barn, the stallion in tow, when Brent spoke up.

"You haven't asked if Pa's around."

Matt took a tighter grip on the reins. "I figured he was. My luck's good, but not that good."

"He's out on the range. At least he's supposed to be. He ought to be back before long. He hit the bottle hard when he first came home, but lately he's been letting up some. I wouldn't say he's a reformed man, but he has changed." Brent hesitated a minute. "He'll be surprised to see you. Right from the start he's been saying you wouldn't return. He's the one got the rest of us thinking maybe you wouldn't."

Matt felt a grim satisfaction at the news. If anyone was going to doubt him, it would be Jack.

"I hate to disappoint him, but I'm here. And I don't plan on going away again anytime soon."

This time he didn't stop until he was inside the barn, his coat on a peg, a kerosene lantern lit and resting on a post. He had a choice of stalls, the barn being empty at the moment. He picked the one at the far end, thinking that when winter came, it would be the least likely to get cold.

Rough slats formed the walls, and there was only a thin scattering of hay on the hard dirt floor. It must be quite a comedown for the thoroughbred, from the luxurious Kingbridge Stables at Newmarket, England, to the back of a barn at the Half-Moon.

DC, as Matt was now calling him, had received a little comfort on the way, in the form of a blood bay mare all too eager to lift her tail. Matt allowed himself a thought about the mare's owner. He wasn't certain just how Juliana Rains had managed it, argumentative as she was, but she had brought him a little comfort, too. He smiled to think how angry she would be if she knew.

With that thought in mind, he threw himself into the care of the horse that was supposed to save the family ranch. DC was amazingly docile during the hard currying. Obviously the stallion had spent his energy at the Lazy Q. Whenever a race approached, Matt would have to keep him far from fertile mares.

He was putting away the paraphernalia he'd

been using to care for the stallion when he felt a change in the air, as if a cold wind were blowing through the open doors, whistling down from the northern plains. But there was no movement in the air, no sound. Just an unwelcome chill.

Matt knew its source, as well as if curse words had broken the silence. The time had come, the moment he'd been dreading for more than ten years. Strange, he didn't dread it now. He wanted it over and done.

Slowly he turned to the figure silhouetted in the light at the end of the barn. Thinner and more stooped than Matt remembered him, he stood like a stone man in the open doorway, nothing of warm flesh about him.

Matt let out a long, slow breath. "Don't bother to say it. You're surprised I'm back."

"Why?" his father asked.

The one word was rasped out. Matt could hear the days and months of whiskey-drinking in it, though he doubted that his father was drunk. Not yet, at least. Brent had said Jack had let up on the drinking.

"Why did I come back? Good question, Jack. I'll let you know when I figure it out."

For a minute the two men stared in silence at one another.

Jack coughed and spat on the ground. "Is that all you've got to say to me? I'm your pa, whether you want to admit it or not, and I ain't laid eyes on you since before the trial."

"I didn't think you'd miss me."

"Shows you how wrong you can be. Hell, I thought you could tell me how I was supposed to act in jail. You being a frequent resident and all."

Matt gritted his teeth, something he hadn't done in ten years. But he couldn't get too riled. Give the devil his due. Jack had a point. Too many times to count, he'd been thrown into a Diablo cell for carousing and drinking and shooting up the town. Sometimes the sheriff had let him sleep off a drunk. Usually it was his father who hauled him back to the ranch, but Brent and Quince had done their share of rescuing as well.

Pointing out that he'd been seventeen would serve little purpose. If his family had any say in the matter, he would carry the disgrace of those days all the way to the grave.

"Speak up, boy," Jack growled. "After ten years you oughta have a few things on your mind."

A rare moment of despair struck Matt. There were so many things he could say, but words did nothing but harm. Especially words about the past. No matter how much a man grieved and regretted, some things could never be set right. If Jack wanted talk, he'd oblige, but he'd stick to what was going on now. Shifting through his choices of response, he chose the most incendiary.

"I understand you've got us in debt again."

Jack hissed. "You've seen Brent. He likes to whine. What I've done is begin to make this place what it could be. He about drove it into the ground while I was gone."

Matt didn't bother to argue. As far back as he could remember, his father had a way of looking at things that put himself in a good light.

"Your old buddy Edmund loaned you the money."

"He's not pushing to get it back."

"Not yet."

"Don't you worry about this place. It's mine. I don't plan to lose it anytime soon. And if I did, as I said, it's mine."

Matt couldn't tell if Jack was deliberately trying to provoke him. If that was his plan, it was working.

"Only because Brent worked hard to keep it."

"He claims you helped—when you showed up. Didn't do that very often, did you?"

Jack had never been a man to show gratitude. It was a trait that prison had not changed.

Matt stared past him into the gloom of gathering dusk. Jack would never know how hard showing up had been, except for the visits with Abby. Neither would he know why his youngest son had chosen a solitary course, pushing himself so hard sometimes that he thought he would die from exhaustion. He'd been more afraid of thinking than of aching. He could tell Jack about the thousand lonely nights on the trail when a shared cup of coffee with the other hands or the feel of a woman's soft arms around him would have brought more pleasure than a week of rest in the finest feather bed.

But he'd kept himself apart, a marked man, Hunter sins stretching like barbed wire between him and the rest of the world.

An ugly silence fell between father and son. Jack broke it when he looked beyond Matt to the last stall in the barn.

"You didn't come back empty-handed."

Matt followed his gaze. Lamplight flickered across Dark Champion's sleek black hide and reflected in the eyes he turned on the two men, his aristocratic head held high, as if he knew he was under hostile scrutiny.

Jack slowly walked past Matt, staying a couple of arm's lengths away. His face was gaunt, lined, with a spare covering of gray bristles across his sunken cheeks. More telling, there was no spring in his step the way there used to be. For all his sharp talk, his walk was more a shuffle than a stride.

He came to a halt in front of the stall. "You think you got something special here?" Scorn edged every word.

Matt moved closer, feeling more allegiance to the horse than to his blood kin.

"I know I do," he said, glad the argument between them was about a thoroughbred. It was safer territory than the topic of what was now and what had been.

Jack looked the horse over, bending to give special attention to the stallion's legs. "I got me one that can beat him."

"That's something we're likely to find out before much time passes."

A nasty grin spread on Jack's face as he pulled himself upright, but whatever he was about to say got lost in the cacophony that burst like a tornado through the open barn door, a screeching cat and barking dog racing down the center, chickens squawking in their wake, men shouting, a horse neighing, a whirl of motion bouncing from stall to stall.

Matt went for DC, grabbing for his mane to hold him in place. The stallion neighed and kicked, wild-eyed when the cat, a streak of black, sailed over the side of the stall, dug his claws into the stallion's hard back, then soared onward up the back shelves and into an overhead loft.

Right behind him came the dog, a yellow-brown streak howling as if the end of the world had come, trying to jump but, being earthbound in the way of his kind, unable to pursue his prey beyond the hay-strewn floor. Behind him came a couple of ranch hands, yelling at something Matt couldn't figure out, and over their yells Jack's curses rang in the dim air.

It all happened fast, and ended the same way when DC shifted and lifted his tail. Horseshit flew in all directions, splattering Matt and his father, the dog, and the foreman Taggart, who had been foolish enough to stray too close, ignorant of the stallion's special talent.

The dog whimpered, fell silent, then with tail between his legs put distance between himself and the horse. The pristine cat peered over the edge of the loft at the scene below, serene as could be, as if he'd just been disturbed from a late-afternoon nap.

DC flicked his tail, dismissing the lot of them, studying the hay as if in disbelief that this was the dinner he was expected to eat.

Matt glanced at his soiled shirt and trousers, then at his similarly anointed father. Their eyes met, and for a moment he thought they were going to laugh. But the moment passed. The grimness on Jack's face returned, and the scorn.

"What's going on here?" demanded a new voice.

They looked toward the front of the barn to see Brent enter. At his side was a woman, fair-haired and pretty. Even in the dimness, with her back to the light, Matt could tell just how pretty she was. He had an instinct for such things.

She was also far too rounded in the stomach to be anything else but in the family way.

"Matt here's brought us a talented horse," Jack said. "Ain't never seen one could spread manure the way he can. Fresh and warm. Begging your pardon, Crystal, I'm trying to keep this as genteel as I can."

"Don't try so hard, Pa," Brent said. And then to Matt: "Guess this is as good a time as any to introduce my wife. Crystal, this is Matt."

Stepping closer to the lantern light, she smiled. It was as pretty a smile as he'd seen in a long time. "Hello, Matt," she said in a soft voice.

"I'll be damned," he managed.

"That's for sure," Jack said.

"I've heard about you," Crystal said. She didn't make it sound as if what she'd heard was bad.

Still, it couldn't have been good.

"I'm sure you have. You care to comment on how I wasn't supposed to come back? Everyone else has."

"Not especially. I'm just glad you're here."

Matt looked at his brother. "I'll be damned," he repeated. "You got married."

"He ain't the only one," Jack said. "Quince got him a wife, too."

Matt shook his head. "I've been gone not much more than six months, and look what's happened. Next thing you know, you'll be saying

56

Baby Sister's found herself a man and gone to wearing dresses."

No one said anything.

For the first time in ten years Matt felt the need for a drink.

Chapter Four

She'd been living in a world made of glass.

Juliana saw that now. In the past two years, surrounded by her late husband's autocratic family, and before that by her husband himself, she had been able to see reality only through the distortion of walls that isolated her from the truth.

When the first letter arrived, cracks began to appear:

Dear Juliana, I regret to inform you that, following a sudden and brief illness, your mother passed away peacefully in her sleep. Please accept my condolences. We share the grief of her loss.

Short and to the point, it was signed Edmund Montgomery. As if she might have forgotten his full name. Stunned, she had read the words three times before grasping what they meant. Her mother couldn't be dead. All her letters spoke reassuringly of how fine her life was. When the truth finally hit Juliana, she was overcome by grief, sharp and unrelenting, though mother and daughter hadn't been near one another in years. In that instant she'd felt more alone than when her husband died.

Then came the terrible second letter, actually written before the first but arriving weeks later, shattering her world completely. It rambled, skipping from subject to subject, rarely a thought completed before going on the next, her mother's usually steady handwriting now spidery, the normally pristine paper of her correspondence blotched with ink.

It began with talk of love, of a mother's love that would never die, exaggerated words as if she had never told her daughter how she felt. On that first reading, and on dozens ever since, Juliana had wept, wishing she could tell her mother that though the miles and years had separated them, she always knew. But that great separator, Death, had come to muffle whatever she could reveal to her mother now.

And so then, as now, she whispered the message, hoping Iona could hear her in her heavenly home.

As painfully sweet as the talk of love had been, the worst of the letter was yet to come, the incoherent rambling, the repetitions, the hints of what Iona Montgomery's life had really been. Juliana had never read anything like it before.

. . . today has not been a good day.

Edmund takes care of me . . .

I need more medicine, then I'll feel better.

. . . the doctor doesn't understand, not like Edmund.

He's given me everything.

. . . he knows what I need.

. . . medicine . . .

I'm to blame.

The latter was scrawled more than once, as were references to the unnamed medicine.

"To blame for what?" Juliana cried, as she had so many times over the past days, but there was no one in the room to answer. She was alone in the ranch house, sitting on the edge of her bed, the oft-folded letter clutched in her hand. There was no one to see her tear-streaked face.

"What medicine?" Her voice fell to a whisper. "What doesn't the doctor understand?"

The worst questions she directed at her step-father. "What did you give her? What did you do to her? Did you truly understand?"

The answering silence screamed at her, its echoes pounding in her head. She stared at the other letters spread across the quilt, cheery messages written by her mother through the years. Juliana had saved them all, clinging, she now saw, to every reassurance that all was well in Texas, that her stepfather treated her mother right, that in her second marriage Iona Sullivan Montgomery was as loved and cosseted as she had been in her first.

The letter from her stepfather—the terse announcement of his wife's passing—was resting off by itself, too offensive to be included with the others. Too cold. Too brittle. Holding it hurt her hand.

She should have hurried back to Texas the instant she received it, but at the time she had seen no purpose. Her mother was dead. Whatever comfort she could have brought, whatever love, whatever respect, should have been given while Iona was alive. And so she had nursed her grief in the silence of her Saratoga home.

The purpose came when Abby Hunter finally got around to sending Iona's last letter, as an afterthought before leaving the family's Half-Moon Ranch with her new husband. When Juliana arrived on the stage from San Antonio two days ago, she'd learned of the marriage and of the young woman's subsequent departure.

How long had the new Mrs. Tremain held Iona's letter? Weeks? Months? It was not dated, yet Juliana felt sure it had been written shortly before the end. No one who wrote with such aching desperation could hold on to life for long.

Yet the letter had been set aside, then mailed as an afterthought.

The Hunters, she was learning, were not the

friends Iona had described. Had the dying woman had anyone in Diablo she could have depended on? With her daughter a thousand miles away, she must have been desperate for someone. That distance, that desperation, lay at the heart of Juliana's shame.

. . . a sudden and brief illness . . .

She knew in her heart that with those words Edmund Montgomery had lied. Why? The question burned in her mind. Only Edmund knew. As much as he repulsed her, there was no staying away from him now, no avoiding the encounter that had become inevitable the moment he took Iona as his bride and shipped off her only child.

Juliana's mission was clear: to find out the truth of her mother's death, and, a far more formidable task, to ease the burden of guilt that robbed each day of the sun, each night of peaceful sleep.

If justice was called for, she must seek it out as well. She'd vowed to do just that back in Saratoga, a vow renewed over her mother's grave when she arrived in town two days ago. Standing alone in the Diablo cemetery, she'd wanted to feel her mother's presence and her forgiveness, but there had been only a damp chill and a sharp breeze blowing over the headstones.

The sound of hammering drifted through the open bedroom window, stirring her from her reverie. At first she thought, foolishly, it was the throbbing of her heart. How lost in thought she was, how removed from her surroundings. In no more than an instant she realized the noise was far more palpable than any heaviness inside her, a harsh reminder that a world of ordinary occurrences existed outside her window.

The hammering seemed to be coming from the front of the house. She doubted that Kane was its source. At this late morning hour, her lone ranch hand was supposedly out somewhere repairing fences.

She could not ignore the disturbance. With a sigh, she set the letter aside and hurried down, not bothering to pin back her hair into its normal respectable knot, forgetting the evidence of tears on her cheeks. She went tilted out the front door to a scene that stole her breath. Matt Hunter, shirtless, crouched beside the back wheel of the wagon he had abandoned yesterday, thick black hair bound by a leather thong at the back of his neck, his jeans-clad rear resting against the heels of his boots.

She stood at the edge of the front porch, knowing she should speak. Instead she watched the play of muscles as he set the hammer aside and gripped the wheel, propped by a wooden log a foot off the ground, canting the wagon to an unnatural tilt.

Juliana felt a little tilted herself, the view throwing her from her usual composure and disinterest in men. Matt Hunter's shoulders were broad, his skin taut and slick with a fine sheen of sweat, scarcely a shade paler than his brown hands. With smooth, deft movements he slipped the log from its position under the wagon, easing the wheel downward until it rested on the ground. He had to be very strong to handle such a task from his position.

And she had to be very weak to notice. Still, she watched. It was a long time, yet far too short, before he stood and faced her.

At first she saw only the fine dusting of chest hairs across the contours of his chest. Black hairs. She had grown used to gray. And to contours not nearly so tight or sharply defined as the ones she gazed at now.

Then she looked into his hazel eyes, which were assessing her with a mocking light as unsettling as his chest. She could have sworn the porch moved.

"Good morning, Mrs. Rains," he said with a nod. He looked at the sky and at the sun almost directly overhead. The muscles of his neck were taut. "Closer to afternoon, I'd guess. I hope I didn't wake you."

He was disturbing her, all right, and he knew it.

"I am an early riser, Mr. Hunter."

He acknowledged her words with a nod, but he did not return to his work. Instead he looked at her. She smoothed her hair back from her face, wishing she had taken time to bind the long, thick strands into a knot. He seemed inordinately interested in the movement of her hand as it touched her cheek, then in the fit of her gown, a pale yellow close to the color of her hair.

She became painfully aware of how isolated they were. Whenever she was close to him, why did she, the most peaceful of people, think about needing a gun?

"Are you almost done?" she asked.

"I believe so. The axle needed bracing, that's all. I figured it ought to be repaired right away. There's no telling how much rent you'll charge if the wagon stays here very long."

"Rent?" she asked, then remembered she had said he would have to pay for the use of her land. But that had been because he wanted to charge her a stud fee after his stallion had assaulted her mare.

More memories rushed in—of the horses mating, of Matt standing at the corral fence taunting her with his insolence.

She ought to bid him good day and hurry back inside. He was not only a Hunter, but the wildest one, the most dangerous of his generation, the most unpredictable. It had been so when he was a youth. She could sense that the wildness had not been burned out by the years, perhaps because he dared to work half naked close to her front door.

As if he could read her thoughts, he reached for the dark work shirt that hung over the side of the wagon. A force she did not understand kept her in place, her hands gripping the porch rail as he eased into the shirt and tucked the tail inside the band of his denim trousers.

"You'll pardon my appearance," he said, as politely as if he had come to tea without a properly tied cravat.

"I didn't notice."

His lips twitched at the absurdity of the lie.

"All right, I noticed," she said. "But it makes no difference to me if you choose to go around like a savage."

"It's a borrowed shirt. I didn't want to mess it up."

"If you're in need of clothing, I'm sure I can find something of my husband's."

"Are you always so generous?"

The question was laced with insinuation.

She let her gaze drop, for a moment remembering the look of his bare chest.

"To one so obviously in need."

"Don't waste your charity. My clothes are in the wagon, along with just about everything else I own."

She peered behind him into the shallow bed of the wagon. A piece of worn luggage, some boxes, a sack of feed were all she could see.

"Everything?"

"Except for the horse. And what I was wearing yesterday, of course. If I had that shirt on, you'd be begging me to get undressed."

She did not bother to make sense of his words.

"Do you usually go around with all your possessions?"

"I've been traveling."

"I see," she said, not really understanding.

"To England."

"I should have guessed," she said, not believing him for a second. And he knew it. She could see that her doubt rankled.

"I bought Dark Champion at a stable in Newmarket."

The hard edge to his voice told her he spoke the truth. Despite herself, she was impressed. That area of England had a reputation for horseflesh that outdid even the stock of Saratoga.

She wanted to ask where he got the money for such a journey and such a purchase, it being common knowledge that Hunters were always in debt. But that would be rude, and she was too well-bred. Still, she wanted to know.

"How's the deflowered mare?" he asked.

Matt clearly had no such compunctions about rudeness.

"Pepper is fine. How did you pay for the horse?"

He didn't seem surprised she'd asked, and she wondered about the kind of treatment he was used to, and about the way he would treat a woman when he caught her alone and vulnerable.

"I earned the money," he said in a challenging voice, daring her to question him further.

Juliana did not hesitate to do so. "Robbing banks?" she asked.

"Horseraces."

"Riding or gambling?"

"Both."

"Robbing banks would be more certain."

"Sometimes I'm lucky."

"With horses."

"Definitely more than with women. Horses are far more predictable."

He began to walk across the yard toward her, an unnerving deliberation in each step. The way he was watching her, eyes dark and glinting, his lean face set in an unyielding expression, he unnerved her as much as when he'd been half naked. She took an involuntary step away from the rail. When he walked onto the porch, the boards creaked under his weight.

"I'm hoping Dark Champion is both predictable and lucky. Look at the way things turned out for him yesterday."

"Mr. Hunter—"

"Pepper, too. Fine mare you've got there, and

fortunate, too. She scents the air, and the next thing she knows, a descendant of Eclipse is coming to her rescue."

Juliana was momentarily taken aback.

"Eclipse? The famous Arabian?"

"It says so in the papers I got from the countess."

Juliana rubbed her forehead. Everything was wrong in this encounter, from the way he looked right down to what he said.

"You bought the stallion from a countess?" she asked.

"Yep. Of course I had to stay outside the castle, Her Ladyship being afraid I'd soil the carpet and stink up the place."

She'd been right. The years had taken the boy out of him but not the devil.

"Are you having a good time?" she asked.

A darkness settled on him, as if he were standing under a cloud.

"I don't have good times, Mrs. Rains."

It wasn't a complaint, but a statement of fact. The death of his mother, the guilt of his father, must have affected him more than she would have guessed. Despite herself, she felt sympathy for him, and a kinship because of their separate losses.

An image of him as a youth flashed in her mind, black hair wild, a grin on his narrow young face, arms and legs moving loosely as he strode down the streets of Diablo, and her heart caught.

"You used to," she said, her voice softened. "Have good times, I mean. That's just about all you had."

"I'm sure that's what it looked like."

He touched her shoulder. She jumped; he removed his hand, then touched her again. This time she held still. The pressure on her was light but warm, very warm, as if his fingers emitted an extra degree of heat.

He studied her face with an intensity that caused her stomach to knot. Surely the dried tears were not still evident on her cheeks. She would not want him to know she'd been crying. Such feminine weakness was not something he would understand. Or tolerate.

"You were always the little lady," he said. "I wondered if you ever smiled."

"I didn't know you noticed me."

"I noticed you."

The words confused her. She didn't know what he was saying, what he was thinking. The world around them blurred, and she became aware of only the two of them, of the way they used to be, youngsters who watched each other from a distance, and the way they were now, a man and a woman drawn to each other by a strange and powerful force.

She swayed toward him, as if to touch him

more, then straightened, horrified by what she had almost done.

"Please move away," she said.

To her surprise, he did as she asked, standing at arm's reach.

"Unpredictable," he said with a shake of his head. "I thought at the first touch you would slap me."

"You were testing me?"

"Not really. I was . . . touching you."

"Don't do it again."

"Not unless you want me to."

"I can't imagine that ever happening." She was lying, but he didn't have to know it.

"We live in a strange world," he said.

"Where horses are predictable and women aren't."

He came close to a grin. It was the grin of his youth. She would have liked to grab hold of the rail once again, but he stood in the way.

"Right," he said. Then all hint of a smile died. "I was sorry to hear about Mrs. Montgomery. Brent told me last night."

The simple expression of sympathy chilled whatever warmth was passing between them. Juliana's world came into focus, with all its hurts and harsh realities. She bristled. How could she have forgotten her mother for even a second? How could she have forgotten why she was here?

She felt as if she had betrayed Iona Montgomery all over again.

"What exactly did your brother say?"

"That she'd died, that's all. And that she'd been ill for a long time."

More proof that the truth of her mother's condition had been kept from her.

"Were you really sorry? I didn't realize you knew her."

Matt Hunter was not stupid, nor completely insensitive to the coolness in her voice, and his eyes narrowed. "Not as well as Abby, of course."

Abby, the one who for weeks had held back the last message Juliana would ever receive from her mother.

"How close was your sister to her? Mother mentioned her in her letters, but letters can be deceiving."

"What's got your back up, Mrs. Rains?"

You. You made me forget. "You haven't answered the question," she said.

"Neither have you." He looked from her to weed-choked beds where flowers had once bloomed, then to the paint flaking from the post by the front step.

"What brought you back here now?"

She read the implication in his words. He might as well have added *since your mother is dead.*

She would have stopped breathing before she told him the truth.

"This was once my home. It was only for a brief time, but perhaps it could be so again."

"It's not been cared for."

"My husband hired a couple to care for the ranch, and I continued with their services after he died. They left without notice, but I don't know exactly when. Apparently, they did not do a very good job while they were here."

"So you're going to bring the Lazy Q back to prosperity."

"Yes." She surprised herself by meaning what she said.

"And more." Here came a bigger surprise. "My father's land lies between here and the Half-Moon. I would like to buy it from whoever is the present owner. Mother indicated in one of her last letters it had changed hands."

As preposterous as the idea was, she realized it must have been at the back of her mind for a long while. Somehow, reclaiming the land on which she was born had become wound up with finding the truth about her mother's last days.

Matt grew very still.

"I just found out about the new owner last night," he said.

"And it is?"

"Jack."

"Jack who?" Then the truth hit her. "Jack Hunter? Your father? Hunters own the Sullivan ranch?"

"It's part of the Half-Moon now."

"But that's intolerable."

"Why? Because he's a no-good, rotten, lying bastard?" Matt's voice was laced with bitterness. He knew she wouldn't answer. She couldn't even tell if he believed the words himself.

She responded with the first thing that popped into her head. "Because he couldn't afford it."

It was the wrong response, if she wanted to get any information out of Matt. She could feel him withdraw from her, though he scarcely moved.

Men were creatures of pride. She'd learned at least that from her marriage. Matt Hunter could, she did not doubt, criticize his father as much as anyone. But that criticism was acceptable only within the family.

He stepped off the porch, glancing back at her over his shoulder. "Get used to the fact we're neighbors, Mrs. Rains, as intolerable as the situation must seem. I put the mules out to pasture while I worked. I'll go fetch them and be on my way."

She watched as he disappeared around the corner of the house, his stride long and brisk, his sudden leave-taking as disturbing as the unexpected sight of him had been. He had been in her presence for what seemed an eternity, but had left too abruptly, too soon.

Refusing to gawk at him while he hooked the team to the wagon—she had done quite enough gawking for the day—she turned quickly and caught sight of her ranch hand standing in the shadows at the far side of the house.

Grizzled, scowling, his clothes loose-fitting and in need of a thorough scouring, Kane looked like a man who lived in shadows. He made her jump.

"I thought you were out working on fences," she called, when she could speak in a strong voice. She reminded herself she was the boss. She needed to remind Kane, as well.

"I came in for supplies," he answered, his voice as coarse as his appearance. "I'll be heading out again soon enough. Unless you need me around here."

He couldn't have meant anything other than work. Or could he? Matt Hunter truly had gotten her on edge.

"I need the fences repaired."

He stared at her for a moment, his features hard and unreadable. Just when she thought he would snap out something about repairing them herself, he nodded and walked away, like Matt disappearing quickly from view. She rubbed her sleeves, chilled as if a winter wind had blown across the porch, though the day was mild. Inexplicably, she felt threatened, though by what she could not have said. She also felt more alone than she could ever remember, worse than when she'd learned of her mother's death.

Shaking off the feeling as best she could, she went inside, hurrying back to her letters and to the formulation of a plan concerning how she could proceed in her investigation.

For a brief while she had allowed herself to think of matters other than her mother. She must not make that mistake again.

Chapter Five

In the early afternoon Edmund Montgomery came to pay his respects, or so he said in the note he left inside Juliana's door. She was out exercising Pepper at the time, trying to put Matt Hunter out of her mind, returning after Montgomery had gone.

As she read the note, she admitted to relief that she'd arrived too late to see him. She had to face him sometime, and she would. But not yet, not until she got better control of her emotions and learned a little more about her mother's final illness.

I am sorry to have missed you, her stepfather wrote. *I will return, or perhaps you can call on me at my office in Diablo when you are next in town.*

She had no intention of doing so. Let him wait awhile and wonder what she was up to.

And why did he suggest his office, when the home he had shared with her mother was close by, high on a hill directly behind the bank? Juliana had never been inside—he'd built it after she was married and gone—but she'd gotten a glimpse of it when she arrived in town.

If he thought he could keep her from the place where Iona had passed her last years, he was more stupid than she had thought. Edmund Montgomery wasn't stupid. Greedy, self-centered and arrogant, yes, but not stupid.

She would eventually get there. Eventually she would enter her mother's room.

But not yet. To face the challenge of that house, that room, she had to be prepared.

Her caution did not mean she would long remain in isolation at the Lazy Q. Which was hardly isolation, not the way Matt Hunter kept dropping by. Later that same afternoon, when the stable hand from Diablo delivered the horse and buggy she had ordered by telegraph from Saratoga, she decided on her first excursion: a visit to the office of Sam Larkin, Diablo's lone attorney.

And then, when she had gathered what information she could, she planned a confrontation with the doctor who had tended her mother at the end.

But first the attorney. Although she scarcely knew him, Larkin had taken care of her interests since her father's death. He had also been the one to hire a ranch hand to help her out in her first days back. Among the questions she wanted to put to him was, why Kane? The man was as unpleasant a sort as she had ever met, and he didn't mend fences worth a tinker's dam, something she'd discovered on her ride with Pepper.

She left shortly after dawn the next morning, making the brisk journey into Diablo in under two hours. Cheeks flushed, she stopped the carriage in front of Larkin's law office in the center of town. Next door was the bank; she did not spare it a glance. If Edmund Montgomery happened to see her arrive, he could decide whether or not to seek her out.

As she stepped into the lawyer's cramped waiting room, she felt an unexpected knot in her stomach. She could not shake the feeling that from this moment on, everything she did, everything she said, would affect the way she lived for the rest of her life. It was an unsettling sensation. Added was the feeling that this day would most likely not go any more smoothly than the one before.

If only she had the confidence to match her determination. She hoped it would come with time.

Standing straight, brushing her wrinkled skirt, she rapped sharply on the office inner door. She swore she heard movement behind it. "Mr. Larkin, it's Juliana Rains," she said loudly. When there was no response, she knocked again. A full minute passed before Larkin opened the door.

"Mrs. Rains, what a pleasant surprise to see you," he said, greeting her with a broad smile.

He was lying. He wasn't in the least pleased. Otherwise, why the bead of sweat on his brow? And what had he been doing that took him so long to let her in?

She answered him with a nod.

"Do come in," he said, gesturing her into his inner sanctum.

Her green silk gown rustling with each step, she swished her way inside, glad to abandon the dark and stuffy waiting room where potential clients had to bide their time until Larkin saw fit to see them. In contrast, his office was finely appointed with oaken desk, comfortable chairs, and windows that opened onto a small garden at the rear.

Beyond the garden, the land sloped sharply upward. At its peak sat the Montgomery house, the place where her mother had lived and died. Juliana had given it a cursory glance before, finding the sight too painful for prolonged inspection. But she had toughened up a little in the past few days, and without apology to Larkin stared openly at it now.

Unlike the other structures in Diablo, it was made of red brick with a steep shingle roof, dormer windows and bright white columns across a wide front porch, a lordly edifice far grander than anything else in the town.

Or maybe she was thinking of its owner and, she supposed, lone occupant.

When her father was alive, and the three of them lived on the Sullivan ranch, her mother had always kept well-tended flower beds. Juliana saw no sign of them at the house she had shared with Edmund.

With a sharpened sense of sadness, Juliana pulled her gaze back to the room in which she stood. A closed door at the side drew her momentary attention. A secret listening post? She brushed the speculation aside. It would do little good to imagine culprits everywhere she went.

Settling into a chair in front of Larkin's desk, she watched as he sat. He was in his early forties, she estimated, tall and rail thin, with sparse sandy hair combed away from a gaunt face, sideburns and a full moustache compensating for encroaching baldness. Possessing a humped nose and mottled skin, he was not a handsome man. For which she was grateful. In her experience, handsome men were usually not what they seemed.

What Larkin seemed at the moment was nervous. He was straightening the few papers on his desk, muttering something about having nothing by way of refreshments to offer, when she broke in.

"Tell me everything you can about my mother in the days before she died." She spoke in a rush, giving no hint of the turmoil tearing at her.

He stopped the straightening. "I beg your pardon?"

She didn't bother to repeat the request. "Everything," she said.

"I . . . I hardly saw Mrs. Montgomery. She usually kept to her house."

"She must have been very ill."

"I assume so. She died, did she not?"

His tone was brusque—more evidence he was edgy—and he immediately shook his head, his insincere smile replaced by insincere sympathy. "Please forgive me. That was uncalled for. Of course you want to know about your mother's last days. It's just that I did not know her well."

"You should have, handling the legal matters after my father died. And after her remarriage."

This time she did not try to keep emotion from her voice. Everyone in the county knew her opinion regarding Iona Sullivan's choice of a second husband.

"But we had few personal dealings," Larkin said. "Edmund Montgomery handled most of the details."

"I'm sure he did."

"It was only natural, considering how close

they had become. He gave her great support during her time of bereavement."

"During which he married her and took possession of all she had inherited, from my father as well as from her late parents."

"As would have happened with anyone she took as her second husband. It's the law. And she was bound to remarry. She was too young to remain single."

The longer he spoke, the greater his confidence became. Leaning back in his chair, he rested his hands on his middle.

"Your mother let me know she depended upon Mr. Montgomery and trusted him to represent her. You were very young when your father passed"—he made the death sound shameful, when in truth her father had died of a fever—"and perhaps do not remember the way things were. Besides"—here his voice turned critical—"after Edmund, Mr. Montgomery that is, entered your mother's life, you were seldom in Diablo, having chosen to accept your paternal grandparents' offer of a home."

"I was eight years old. They wanted me. Edmund Montgomery did not."

"That's putting it rather bluntly. Your mother and he were newlyweds. Perhaps they wanted time to themselves."

Juliana refused to think of how they might have spent that time.

"Those early years do not interest me. It's the later ones I want to hear about, especially my mother's last days. Please tell me what you remember. It hasn't been that long, only a few months. Did you see her in town? In church? At the store? Did she have friends?"

Juliana threw the questions at him without pausing so that he might answer.

"Really, Mrs. Rains," he said smoothly, "you ought to meet with her widower. Montgomery can help you far better than I. Or Abby Hunter. I beg your pardon, Mrs. Tremain she is now. Your mother was very close to her."

Juliana thought of the delayed letter. "You can be sure I plan to see her as soon as possible."

"Unfortunately, that may be a while. Since your arrival, I've learned she is with her new husband buying furniture in New Orleans. I believe that when they return, it will be to the fort where he is commander."

Stifling her frustration, Juliana smiled. "Rest assured, I'll meet with her eventually. In the meantime there must be others I can talk to. Mother lived in or near Diablo most of her life. It's not a large town."

"Six hundred citizens, more or less."

"Surely there was talk about her condition."

Larkin sniffed and smoothed his sparse moustache. "I am not one to listen to gossip."

"I'm not asking for anything like that. The

health of the town's leading citizen, and of his wife"—Juliana almost choked on the words—"would be of natural concern to anyone. It's not gossip to care about someone's health."

She wasn't being entirely honest. She'd take any kind of talk she could get—rumors, speculation, gossip. Within them might be found a kernel of truth, something she could put to her stepfather when she decided to see him.

"I can only say that when I saw her in church she appeared pale and had clearly lost weight. Naturally, I was concerned. But I did not know her well, and did not feel I could inquire as to her health."

"What about Dr. Gibbs? He attended her, did he not?"

Larkin straightened. "Well, there you have another problem. Dr. Gibbs is no longer a resident of Diablo."

She stared at the lawyer in disbelief. "Since when? He was here when my mother died, wasn't he?"

"Most certainly. He left not long after, I believe." Larkin cleared his throat uncomfortably.

"Where is he now?"

"I don't know."

"Who does?"

"I don't know."

She drummed her fingers in her lap, her dismay turning to anger. All of this seemed too coincidental—the lone lawyer pleading ignorance to everything she asked, the doctor disappearing, Abby leaving the state. And behind them all was the shadow of Edmund Montgomery. If she were to look for culprits, she need look no further than him.

"Didn't Dr. Gibbs have close friends? Someone he might have told about his plans?"

"Dr. Gibbs kept to himself, except, of course, when he was tending patients."

"So the one person who might tell me of my mother's last days has disappeared."

"That's putting it a bit strongly. Dr. Gibbs saw the need to move on, or so everyone in town assumes."

"That's the gossip."

"You really ought to talk to your stepfather about all this. He dealt with the doctor. He tended your mother. He's the one to see."

"I plan to." And, she thought to herself, sooner than she had wanted.

Again Larkin cleared his throat. "Is there anything else I can do for you? I do truly want to be of assistance."

She thought of the grim-faced man he had sent to help her at the ranch. If she asked about him, she would probably get something about Kane's being the best the lawyer could find on short notice. If problems developed, she could hear Larkin say, she must let him know right away.

Larkin was, she had discovered, very good at offering help but delivering none.

"You've already done enough," she said.

He stood, ready to escort her to the street. She kept her seat.

"There is one thing more. Jack Hunter has bought my father's land." She didn't put it as a question.

Reluctantly Larkin sat back down. "I believe he has. From the owner who bought it from your mother."

"She didn't sell it, not on her own."

"No, of course not. Any transaction concerning the Sullivan ranch went through Montgomery, as you well know."

"Oh yes, I know. As her husband, he controlled everything she owned."

"Technically, yes. We've already covered that. But if she had objected to the sale, I am certain he would have honored her wishes."

As far as Juliana knew, Iona Sullivan Montgomery had never objected to anything her second husband said or did or thought. When Juliana was freshly grieving over the loss of her beloved father, begging her mother to stay with her on the ranch, understanding even at that young age the power Montgomery had over Iona, she had felt his animosity. And she had hurt all the more when her mother chose him over her only child.

At the time, she hadn't thought all this through. Her father's parents had been loving and eager to raise her. But as the years passed and her visits with her mother grew further and further apart, she had begun to blame the new husband, and to try to understand why Iona hadn't fought to keep her daughter by her side.

The memory still hurt her. But it did not ease the guilt over her absence during the past few years.

"Where did Hunter get the money?" she asked.

"Really, Mrs. Rains, I can't reveal any of Jack Hunter's dealings. He is my client, too."

"I want to buy the land back from him."

"I hardly think he will sell."

"Everyone has a price."

"Jack Hunter is not like other people. Ten years in prison did not soften him, nor make him more amenable to, shall we say, discussion."

She thought of his son and how he had described him.

. . . he's a no-good, rotten, lying bastard . . .

"I don't plan to discuss it. I'll make him an offer he can't refuse. I have sufficient funds, as you well know."

"Of course you do," he said. "That's not the issue."

"You're not being very helpful, Mr. Larkin."

"I can do no more than my best."

Which, Juliana was learning, was not very good.

Suddenly the room seemed robbed of air. She could not breathe. She stood, and he followed suit.

"Thank you for your time, Mr. Larkin," she said. "Don't bother to see me out. I'm sure you have other business to tend to."

When she left, she had to force herself not to run out to the street.

Sam Larkin stared after her. He felt cold and hot at the same time. Why had she really come? What was she up to? If she had cared about her mother, she wouldn't have stayed away so long. Such was the talk in town, and he believed it.

Maybe he should have told her the truth.

Your mother was the town drunk. She drank herself into the grave.

But that would have been too blunt, too honest. As a lawyer he had learned that honesty was not always the best policy. Besides, the bearer of bad news was too often blamed for the news itself. Let her learn the truth for herself.

Slowly the side door opened, pulling him from his thoughts, and he turned to face the man who entered his office.

"Well, well," Edmund Montgomery said in that slick-smooth way of his. "Our little girl from back East is stirring up trouble already."

Sometimes Sam's hatred for the banker was so consuming, he came close to letting it show. He would have now, but he had other matters on his mind. He took a handkerchief from his pocket and wiped his brow.

"You told me she wouldn't come back," he said.

Montgomery's eyes narrowed. "I was wrong."

"So what do I do now?"

"Nothing."

"But what if she . . ." Larkin couldn't put the rest of the question into words.

"If she asks about the trust fund? The money that was her only legacy from her father? You should have thought about the consequences when you started embezzling."

"You've always put too harsh a name to what I did. I invested the money, which she knows."

"Does she know it was in horses and cards and women?"

"Not women," Larkin answered indignantly.

"I keep forgetting. You pay for them yourself."

Larkin swallowed. His sexual pastimes were not a subject he could ever discuss, especially with the man smirking at him now. Oh, how he would like to smack his fist into that face.

"Besides," he said, drawing himself to his full height, "I have documentation to show where the money has gone."

"Your so-called documentation wouldn't fool

a fool. And Juliana Rains is hardly that."

Montgomery always tried to cast things in the worst light. And he never, ever let a man forget his mistakes. The lawyer felt his back was to the wall. There was only one thing to do.

"No, she's not a fool." He spoke softly, slyly, going on the attack himself. "You heard her questions. They weren't about money. They were about how her mother died."

Montgomery took a step toward him, and another, until they were so close he could feel the man's hot breath on his face. Observing him was like watching a snake uncoil. Larkin's courage began to fail.

"My dear wife suffered a combination of ills," Montgomery said, "not the least of which was an addiction to sherry. Her problem was widely known around town."

"Alcohol wasn't her only addiction," Larkin managed, unwilling to give up the attack so soon. He was talking about something he only suspected, but he could see by the flare of rage in Montgomery's eyes that he had hit close to the truth.

"How dare you hint of such a thing?" Montgomery's voice was like a razor, each word slashing at his listener, cutting to the bone. Larkin could feel the hate in him, a hate so strong it rendered his own inconsequential. For the first time since they had begun their unfortunate relationship, the banker seemed close to being out of control.

If Montgomery were holding a gun, Larkin knew he would now be dead.

Instead, the banker—town leader, deacon in the church, benefactor to widows, holder of every mortgage in the county—smiled. It was not a sight Larkin wished ever to see again.

"My wife died of her own weaknesses. And so might you, Sam. Your weakness for talk."

"I . . . I'm sorry," Larkin stammered, turning his hatred onto himself.

"You had better be more than sorry. I've only to speak one word to the sheriff, and you'll find yourself so deep in jail you won't see the light of day for years." Montgomery looked beyond him to the well-tended garden outside the back window. "You like beautiful things, Sam. Ask Jack Hunter how much beauty you'll find in a cell."

His cold eyes shifted for a moment to the door through which Juliana Rains had departed.

"As far as my inquisitive stepdaughter is concerned, she'd better be careful or she'll find herself in far worse trouble than jail."

"You wouldn't—"

"Don't tell me what I would or wouldn't do," Montgomery hissed. "No one does, least of all a spineless, sniveling thief like you. Kane's at her ranch, isn't he? At least you managed something right. Maybe what dear Juliana needs is a warning. Maybe it's time Kane earned his keep."

Without waiting for a response, he slammed his way out of the office, leaving Larkin to sweat and sink weakly into his chair. After a moment, when he could think, he stared around the office he had furnished with such care. Nothing in his vision held much value for him, not now. For the first time since establishing himself as Diablo's lone attorney twenty years before, he considered the possibility of following in the doctor's footsteps and getting the hell out of town.

Matt Hunter caught sight of Juliana the moment she exited Sam Larkin's law office.

"Hell-o," he said, dragging out the word, knowing she couldn't hear him. He stood in the shadows beside the Lone Star Saloon, across the street on the corner of the next block.

Her unexpected presence took his breath away. She looked good. No, he amended, she looked great. Green silk rose smoothly across fine breasts, then tucked into a small waist, the full skirt hiding what he figured to be equally fine hips. She had her hair twisted up under a fancy little bonnet, but there were wisps of yellow gold framing her face and slender neck. The sight of her made a man wonder if a solitary life was the best way to exist.

It was a crazy thought. If he were foolish enough to follow in the footsteps of his brothers, she was the last woman he should take as a wife. She knew too much about the Hunters. And she didn't like them. She'd made that clear enough yesterday on her porch.

There had been a moment when he touched her . . .

He should have kept his hands to himself. But he was human. And he hadn't touched a woman in a long, long time.

When he did, when he finally chose someone to give more than just a brush on the shoulder, it wouldn't be a woman from Diablo. Once the Half-Moon was clear of debt—again—everyone in town, and at the ranch as well, could eat Matt's dust.

Even as he told himself all these things, he watched her stand at the edge of the street, as if caught in indecision. An expensive-looking horse and a shiny new carriage were hitched in front of the office. Instinct told him they were hers. They went with the silk dress.

He was debating whether to cross over and speak to her when a stranger stumbled into view in the middle of the street, not bothering to avoid the horse droppings, letting the few riders and carriages passing through town make their way around him. Ill-fitting, grimy clothes hung on his burly frame, his swarthy skin made darker by a scraggly gray-and-black beard.

As he passed Juliana, he stared at her a moment. Matt's gut tightened, but the stranger kept on staggering toward what became obvious as his destination: the Lone Star. If he spied Matt, he gave no sign. Instead, after several tries he managed to step onto the walkway, stopping in the open doorway of the saloon, swaying and almost losing his balance as he blinked into the dimness of the interior.

"Jack Hunter, you old bastard," the man shouted, his voice carrying down the street. "Is that really you? I ain't seen your ugly face since prison." With a whoop, he lurched inside.

Matt's first thought was that he'd been right about where he would find his father. His second was to wonder why in the devil Juliana had perked up at the man's words.

And why was she striding with sudden determination toward the saloon? Behind her he watched a second figure emerge from the lawyer's office. What was Edmund Montgomery doing there? He must have been present during Juliana's visit. The office had no back door.

Somehow he couldn't picture stepfather and stepdaughter having a tearful reunion. Maybe they were scrapping over whatever Iona Montgomery had left behind. He pushed the idea from his mind. He couldn't picture the woman he'd talked to yesterday engaging in such a squabble.

He could be wrong. He did not know her very well.

That became even clearer when the very dignified, sophisticated Widow Rains stepped carefully across the street, onto the walkway and, with only an instant's hesitation, into the saloon. It was the last place in Diablo she ought to be visiting. Maybe, like her mother, she was a tippler. Nope, that couldn't be it. If she was, she'd drink brandy or sherry from a crystal decanter in the privacy of her home.

He knew what had drawn her there. Jack Hunter, current owner of the land that had once been her father's pride and joy. At the best of times, Jack was trouble. Drunk, he would be impossible.

With a shake of his head, thinking he ought to be running the other way, Matt followed Juliana into the saloon.

Chapter Six

Unnoticed, Juliana stepped into the shadows of the saloon, breathing in the stale, smoky air. Only a few feet away, Jack Hunter leaned against the bar, his lined face bristled, gray-streaked hair ill combed, his clothes loose-fitting on his once powerful frame. He had aged, Juliana thought, far more than the ten years since she'd seen him.

Prison had taken its toll. But, no doubt, so had the memory of killing his wife. Talking with him, dealing with him, would not be easy. But she had no choice.

Beside him, his back to her, stood the stranger who had hailed him from outside.

"Here I thought I was without a friend in this godforsaken town," the stranger was saying. "I'd forgotten you came from these parts. When'd you get out? It was after me."

Juliana could not hear Jack's muffled reply.

The stranger dragged a dirty sleeve across his mouth. "Picked up a thirst, I did. How about buying a fellow convict a drink?"

She read the dismay on Jack's face. He gestured toward the bartender, a portly man who, after a brief hesitation, poured the stranger a shot of whiskey. He downed it fast, then set the glass heavily on the worn wooden bar.

"We was jail buddies for a time, old Jack and me," he said to the bartender, loud enough for anyone in the saloon to hear. "He's the best one I ever had. I ain't keepin' it a secret. I've had more'n a few."

That was clearly Jack's cue to buy another drink. Impatient, Juliana stepped out of the shadows into the Lone Star's murky light.

Jack caught sight of her right away. Unfortunately, everyone else in the saloon did so at the same time. The place had been noisy, filled with the sounds of a dozen gamblers and drinkers slouched at the tables. No more. They sat mutely now, watchful, eyes on her, waiting for a show to begin. The stairway at the side of the room led up to a railed landing, at the back of which were several closed doors. Two women stood by the rail, silently staring down at her. Juliana began to question whether invading the Lone Star had been a good idea.

"What the hell are you doing here?" Jack growled.

She started, then realized he was looking past her. She glanced over her shoulder. Matt Hunter filled the doorway. His face was in shadow, but there was no mistaking the tall, lean, long-legged man for anyone else. No one could stand in a doorway quite like Matt. No one could steal her breath quite so fast.

But that didn't mean she was glad to see him. Without saying a word, he seemed to be criticizing her for being where she was. He could criticize all he wanted. There was no notice under the Lone Star sign saying *No women allowed*, no similar message over the bar. Considering the looks she was getting from everyone but the Hunters, she figured women were welcome.

Matt gave her a curt nod, then looked at his father. The air between them crackled as they stared at one another in cold assessment, without warmth, more like enemies than father and son.

Juliana felt the tension, and for a moment it became hers, too, a sick feeling that real trouble was here and not about to go away.

These were Hunters, she reminded herself, part of a family torn by problems as serious as any she faced. She was here for one purpose and one purpose only. Caught between them though she was, she must not get involved; she must not care.

"We need to step outside," Matt said, a flick of his eyes in Juliana's direction bringing her into the *we*. Though he wore his hat low on his forehead, she could see the look he gave her. Her stomach tightened. She wasn't afraid of him. So why did he shake her so?

"I don't need you telling me what to do," Jack snarled. "You want to run along with the little lady, you do just that. I'm having a drink with my old buddy here."

As proof, he gestured to the bartender for another round.

But his son wasn't done with him. "You don't even know his name."

"Sure I do. It's Joe."

"Harry," the stranger corrected.

Jack ignored him. "Set him up with another drink," he said to the bartender. "And pour one for me."

Juliana could hold her silence no longer. "Mr. Hunter," she said, "you and I have to talk."

Jack looked from her to his son, then back to her. "You two working together?"

"No," Juliana said hurriedly.

"Maybe," Matt said.

Jack shook his head in disgust. "Get your stories straight. Naw, just get the hell out of here." He turned back to the bar and tossed down his waiting shot. "You sure are letting a bunch of riffraff in these days," he said to the bartender.

Juliana could not be so easily deterred. If only Matt weren't here, stirring up his father, this might be easier. But nothing was going to come easy to her now. Those days were gone. Silently wishing him away, fighting a rising dismay that was close to alarm, she took a couple of steps deeper into the saloon, the only sounds the swish of her skirt and the pounding of her heart.

"Mr. Hunter," she said, "I came in here to talk about my father's ranch."

"No such place around here anymore." He looked at the bartender. "You ever hear of one, O'Malley?" The bartender shook his head.

Juliana bit back a retort, struggling to keep her tone reasonable. Where the Hunters were concerned, being reasonable was hard.

"All right, the part of the Half-Moon that was once the Sullivan ranch."

Jack licked his lips, catching the last taste of whiskey. "Fine piece of land. Got it real cheap."

"I want to buy it."

She tried to talk softly, keeping the offer between just the two of them. But she felt dozens of eyes on her. And she felt the presence of the man at her back.

"It ain't for sale," Jack snarled.

"I'll double what you paid."

That stirred some talk. She ignored the buzz.

"You hard of hearing? I said it ain't for sale."

She took a deep breath. "Triple. But that's it." She wasn't sure if it really was, but she had to call a halt to this absurdity sometime.

The offer brought more buzz, more stirring.

"Juliana," Matt said behind her, "let it go."

He didn't understand. He didn't feel her desperation. That land was hers by birthright, no matter who held the deed.

Harry, Jack's onetime jail mate, let out a crude snort. "Damned if you ain't the luckiest one, Jack. Get ten years for murder when most men woulda been hanged from the nearest tree, and now here's a purty little lady throwin' money at you. Don't that deserve another drink?"

At that point Matt got into the action. Stepping around Juliana, he took Harry by the collar, slapping a hand on one arm, and turned him from his father.

"It's time you left."

"See here—"

"What we've got," Matt said, ignoring the protest, "is a private conversation going on. As I said, it's time to be moving on." He thrust a folded greenback into Harry's shirt pocket. "There's a restaurant across the street. Get yourself some grub. I'd be much obliged."

He spoke politely, all the while shifting the man around Juliana and toward the door. Harry wasn't small, but Matt moved him like a stuffed toy. He also wasn't giving him much choice about leaving.

The man's protests outside the saloon soon died, leaving Juliana and the Hunter men staring at one another. Matt's eyes cut into her; Jack studied her with a smirk.

Juliana concentrated on Jack.

"Mr. Hunter, let's be frank here. You need the money. I need the land. It's a fair exchange."

There she went, she thought with instant regret, stomping on a man's pride again.

Jack spat on the floor. "I ain't the fool folks think I am," he said, talking loud, letting everyone in the saloon hear. Then he sneered at Matt. "That's something for you t' think about, son." All the scorn in the world was in that *son*.

His gaze shifted back to Juliana.

"And as for you, missy, you got money, all right. You married a rich old man, probably drove him to his grave, and then you have the nerve to come in here being Miss High and Mighty after all these years." His eyes narrowed. "Where were you when your ma was dying?"

He might as well have stabbed her in the heart. She gasped, unable to come up with a reply.

Jack stumbled toward her, drunker than she'd thought, but his drunkenness didn't ease the crushing wound of his words.

"That's it," Matt said, "we're leaving," but she was too stunned to move.

A gambler from the nearest table threw himself into the situation.

"Jack, take it easy," the man said. "And as for you, little lady . . . you got money, I've got land to sell." Pushing himself out of his chair, he headed for her. "Come sit a spell and we'll talk about it. I always like talkin' with a pretty gal."

"That-a-way, Ned," a voice called from out in the saloon. "When you get finished, pass her on back."

A few catcalls rang out, along with ugly laughter. Ned grabbed her by the arm at the same instant Jack fell against her, and the next thing she knew, she was on the floor with the two men in a tangle of skirt and trousers, Matt hovering over them, throwing out swear words she'd never heard.

Somewhere in the smoke, someone yelled, "Hot damn, we got us a fight."

Struggling to stand, Juliana couldn't get her feet under her. Matt took care of that, lifting her as if she weighed no more than a kitten, tossing her over his shoulder and heading for the door, leaving behind the whooping crowd.

Outside, he didn't stop until he was standing by her carriage in front of the lawyer's office. With little more gentleness than he had demonstrated when he picked her up, he set her on the ground, staring at her from under the brim of his black hat. How he'd managed to keep it on, she couldn't imagine. She realized he could get more fury in his eyes than any man she'd ever known.

If Juliana had been a meeker woman, she would have trembled at that fury. Instead, gathering her wits about her, she glared right back.

"How dare you," she hissed.

"I dare a hell of a lot more than that." He shook his head in disgust. "There's quite a fight going on in that saloon. Want me to toss you back inside?"

Matt Hunter had a maddening way of keeping calm at the same time as her temper blew. Silently she counted to three. It was as far as she got before exploding again.

"What I want is for you to stay away from me." She brushed at her skirt. "Everything would have been fine if you hadn't come in and riled your father."

"Jack was drunk." The venom in his voice stopped her for a second, but he kept on. "He wasn't up to serious negotiation. Except with a whiskey bottle."

"Once I determined that, I would have left and caught him at a better time" she said.

"He's not a kind man. He doesn't have a better time. And what the hell were you thinking, going into the Lone Star?"

"I went in to speak to your father about a private matter." She blew at a stray lock of hair that had worked its way from beneath her bonnet. "Surely you heard what I said."

"All of Diablo probably knows by now. You've got more money than good sense. Back there in the saloon was just a taste of the kind of trouble that'll bring you."

She waved a hand in disgust. "This is getting us nowhere. Now if you'll kindly go away—"

Gunshots from the saloon stopped her. A pair of brawling men fell through the open doors and rolled onto the street.

Muttering under his breath, Matt picked her up none too gently and placed her inside the carriage, then pulled himself up beside her. With a slap of the reins, he guided the horse into the street and away from the saloon.

"What do you think you're doing?" She was practically yelling.

"Getting you out of town."

"What if I don't want to go?"

"I don't imagine you do. You're not acting real smart right now."

He reined to a halt in front of the general store, growled an order for her to stay where she was, and hopped from the carriage. She peered around and watched in dismay as he hitched his horse to the rear.

He was back in half a minute, once again slapping reins.

"What about your father?" she said. "He's back there where the shooting's going on, or have you forgotten?"

"Jack can take care of himself."

He spoke flatly, his jaw set, his eyes straight

ahead. Matt Hunter was a stubborn man, not Juliana's favorite kind.

She settled back in the carriage. Angry, frustrated, upset over the land, she admitted to herself that getting out of town wasn't such a bad thing. But she would walk to the Lazy Q before letting Matt know.

Tossing his hat at his feet, he ran a hand through his hair and concentrated on the road ahead. He acted as if he abducted women every day. For all she knew, maybe he did.

They'd gone no more than a mile when her anger began to ease, and she remembered Jack's hateful words.

Where were you when your ma was dying?

Where indeed. Her eyes burned with tears she could not shed, not until she was alone. Jack Hunter had asked nothing she had not asked herself a hundred times. Only he had asked the question openly, where the world could hear, reminding anyone of her neglect, of her sin. It was as though she'd been disrobed in public, all her flaws and weaknesses exposed.

In her planned visits to Diablo, she'd wanted to hear gossip about her mother. Now she herself would be the topic of that gossip. The irony of it was more than she could bear.

If she'd hoped to slip into town, ask discreet questions, absorbing rumors or whatever she could learn, gratefully thanking those who could

107

help her, those who would tell her what she needed to know, that hope was dead now.

Somehow Edmund Montgomery had mistreated his wife, or at the least had allowed her illness to go untreated. The discrepancy between the years of cheerful communication from her mother and that last rambling, frightening letter told Juliana so. But proving it was going to be harder than she'd imagined.

In her first skirmish with her stepfather—though they had yet to face one another—Edmund had won.

The ride to the ranch took a lifetime. Juliana and Matt spoke little, except once when he halted the carriage beside the road and asked if she needed to get behind a bush.

"No," she said, unwilling to admit that she did, and even more unwilling to show gratitude for his concern. It was a foolish consideration, but she couldn't help herself. She might not be her own worst enemy at the moment, but she was also not her own best friend.

Matt Hunter would never understand her situation, one that went beyond her current quest, her public humiliation. All her life she had been under the supervision of other people—her parents, her grandparents, her husband, all older, all very much in authority. After she was widowed, able at last to make her own decisions, she had remained in Saratoga. In doing so, she had made a mistake. And now she was here to make amends.

Thus far she'd handled matters so poorly she could hardly contemplate it. And look at her now, captive in her own carriage, sitting much too close to a good-looking rascal—an overbearing rascal at that—wearing leather the color of his skin, a white shirt, a red bandana at his throat, nothing newly purchased, all of it showing signs of long use. Including the strong hands on the reins.

Sure of himself, scornful of his father, he was everything she was not.

He hopped out and headed for a stand of trees. When he emerged, he took what she considered a slow stroll getting back to the carriage, casting his dark gaze around as if he saw things she couldn't see.

"This is good land," he said when he settled in beside her. He spoke as if they'd been considering the pros and cons of the Texas hill country over the past few miles. Instead, she had bitten her tongue a dozen times to keep quiet, trying to sit upright in a carriage that, despite its expensive springs, kept jostling her against him.

He had hard shoulders, powerful hands; everything about him was strong and capable. She almost wanted to touch him more, to talk to him, to find out what was behind that hard, enigmatic character he showed the world. His comment about the land was the first sign of softness in him she'd ever seen.

Glad to think of something else besides his presence, and her own miserable state of affairs, she looked where he had looked, at the rolling hills, the shrubs, the oak trees growing stubbornly out of the rocky soil. There was good grassland tucked in those hills, along with a web of shallow creeks, both a boon to the early travelers who had forged the trail.

She liked the ruggedness of the landscape, so different from her husband's home back East. Not long ago, Comanches roamed these hills, and pioneers headed west across them, people with dreams, people running away. Even today, a hundred years after the beginning of the nation, this portion of it was barely civilized, very much like the man beside her, hard and uncompromising, enticing and forbidding, bearing scars of a violent past.

Matt might never admit to the scars, but he had them. Otherwise he could not hate his father as he did. She could not judge him. There was no disputing what his father had done.

The sun was halfway down the western sky when he reined the carriage onto the narrower lane leading to the Lazy Q. She had not yet managed to put her influence on the ranch, the land, the house, to make them feel truly and rightfully hers. But she had to. She had to take away its shabbiness, the atmosphere of having been abandoned. Her reason was simple. She had no place else to call home.

Whatever sympathetic understanding she had directed toward the man beside her, it evaporated when he reined the carriage to a halt at the back of the house, close to the barn.

In the shadows, the air was cool. She rubbed at the silk sleeves of her gown.

"You should have worn a coat." He said it critically, as if the ride with her had been no more than an unwelcome chore. She blushed to remember what she'd been thinking about him.

Why tell him she had meant to wear that coat? In a rush to get to town, she'd left it hanging on the hall tree by the front door.

Jumping down from the carriage, he looked around him, at the house that needed paint, at the eaves requiring repair, at the hard-packed, weedy ground. Last, he looked back at her sitting above him in her fine silk dress which should have been covered by wool.

"You're going back East, aren't you? I don't think you'll make it out here."

In that instant, with him repudiating all she'd been thinking, all she truly wanted, the Lazy Q became home for sure, the best one in the world, the only place for her. Anger was pushing her into the knowledge, but a sense of rightness was helping her accept it as the truth.

"I'll make it, all right, Mr. Hunter. I was born in Texas, in case you've forgotten, and I'll be buried in its soil."

"With the way you're behaving, that could be sooner than you're planning. Don't count on me being around all the time to rescue you."

She gave up on getting the last word. Ignoring his extended hand, she got out of the carriage on her own. She made sure her shoulder didn't brush against his as she hurried around him. They had touched one another more than enough on the ride from town.

"Don't spend any time worrying about me," she said. "I'll be fine. No, better than fine, if I don't have to deal with Hunters more than once a decade."

Without a backward glance, she hurried inside the house, waiting in the kitchen for the sound of his departure before going out to tend the carriage horse. What she heard was something far different, the noise of his unhitching the horse himself. Opening the back door a crack, she watched as he led both her animal and his to the water trough, then set them out in the corral to graze. He moved quickly, deliberately, taking care of the chores in short order. When he headed for the house, she closed the door and backed away. What did he think he was doing?

What he did was open the door and walk right inside, crossing the room in a couple of strides and taking her by the shoulders.

"Here's one Hunter you're going to have to deal with, Mrs. Rains. You forgot to thank me. I'm giving you another chance."

Before she could yelp or scream or fight, he bent his head and covered her lips with his own.

Chapter Seven

Matt meant to kiss her fast and leave. Juliana Rains was far too much of a temptation, sitting beside him the way she had for the past two hours, their shoulders touching, her fine womanly body a constant distraction, the tilt of her head defiant and yet somehow vulnerable.

Out in the open he hadn't smelled sage the way he usually did; he'd breathed in the flowery sweetness of her.

Whoa, boy, he'd had to tell himself when the old urges built in him. He already had enough complications in his life without adding her.

But how was he to know she had the sweetest lips he'd ever tasted? That beneath his hands he would feel the life throbbing in her, feel it flow into him, stirring up serious needs he hadn't experienced in a long time?

She tried to twist away, but she didn't try hard

and she didn't try long. If she did, tough as it would be, he'd let her go. But she didn't, and he began exploring her with his tongue. Her mouth was wet and warm, her lips soft. He couldn't stop himself from holding her tight against him, feeling her breasts against his chest, remembering the tiny waist and flare of hips beneath the rustling green silk dress.

Somewhere in the kissing and touching and feeling, they both went wild. His hands slipped easily down the fabric of her gown, cupping her breasts against his palms. Her waist, her hips, her thighs—he explored them all, wanting to know everything about her at once. In response, she gripped his arms, then stroked his neck, tugging at the bandana before trailing her fingers across his face and burying them in his hair.

He moaned in pleasure, she cried out softly, both of them steaming, breathing hard though they refused to break the kiss. The built-up tension of the past years exploded within him. He needed release. He needed her now, here, on the floor, the table, anywhere he could get her.

The last thought brought him to his senses. What was he doing? What was he doing to her? He broke the kiss and held her close, his body aching with need. Oh, yes, she was a temptation, the most compelling one he could remember.

She trembled against him, then suddenly pushed him away, one hand pressed to her lips as if to suppress a scream. Her amber eyes stared up at him, not with passion but with horror. For just a moment he wondered what her married life must have been like.

"What have I done?" she whispered, more to herself than to him.

Matt took a deep, slow breath. "You didn't do it alone."

"But I never . . . I . . . I don't . . ." She broke off, floundering.

She looked lost, afraid, a wild animal caught in a trap. What the hell had she thought was happening? Matt cut back his irritation. He knew the answer: Like him, she wasn't thinking at all. He wasn't much of a gentleman—far from it—but he couldn't let her go on. Wanting to strangle her, he also wanted to hold her gently, to tell her that nothing had really happened, nothing to bring her real harm.

At the moment, with the wild light in her amber eyes, he figured she'd prefer the strangling. He'd never seen someone so close to panic. Crazy. A moment ago she'd been ready to take off her clothes.

"Under ordinary circumstances, maybe you don't," he said sharply, knowing it was like a slap in the face, "but today, Juliana, you did. Almost."

"You bastard."

That was better. She was getting control.

"You're not the first to notice," he said.

"Get out of here."

He looked around. Everything about the kitchen seemed cold, sterile, unlived in. He studied her, the bonnet inadequate for the Texas sun, the golden hair that had pulled loose from its confines, the full lips moist and swollen from the moment's kiss. And those strange, beautiful eyes. She looked stubborn, angry, defiant, hardly a woman who'd been probing him with her tongue only a minute ago.

But she also looked unprotected, alone, needy in ways even she might not realize. He was thinking a little crazy himself, but he knew he was right, though he couldn't have said how or why. She was a woman with troubles that went beyond a need for sex.

In that, they were alike.

"Are you going to be all right?"

"I'll be fine as soon as you're gone."

He gave her a two-finger salute. "I do like to give a woman what she wants."

Without waiting for a response, he gave her what neither of them really wanted. Hard as it was to do so, he left.

Juliana stood in the suddenly tomblike kitchen and listened for the sound of Matt Hunter riding away. It took him a few minutes to get his horse from the corral. She didn't move, she didn't let herself think until she heard the pounding of hooves on the hard-packed ground. Only then did she make her way upstairs to her bedroom.

Sitting on the side of the bed, she touched her lips. She could still taste him. She could smell the aura of the outdoors that hung on him, could feel his arms around her, could feel the power of his embrace. In the past minutes something new had happened to her; a driving force had erupted from deep within, like steam compressed far too long without release.

She had never been more afraid, not of him but of herself. What almost took place on the kitchen floor was wrong, all wrong—the timing, the baseness, the immorality. But, oh, the lingering taste and scent and feel taunted her with a primal urgency that she could not dismiss with any amount of rationalization. She had wanted him. Alone, ashamed, she still did.

Could he possibly understand the depth of that want, the fierceness of it? And how could she ever face him again?

She struggled for sanity, forcing herself to recall all that had happened today, from the visit to Sam Larkin to the brawl in the saloon and the long ride home. It had been a day of frustration, of futility, of public shame. Despite it all, inevitably her thoughts returned to Matt's kiss. It wasn't the most important moment of the day, yet it was the moment that lingered in her mind.

Never in all their years of marriage had Harlan

kissed her like that. Early on, he'd told her she was too young, too inexperienced to arouse him, forcing him to seek relief in the arms of whores.

Their lovemaking—hardly an accurate term to describe what they did in bed—was perfunctory. During the act itself, he frequently hurt her. When she tried to draw away, he claimed the pain was her fault. "You're supposed to be wet," he told her. She'd hardly understood what he meant. Years later, her understanding had begun.

Matt. She buried her face in her hands, wishing away the sting of shame in her cheeks. He should not have invaded her kitchen, should not have touched her, most certainly should not have kissed her. She was honest enough to admit that after the first few seconds, he'd done nothing she hadn't wanted him to do. Worst of all, she'd let him know it.

"Oh, Mama," she said to the empty room, "is that how Edmund made you feel?"

The idea, coming out of nowhere, repulsed her. But it would not go away. If Iona had experienced anything like the brief, mindless passion of her daughter, her second marriage became a little more understandable. Not right, never that. But understandable.

Enough, Juliana told herself. A woman could go through only so much self-flagellation in one day. Changing from the green silk to a plain black gown, she hurried out to the corral to see that the carriage horse had been properly taken care of. And to stroke her beloved Pepper's neck and tell the mare about her day. Naturally, she left out a few parts. The mare might not be so innocent anymore, but there were some things Juliana had to keep to herself.

Kane watched the mistress of the Lazy Q as she talked to her horse. He'd already decided she was a little tetched, expecting him to handle all the chores. She didn't say much to him, or complain, but he had a pretty good idea what was on her mind. It would take a half dozen men working dawn to dusk to get the place anywhere near in shape to be called a working ranch.

Kane didn't work that hard for anyone or anything, and it didn't matter how much money Edmund Montgomery was slipping to him over and beyond his Lazy Q pay. Besides, he was supposed to be creating trouble. That was work enough for him, and a job he enjoyed. He was good at it. He figured a man ought to feel good about what he did. It wasn't his fault the Hunters kept fighting back.

Juliana Rains was a different situation. He didn't figure she'd have their spirit or their luck.

What he needed to tell Montgomery, though, was that something was going on between her and Matt Hunter. If Matt wasn't already poking it to her, he would be soon. Damn. Hunters had all the luck.

Leaving the barn, he waved in the direction of the corral, then slowly made his way to the carriage. Fancy new rig, expensive, leather seats. But the undercarriage would be like most buggies, a little stronger maybe, built to take the jolts on Texas roads.

But that didn't mean it couldn't be fooled with. An axle was an axle, he figured. A man who knew how to weaken one of them would know how to weaken them all. And Kane knew. As soon as Montgomery gave the word, he'd be applying his skills to this one.

He chuckled to himself as he pushed the smooth-rolling carriage toward the barn. He didn't give a damn about mending fences. Mending anything, to tell the truth. He preferred breaking things down. Pulling wings off flies, which he'd done as a child.

He didn't fool with flies now. He liked pulling people apart. People with land, people with money, people who thought they were better than anybody else.

People like Juliana Rains.

Chapter Eight

Matt devoted the next couple of days to Dark Champion, working him in one of the Half-Moon's distant pastures, establishing a rapport, letting him know who was boss. Horses were social animals, even a cussedly independent one like DC. Isolated from the herd, he had no choice but to depend on his human owner for companionship, sidling up to him in the field, letting human fingers rub his nose and scratch behind his ears.

The riding went even better. Matt never let DC open up completely. Instead, reining back on the stallion's tremendous power, he cantered and loped about the countryside, going on instinct, figuring the horse, like the man, had to get used to being in Texas.

Having a horse as his only company suited Matt just fine. He bunked with the men, stayed away from the ranch house, and except for a couple of distant waves in Brent's direction when he was heading out to the pasture, avoided all members of the Hunter clan.

If he thought of anyone at all, it was Juliana. She and her mare were the topic of several conversations he had with DC. The stallion was a good listener. He never disagreed.

"Women," Matt said the first day as he was grooming the horse; "they do unsettle a man."

He thought of one particular woman who'd curled herself in his arms. DC bobbed his head.

"Take Pepper, for example. There we were riding along, all peaceable like, and the next thing you know, the wind shifts and you're kicking that poor trailer to hell and gone."

DC laid back his ears. It could have been because Matt was scratching them at the time, but maybe not.

"Then there's her mistress, a contrary female if I ever saw one. Looking all delicate and dainty, then strolling into the Lone Star like she went there for a shot of whiskey every day."

Juliana hadn't seemed particularly delicate or dainty when the two of them had been alone in her kitchen. She'd been all woman. Holding her in his arms, he'd felt a power that might equal DC's if it ever got totally unleashed.

He didn't dwell on the details of what might happen; he also didn't let himself consider who might do the unleashing. He couldn't be the one. He had a plan, but when it was over, he figured he'd be moving on. At heart he was a rambler and a rover, an outcast to those who knew him best. Or thought they did.

Still, Juliana Rains hung on in his mind.

Over those two days Matt was generally feeling good about things, as good as he ever felt. Trouble started when he shifted the stallion to the field where a herd of Half-Moon horses were grazing. There were two dozen of them, mixed breeds, a few mustangs, mostly mares and geldings. And one other thoroughbred stallion. The racehorse Jack had bragged about that first day in the barn.

That night in the bunkhouse Curly had elaborated.

"Fancy Dancer's his name. Your pa bought him off a man drifting through, or so the story goes. Me, I try to stay out of matters don't concern me."

"Good thinking," Matt had said. "But I'll bet you tonight's supper Edmund Montgomery supplied the money."

Curly had been around the Half-Moon for as long as Matt could remember. He didn't try to deny he was privy to a fact or two.

"You'd win the biscuits, that's for sure, and welcome to 'em. Since Miss Abby took our cook away, Hank ain't quite got the hang of makin' 'em."

Under his breath, Matt muttered a few curse words at Montgomery. His father had done no more than he himself had, buying a racehorse to help out the ranch, but Matt had paid with cash he'd earned with hard sweat. Jack had gone to his old buddy the banker, the one who had already tried to foreclose on his land.

"It caused a mite of trouble between your pa and your brother," Curly added. "Now that's all I'm saying."

It was enough, although on subsequent nights Matt learned Jack had raced the animal twice and won. True to form, his father had also spent the winnings in town, buying rounds of drinks at the saloon.

When Matt let Dark Champion into the pasture, the trouble came right away. Fancy Dancer, a fine-looking chestnut, lifted his head, nostrils flared, ears back, declaring war on the newcomer.

DC ignored him, turning instead to an unoccupied few square yards in the field. Dancer was not about to be ignored. He made right for DC. Confronted, Matt's stallion was not a horse to back down, and he held his ground. As the horses faced one another, the challenge was clear. Only one of them could be dominant in the herd. Fancy Dancer did not want his position of authority usurped. The other horses backed away, shifting nervously, as if they knew a fight was about to take place. Sitting astride the gelding he'd used before he left the country, Matt could do little but watch.

DC's dominance did not come right away. It took some baring of lips and showing of teeth, some shifting around of the hindquarters, letting the chestnut know he was ready to bite and kick, letting all the horses know he was the more aggressive of the two stallions.

DC and Fancy Dancer circled one another, ears back and necks extended, snorting and squealing, kicking up grass and dirt. The air smelled of horse and fight. Matt's gelding shifted skittishly and Matt had to hold tight to the reins. This wasn't an idle dust-up, one male strutting himself before another. A horse, especially the racing kind, had to keep his confidence, otherwise he'd be letting other horses pass him by.

The scene was one of battle, although other than brushing shoulders a couple of times, the stallions did not actually touch. Just when Matt thought teeth and hooves were to be put into play, Fancy Dancer backed away and, as if nothing had happened, began cropping grass twenty yards from the victorious DC. Matt sat back in the saddle and grinned. It was more emotion than DC showed. The English horse trotted to another part of the field and, like the loser, turned his full attention to eating.

Changes among the other horses were subtle, mostly a shifting toward parts of the field closer to DC. If hard times came, instinct told them, he was the one to lead them to food or water or safety, whatever was needed for their survival.

DC himself gave no sign he noticed them. Instead, he kept cropping grass, lifting his head every now and then to stare about the landscape, as if reminding himself of his whereabouts. Whether he was contented or not at his new home, Matt had no clue.

That evening, while Matt was in the stable rubbing down the gelding, trouble came again, this time from a far more usual source: Jack Hunter entered the barn cussing. Right behind him trotted the ugliest dog Matt had ever seen, the lop-eared, mangy mutt that had chased the cat into the barn on Matt's first night back.

"Fine dog you got there," he said without stopping the rubbing.

"Cat ain't mine," Jack growled.

"Cat?" Matt asked.

"Short for Catfish. Abby gave him to me as some kind of joke. He's a bottom feeder for sure. And don't change the subject."

Matt took off his gloves and tossed them aside, then turned to face his father. Like DC, he wasn't interested in a fight, but also like DC, he wouldn't run away from one.

"You lost me. What subject?"

"That damned horse of yours. What'd he do to Dancer?"

"He introduced himself, that's all."

"What kind of animal did you bring back to the ranch?" Jack didn't wait for an answer. "I ride out to bring Dancer in, and he's off by himself, like he was ashamed or something. Damned animal wouldn't come when I whistled."

He went on to describe rounding him up and bringing him to the corral. The longer he talked, the redder his face became and the wilder his gestures. By the time he stopped, he was sprinkling curse words liberally among his comments.

Matt took it as long as he could. Grabbing up his hat and coat, he walked slowly and deliberately toward his father, facing him straight on.

Jack watched him carefully but held his ground, a bent man far too old in appearance for his years. There was a mean and hateful light in his eyes. Matt should have been shaken by the hate, but he'd grown tough through the years, always knowing how his father felt about him. Too, he could smell the whiskey on his breath. When he was drunk, Jack Hunter was capable of almost anything. He'd proven that ten years ago.

"What I did, Jack, was try to save your sorry hide. This ranch is about to go under, or don't you have the good sense to know it?"

"That's no concern of yours. The Half-Moon does not belong to you and never has. Get your ass off my land pronto." He swayed and there was spittle on his lips, but his voice was as strong as ever. And as full of rage. "If I find you on it again," he growled, "I'll give my men the order to shoot."

Matt stared at his father long and hard. Here it was, the final break. He should have felt something—anger, pain, desolation. But all he felt was the inevitability of what his father had just done. Matt's problem was he hadn't seen it coming.

Settling his hat low over his eyes, tossing his coat over his shoulder, he smiled at his father. "I was told you thought I'd stay in England. I guess I should have. It's for damned sure I've never had a home here."

Stepping away from Jack, he made for the front of the barn. Brent was blocking the way, and behind him stood his wife, Crystal.

"He's drunk, Matt," Brent said. "He'd just about given up the bottle, but over the last few days he's been hitting it pretty hard. Ignore him."

"He's not so drunk he doesn't know what he's saying."

Brent looked ready to argue, then shook his head. "What are you going to do?"

"Get off Jack's land. I wouldn't want you

shooting at me, Brother. Your aim's too good."

Crystal stepped up beside her husband and held onto his arm. "You can't go," she said, her blue eyes wide and moist and sincere. "You're my brother, too, as much as you are Brent's, and I need you here."

Brent covered her hand with his. "She's right, Matt."

"No offense, Crystal," Matt said, "but you're both wrong. With the baby coming, you don't need me around stirring things up. That's what I do. It's what I'm good at. Ask Brent. I bought Dark Champion with my own money, so I'll be taking him with me. Jack's right. I don't have anything else around here I can claim as my own. I'm donating the wagon and mules to the Half-Moon. Consider them payment for my grub."

Without a backward glance, he headed toward the bunkhouse to gather his few belongings, including the saddle he used when he rode DC. After that, he would be leaving the Half-Moon Ranch with its ugly memories and unsettled troubles for the final time.

And where was he going? For the first time he wasn't in the mood to travel west, to roam and pick up jobs where he could, living with strangers, most often being by himself. But what was his choice?

An idea occurred, a really crazy idea, way beyond most of what he'd come up with lately. And it wouldn't go away. Matt could almost laugh at himself. Hadn't he always been a little crazy in the head? Growing older, he wasn't changing; he was becoming more of what he'd always been.

Juliana awoke early, expecting to welcome the woman she'd hired to serve as housekeeper and cook. That first day in town she'd bought supplies, but things were about running out. The woman was supposed to bring a big order from the general store.

But she didn't hear the woman outside her bedroom window. Instead, a far too familiar voice drifted into the room from the corral.

What could Matt Hunter possibly be doing at the Lazy Q? There was only one way to find out: Go down and ask.

She dressed quickly, taking time to pin back her hair, then hurried down to the kitchen. Someone had put on coffee, and she could smell biscuits baking in the oven. Unless a cooking angel had drifted down to help out her pitiful attempts, she could think of only two humans who could have done so. Since she doubted Kane would go out of his way for his own mother, that left Matt.

Which meant he had been in her house while she was upstairs alone and asleep. How dare he? But then she remembered the last time he had been in her house, in her kitchen, standing about where she was now. Matt Hunter dared a great deal.

Slamming out the back door, her heart beating much too fast, she made for the corral. He was standing with his back to her, a crop in his left hand, hat pushed to the back of his head, his attention directed to the stallion Dark Champion. She stopped for a second and felt a funny twist in her stomach.

Juliana wanted to shake herself. Just because Matt looked as good from the rear as he did from the front was no reason for her to feel anything but irritation. He was a man and he was a Hunter. She shouldn't let him affect her so.

The trouble was, he kept getting in her way, inserting himself in her life. What was she supposed to do? Ignoring him was out of the question.

She was halfway to the fence when he turned to look at her. For a moment that was all he did, and she could do nothing but look right back. With his dark, chiseled face and penetrating eyes, he looked lean and lost, she thought, stopping in place. Then she wondered how she could have come up with such an assessment. If there had been anything lost in his expression, it was gone now. Rather, he looked as if he were challenging her to some kind of confrontation.

Remember the coffee and the biscuits, she told herself. She would confront him, all right, but she would do it genteelly. She would keep her control.

He thumbed his hat, which she supposed was gentlemanly for him.

"Good morning, Mrs. Rains," he said. "I guess you're not much of an early riser."

Since the sun had barely cleared the horizon, she figured she was up early enough.

"What are you doing in my corral?" she snapped.

So much for gentility.

"Working with DC here. You want us out? We can oblige."

"That's not what I said."

"So we can stay."

"I didn't say that either. I want to know why you're here practically at dawn. And why you made coffee and biscuits."

"No one else did. And the corral wasn't being used."

He spoke matter-of-factly, as if explaining everything.

Before she could respond, he set down the crop at the edge of the corral, pulled off his gloves and dropped them by the crop, then leapt over the fence with an ease and grace no man had the right to possess. To her surprise, he walked past her with a one-word explanation: "Biscuits."

Stopping to wash up at the pump, he strode

through the back door. Having no choice, she followed him inside. As if he owned the place, he grabbed a towel and removed the biscuits from the oven, set the pan on the table, then grabbed a couple of plates from one of the cabinets, along with two cups. He poured the coffee, put everything beside the biscuits, then turned to the stove.

"You got any eggs? Ham? Bacon?"

Without her saying a word, he found the last of the eggs in the icebox and cracked them into a pan. Within a few minutes, he was dishing them up onto the plates.

"I can take mine outside if you don't want to eat with the help."

Juliana rubbed at her temples. "The help?"

"I won't charge much. Mostly a roof over my head and some grub. Which I'll fix if you need me to, but I've run out of things I can cook. You might grow tired of biscuits and eggs every meal."

Juliana sat down hard beside the table. "You're out of your mind."

"I've been called worse things than crazy. But I'm honest and hardworking. And it's plain to a blind man you need someone to do some work around here. I need a place to stay for a while. Seems like a good trade for us both."

"What about the Half-Moon?"

He'd been speaking almost jocularly. At her

question, it seemed as if a curtain came down on him, blocking out his light. Suddenly she realized that for all his good spirits of a moment ago, there had been a tension to him he was barely holding under control.

"Let's just leave it that I need a place to stay. I earn my keep. I always have, at least for the past ten years. I don't plan to stop doing so now."

She pushed her chair away from the table and stood. "No. It's out of the question."

"I won't touch you again, if that's what you're afraid of."

The blood rose fast in Juliana's face. "Mr. Hunter, that was a terrible thing to say."

"Okay then, I will touch you."

She stared grimly at him. "Do you get your face slapped often?"

"No."

"It ought to be slapped now."

His eyes narrowed, and she knew he was recalling particulars about their last time together in the kitchen. She was recalling them, too.

"To slap me, you'd have to touch me," he said in that soft way he had that still managed to be all man. "I guess maybe that's what you want after all."

What Juliana wanted was not to have to look at Matt, not to listen to him, not to remember the way he had taken her in his arms and kissed her. The remembering had haunted her for the past days. And nights, too, even more than the days. Now here he was standing a few feet away making the memory all the sharper.

"Get out," she said.

"Sure thing."

She stared at him in surprise. Ejecting him could not be so easy. She found out right away it wasn't.

"I'll take my grub out back and give you time to think over my offer. Eat your food while it's warm. Then come on out and give me the word. There's lots of things I want to get to, and the day is getting away from us."

He left her standing practically open-mouthed. She needed a few deep breaths to get herself under control, to clear her mind, to take in what was going on. She would give him a few minutes, then go out and send him on his way, that's what she would do. It was the only action possible. Anything different would be insane.

In the meantime the food was getting cold and she was starved, having depended on her own inadequate culinary offerings since she'd arrived. She ate fast, gulped down the coffee in a decidedly unladylike way, and was prepared to go out for a final confrontation with Matt when she heard the approach of a horse and rider.

"Ho, Matt, hold up," a man called out.

Then silence for a minute before Matt said, "Hello, Quince. I should have figured you'd be showing up sooner or later. Come to put in your two cents' worth?"

Quince, the middle Hunter brother, Juliana thought. She held back, feeling guilty for listening in, then figuring she had a right since the conversation was taking place on her land.

"I went over to the Half-Moon to see you yesterday," Quince said. "Sorry it's taken so long, but there was some work I needed to take care of that wouldn't wait. You heard I got married, didn't you?"

"I heard," Matt said, and Juliana could discern the restrained anger in his voice, as if he didn't want anything to do with another Hunter. Strange that she was picking up such nuances in the speech of a man she barely knew.

"Brent told me what happened between you and Pa."

"Jack was only being Jack. And he spoke the truth. It's his place. He can kick off anyone he wants."

"Hell, Matt, you worked as hard as anyone to keep the ranch going. Harder than me, that's for sure. You're as much a part of the place as any of us."

"Quit lying to yourself," Matt said, "and you can damned sure quit lying to me."

"You always were quick to take offense. Pa was drunk. I wouldn't be surprised if he forgot all about what he said in a few days."

Matt's laugh was harsh. "He won't forget. And he wasn't that drunk."

An awkward silence fell. Quince spoke first.

"That horse in the corral—is that the one got Jack so upset?"

"That's the one. The killer stallion from England."

"If you ever race him against the ranch," Quince said, the admiration apparent in his voice, "we're doomed for sure."

"I'm not making any promises. Not today."

The two brothers went on to talk about Jack Hunter, then Glory, Quince's new wife. Juliana backed away from the door, thinking over what she'd heard, and what she already knew. Matt had gone to England to buy a racehorse, had brought him back to the ranch supposed to be his home, and had promptly been told to go someplace else.

The knowledge was sobering, and she had a hard time holding on to her anger. She sighed. Why couldn't things be simple? Why couldn't she clearly make out right from wrong?

Matt was cocky; he'd probably brought a little of his current misfortune on himself. But not all of it. Juliana's heart warmed—a foolish reaction, but she knew what it was like not to have a place to call home. If she didn't act on what she knew, if she didn't do what her conscience and her heart told her was decent, what kind of woman was she?

She waited a few more minutes, making sure the decision she was coming to was not only decent but also smart. She concluded it wasn't, not in the least, but she would stick with it anyway. Harlan had never said she had a fine mind.

Taking a deep breath for courage, she went out back, nodded at Quince Hunter—she would have taken him for Matt's brother anywhere—then looked at Matt.

"The day's getting away from us. We'd both best get to work. There's loco weed growing out in the south pasture. I'd like to start running cattle there soon. See what you can do about getting it ready."

With another nod at Quince, she beat a hasty retreat back inside, thinking that now she had something else to try to forget besides Matt's kiss: the warm, assessing look he'd given her as she spoke, the far-too-familiar regard that twisted her heart into a knot.

Chapter Nine

Using a kitchen knife, Juliana cut the skirt of the ruined amber dress into strips, dipped one of the strips into a pail of soapy water and began scrubbing the top of the stove.

"You make a mess in the kitchen," she said to the absent Matt. "Look at all this grease."

She liked talking to him when he wasn't around; she got less sass that way. But she also had to admit some of the grime was hers, accumulated over the past few days. She definitely needed that housekeeper. Thank goodness she was supposed to arrive today.

So why was she cleaning the kitchen? Juliana laughed to herself. She didn't want the woman to take a look at the work ahead of her and leave. More than just a good housekeeper, she needed the stability of another woman's company. Matt might have ridden out to the south pasture after his brother Quince left, but he seemed very much a presence wherever Juliana went, putting her in an unstable frame of mind.

When she finished with the stove, she was pondering where to store the makeshift cleaning rags when a hard knock rattled the kitchen door. It must be the housekeeper, and from the force of the knock, she was a sturdy woman.

With a smile Juliana threw open the door. "Hello . . ." she began, then broke off. Her mouth dropped open. Standing in the light just outside the kitchen was a man she'd never seen, a big, hairy man, sleeves rolled back to reveal forearms like fuzzy tree trunks, his broad face hidden behind a full beard, his head bald as a rock.

Hat in hand, he bowed.

"Howdy, ma'am," he boomed, taking a step backward. "I've come about the housekeeping job. Name's Mugg Snelling. Dorothea couldn't make it. She's my sister. Got herself hitched, she did, to a traveling man and moved back East. I figured I'd take the position, if it's all the same to you. I know what you're paying, and it seems a right fair sum to me."

Juliana took a deep breath, for him as well as for herself.

"Mugg Snelling?" she asked. It was the only thing she could get out while she gathered her wits.

"That's right. An old and honorable English name, I'm told, though there's some who find humor in it."

She studied Snelling openly, not bothering with subtlety. Under the circumstances, subtlety did not seem called for. He was taller than Matt, well past six feet, and outweighed him by at least fifty pounds. She couldn't begin to guess his age, but his bushy dark beard was streaked with gray.

"I don't understand," she said.

"I don't either, to be honest with you," Snelling said. "She hardly knew the man."

"That's not what I meant. You're a housekeeper?"

"Not by trade. I used to be a trail cook, and before my wife died, may she rest in peace, she taught me a trick or two in the kitchen. Had me doing cleaning and the washing as well, when she was suffering one of her spells. If there's anything else that goes along with the job, I figure I can pick it up without too much hassle."

He looked big enough to pick up Pepper, an observation Juliana kept to herself.

"Lately," he went on, "with the trail drives dying out, I've been working at the stage office in town, caring for the horses and such as needed, but it wasn't anything I took to, lacking variety as it did."

Juliana closed her eyes for a moment and sighed, asking herself not for the first time why

things couldn't be simple. When she'd first returned to Diablo, she had made arrangements at
the general store for hiring someone to help out
with cooking and cleaning—a woman, of course.
Mr. Spindle, the store proprietor, said he knew
just the person, although she was finishing up
employment at the boardinghouse and wouldn't
be available for a short while.

Nothing Spindle said had prepared her for
Mugg Snelling.

"Mr. Snelling—" she began.

"Mugg, if you don't mind. Nobody ever called
me mister." He looked beyond her into the
kitchen. "I see you don't have dinner started. I've
got supplies in the wagon. Let me fetch 'em and
show you what I can do. In the meantime, unless
you have any real objections, you just go on
about what you were doing when I knocked."

He took only three strides to reach the wagon
he'd left close to the kitchen door. She followed,
ready to protest—exactly what, she wasn't sure,
but a protest definitely seemed in order—but
Mugg had already lifted a heavy bundle from the
wagon bed and was headed toward the kitchen.
She had to step quickly to get out of his way.

Then he was back for another load.

"I got some chickens in the wagon as well," he
said, not breaking stride on the back-and-forth
trips. "They're kinda quiet now, but they were
peepin' up a storm on the ride out. I figured you

wouldn't mind my adding them to the supplies. Can't be going into town every time we're wanting an omelette."

An omelette? Surely she wasn't hearing right.

"We'll have to get us a rooster before long. And," he added, "there's a fellow I know can supply us with hogs if you've no objection. Don't worry about the slaughtering. I can take care of that, no trouble. Smokin' the meat, too. If you don't have a smokehouse, I can build you one. You'll find I'm right handy to have around."

He didn't sound like a braggart, but rather a man who was reporting the way things were. She didn't doubt his handiness at building and slaughtering. But she could not possibly hire a male housekeeper half the size of the barn. Could she? With all the dusting and sweeping and mopping required, housekeeping was a woman's job.

The thought stopped her. Running a ranch was man's work, but she, a puny female, planned to run the Lazy Q. She'd be a hypocrite to send Mugg Snelling on his way just because of his gender and size.

While she was pondering the matter, Mugg continued talking.

"Spindle said to tell you if any questions come up about my character, he'll vouch for me. He'll put it in writing if you want."

Juliana stared at him a minute; then a small smile tugged at her lips. What would Matt say when he got a look at the new cook? He'd think she was either foolish or downright insane. But he thought that anyway. Why not give him more proof?

"I'll tell you what, Mugg. You get dinner started, and then later we'll talk about whether you'll be staying on."

Every time Matt had dealings with Juliana, she became more of a puzzle to him. Showing up this morning had been risky; he'd expected fireworks after invading her house while she was sleeping. He almost got them, out in the corral when she first confronted him, and again in the kitchen when he was dishing up the eggs.

Now here he was, hired and out on the job. Something had cooled her down, put her in more of a mind to be reasonable. He suspected it was listening in on his talk with Quince, finding out just what had brought him to the Lazy Q.

Poor Matt, she was probably thinking, kicked out of his home by a drunken father, looking for a place that would take him in.

The idea riled. He didn't want charity. Juliana would find out soon enough he could and would more than earn his keep—for as long as he stayed around, that is. He had some things to think over, things to take care of, and then he'd be gone. He was nobody's fool, and he sure as hell was nobody's victim.

Anyway, ever since his return from England the Half-Moon had been a temporary stop, a place to take care of leftover business. He knew—bitterly knew—it could never be home. That possibility had died ten years ago. He'd planned to stay awhile, making his last contributions to the ranch, but that was before Jack—

The crack of a gun interrupted his thoughts, the bullet kicking up dirt not three feet away, sending him scrambling out of the saddle, landing hard on the ground. Another shot whizzed past his head. He crouched low by his frightened horse, holding tight to the reins as he grabbed for the rifle holstered against the saddle, his eyes all the while searching for who was shooting and from where.

Echoes of the shots rang in his ears. The best he could tell, they came from a stand of trees at the eastern edge of the pasture. He pulled himself back into the saddle, stretching his body low over the horse's neck, and took off toward where he figured the shooter had been. He headed straight into the morning sun, the rifle still clutched in his hand.

He was acting on instinct and the training of years alone on the trail. Nearing the trees, he fired once, hoping he was getting close to the shooter, keeping his horse's stride as he slammed out of the sunlight and into the shadows of the grove. He was rewarded with the sound of a horse taking off fast ahead of him.

Holstering his rifle, he followed the noise, his mount twisting and shifting through the trees, hooves crashing against the debris on the forest floor. A time or two he caught sight of the rider, but never clearly enough to get off another shot. He was gaining on the shooter when his horse pulled up lame. With a curse, he dismounted and spat in disgust, having no choice but to let the coward get away.

The horse had picked up a rock, but a knife soon took care of the problem. Leaving the horse to crop grass in the pasture, Matt returned to the edge of the woods, moving cautiously, looking for tracks. His old luck was with him, and he found not only what he was looking for—signs of a man crouching and a horse moving about— but also a couple of spent shells that hadn't been lying around for long.

He gave special attention to the tracks, looking for something to identify them, but the bed of the grove was too thick with leaves and twigs for him to pick up any distinguishing traits. Pocketing the shells, he went back to the pasture to finish his work, figuring the bastard had done all the shooting he was going to do for the day. But he didn't work with an easy mind, looking over his shoulder as he tramped across the field, jumping when he disturbed a covey of quail that took off without warning in a flutter of wings.

By the time he made it back to the ranch house, he'd lost whatever skittishness the shots had provoked and come up with a full load of anger. The gunman was either a poor shot or was trying to warn him away. But away from what? Digging up loco weed?

As bad as his troubles were with his father, he couldn't see how this most recent trouble had anything to do with the Half-Moon. Shooting from ambush wasn't Jack's way. He didn't want his youngest son dead; he just wanted him gone. If Jack ever tried to warn him away with a few shots, drunk as he would be, he'd more than likely shoot himself in the foot.

Matt was putting his fed, watered and brushed horse into the corral alongside DC and the mare Pepper when he caught sight of a rider coming up the back side of the barn.

The man was a stranger to him, but even from a distance Matt didn't like the look of him. Dark, grizzled, clothes hanging on him like he'd slept in them a night or two, he emanated waves of trouble as visible to Matt as if they were heat.

When he dismounted at the front of the barn, Matt was there to meet him.

"Good evening," he said with a nod. "You have some business with Mrs. Rains?"

The stranger scratched his bristled face, his small, dark eyes steady and unfriendly.

"I might ask you the same thing. Kane's the name. I work for the woman."

"That makes two of us," Matt said, pulling the spent shells from his pants pocket and jingling them in his hand.

"I ain't got no problem with that," Kane said. "There's work enough around here for a dozen men."

"Did you by any chance work near the south pasture today?"

"Nope. I was mending fences to the west. Why? Something happen there?"

Without answering, Matt looked beyond him to his horse. "I see you carry a rifle with you."

"Never can tell when you'll run into trouble."

"True enough. I was riding through the woods near the pasture and came across these." He held out the shells. "Newly spent, looks like, and from a rifle. You wouldn't know anything about them, would you?"

Kane shrugged. "And you wouldn't be accusing me of anything, now, would you?"

"Like what?"

"You're doing the talking," Kane said, "not me."

Something about the way Kane shifted his weight, along with the challenge that burned in his eyes, convinced Matt he had his shooter. He had no proof, of course, but he knew he was right. He also knew that Kane would have killed him if that had been his purpose. He was a gunman, not a ranch hand. He'd been laying down a warning about something, or else playing games. A warning, for sure. Kane didn't look like a man interested in games.

Why had he done it? It wasn't an easy question to answer. To scare Matt off, probably, as if another man on the spread offered some kind of threat.

That thought led to another question. What had gotten into Juliana to hire him?

Matt looked around him in disgust, at the rundown barn, the untended corral, the weed-choked grass. It would take an army of men to get everything in shape, something he'd known that day his wild pursuit of a horny DC had brought him here for the first time.

But the Lazy Q wasn't his problem, and he sure as hell didn't appreciate being used as target practice by Juliana's only other hand. Some things were just too irritating to allow.

He was about to lay down some Hunter rules to Kane when the kitchen door opened. Matt looked around, expecting to see Juliana sashaying out, looking beautiful and feminine and stubborn, stirring up trouble as was her habit.

Instead, still another man was standing outside the house, a big man with strong arms, a full beard and a bald head. He had an apron wrapped around his considerable middle.

NAME: _____

ADDRESS: _____

_____

_____

TELEPHONE: _____

E-MAIL: _____

_____ I want to pay by credit card.

__ Visa   __ MasterCard   __ Discover

Account Number: _____

Expiration date: _____

SIGNATURE: _____

*Send this form, along with $2.00 shipping
and handling for your FREE books, to:*

Historical Romance Book Club
20 Academy Street
Norwalk, CT 06850-4032

*Or fax (must include credit card
information!) to:* **610.995.9274.**
*You can also sign up on the Web
at* www.dorchesterpub.com.

Offer open to residents of the U.S. and
Canada only. Canadian residents, please
call 1.800.481.9191 for pricing information.

If under 18, a parent or guardian must sign. Terms, prices and conditions
subject to change. Subscription subject to acceptance. Dorchester
Publishing reserves the right to reject any order or cancel any subscription.

"Dinner'll be served shortly," the man announced. "I'm dishing it up in the kitchen, Miz Rains not wanting to open up the dining room just yet. She says you two are welcome to join her."

His voice was deep and coarse, matching his size. Nothing about him went with the apron.

Juliana chose that moment to make an appearance, coming out the back door just the way he'd pictured, her plain gingham gown looking fine as silk, her golden hair pinned loosely on top of her head, her amber eyes flashing with what looked very much like a challenge.

"I see you've met Mugg Snelling. He's the new housekeeper at the Lazy Q. Mugg, this is Matt Hunter. He'll be working here awhile."

"Matt Hunter?" Snelling sounded surprised. "You one of the Hunters from the Half-Moon?"

"Sort of. You have any problem with that?"

Juliana stepped between the two, but Snelling was already answering.

"Nope. I'm like most folks, Matt, I just try to get by."

Matt told himself to settle down. Snelling seemed a decent sort, not like Juliana's other hand.

"How about—" he began, looking over his shoulder, but Kane and his horse were gone. Matt looked back to see Snelling returning to the kitchen, leaving Juliana alone with him in the shadows behind the house. She gave him a questioning look, as if she could tell something was wrong.

"You sure are edgy this evening," she said.

"It's getting to be my natural state."

Matt walked closer to her, breathing in her flowery scent, looking at the shape of her, taking in the fine features of her face. He didn't hurry. Enjoying Juliana's presence seemed a small enough reward for almost being killed.

She held her ground. He liked that in her, admitting at the same time that it probably wasn't a smart thing for her to do, not with the way he was remembering the taste of her lips.

And even if she didn't know it, he did need a little comforting. He didn't get shot at every day. The experience had left him . . . how had Juliana put it? Edgy. He was that way, all right.

"You do hire strange people," he said. "A gunman, an outcast and a hairy giant as a cook."

"Mugg's a fine cook," she said, then stopped. "You think Kane's a gunman? He's unpleasant, I'll give you that, but surely not a . . . a killer."

"You get much work out of him?"

"Not much."

"Then get rid of him."

He could see she was bristling. "I will. In my own good time."

"Right now seems good enough. You want me to ride after him?"

152

"I didn't hire you as foreman, Matt. I said I'll take care of him, and I will."

She was a stubborn one. And proud. That was something he could understand. The trouble was, pride sometimes got in the way of acting smart.

"You're the one who worries me the most," she said, doing a neat job of changing the subject. "You get that loco weed in the south pasture?"

"I said I would, and I did. Burned a pile of it." He stared at her lips. "Worked up quite a hunger."

Her eyes darkened from amber to a golden brown. She got his meaning.

"There are some things that won't be put on the table," she said, but she didn't say it right away, choosing to look at him for a second or two, giving him a few ideas she might not appreciate. "Privileges around here include nothing but meals and a place to sleep."

"Where would that be?"

"Not where you're thinking. There's a small bunkhouse on the far side of the barn. I can't vouch for the condition, but since Kane doesn't use it, you'll have it to yourself. Now wash up. Mugg told me the food is best served hot."

She went back inside, head high, loose curls of yellow hair trailing down the back of her neck. Matt stared at the closed door, then back toward the barn where he'd talked to Kane, his perusal moving on to the corral where DC and Pepper were standing close together. His senses were torn between the echoing blasts from the rifle and the sight and scent of a woman too ripe for her own good. And more vulnerable than she realized.

He'd thought his troubles were over when he left the Half-Moon, having been officially relieved of all responsibilities toward the family ranch. But it could be that the real trouble had only just begun.

Close to midnight Edmund Montgomery stood behind his house smoking a cigar and drinking brandy, a habit he'd formed since Iona's death. Not that he missed his wife. She'd been a cloying, whining drunk, too easily made dependent on her opium-laced medicine. Doc Gibbs had helped him get the laudanum, until he could set up a source of his own. Now Gibbs was gone, the spineless fool, simplifying everything by running away.

No, loneliness didn't drive Edmund outside. It was just that the walls seemed to close in on him at times. He had money and respect. Ask anyone—there was no one in town more admired than Edmund Montgomery. But he hadn't gotten what he wanted most.

He cursed the memory of Elizabeth Hunter, his beloved Beth. All those years ago in New Orleans, when they were young, just learning who they were and what life was all about, she should have had the sense to marry him instead of that worthless Jack.

It brought no consolation that her decision had eventually cost her her life.

Three boys she'd brought into the world, not one worthy of keeping, and Jack acting superior with each one, as if he'd done something special besides poking his wife.

And then came Abby, looking like her mother, taunting Edmund with her soft little body, then giving it to that bastard soldier she'd married. Montgomery gingerly touched his nose. It still smarted some from when Tremain had beaten him, and just because he'd laid a hand on his precious wife. As if she were something that shouldn't be touched, when all those years she'd been flaunting herself in front of him, showing sympathy to that whimpering Iona, wearing trousers, letting him see a little of what he could never have.

When the newlyweds finally got back, he'd see that Tremain paid for that beating, and with more than just a broken nose. He owed something to Abby, too. She needed to know what a real man was like.

He took a long draw on his cigar and chuckled, forgetting his failures. The rest of the Hunters would pay, too. He held the mortgages to half the ranches in the county, but nothing, not liquor or sex or money, could give him the satisfaction of grinding Jack and his ranch under his heel.

He was finishing the brandy when he heard a rustling in the shrubs at the back edge of his property. In the moonlight a familiar figure walked toward him, not bothering to keep to the shadows.

Montgomery cursed. "Kane, what the hell are you doing here? You know I don't want us seen together."

Kane came to a halt close enough for Montgomery to smell his stench. "Yeah, well, I figured you'd want to know what was going on with that stepdaughter of yours."

Montgomery glanced at the darkened house. The last thing he needed was for the housekeeper, Hilda, to listen in. With a nod, he directed Kane back toward the shrubs.

"What in hell is Juliana doing now?" he asked when they reached the shadows. "Packing, I hope."

"Nope, settling in. She's got herself a housekeeper"—Kane laughed as if enjoying a private joke—"and another ranch hand."

"You rode in to tell me this?"

"The hand's Matt Hunter. Seems his daddy kicked him off the Half-Moon, so he's sniffing around your family now."

"She's not my family," Montgomery snarled.

"So you don't care about Hunter," Kane said, turning as if to leave.

"That's not what I said," Montgomery snapped.

The banker stared at his empty glass. Hunters had a way of causing trouble wherever they went. If Matt stayed near the unpredictable Juliana long enough, he might convince her to dig in. Damn him. The last thing Montgomery needed was a meddlesome stepdaughter hanging around asking questions about her mama's death.

There weren't many who could tell her the truth, just Larkin and Gibbs. With the doctor gone, that left only Larkin to deal with, and he was mostly talking out of his rear. Montgomery had no doubt he could take care of the mealy-mouthed lawyer when the time came.

That left Juliana, a tasty morsel if he'd ever seen one, a widow ready for the plucking, like her mother had been, only more of a woman, with a spirit that wasn't easily crushed. But that didn't mean he couldn't handle her. He just needed different tactics, and quicker ones. Iona's death had taken years.

Once he was rid of the daughter, he had a feeling Matt would be moving on as well, taking his damned English stallion with him. Jack didn't have the sense to make money out of racing, but his youngest son did.

Edmund puffed on his cigar and looked at

Kane. "You were telling me earlier about this carriage she has."

Even in the dark he could make out the man's grin. "Wasn't sure you was listening."

"Don't be a fool. I was listening, all right. What you were talking about . . . maybe it's time you took care of it."

"Fine by me. When do I get paid?"

"Same as always. You do what you have to do, I'll be by your cabin right away."

And he would, after he was done grieving openly for the loss of yet another member of his family. There were always fools to accept such grief, namely the preacher, most of the men, and all of the women in town.

After Kane left, he crushed the cigar under his heel, then went back inside to pour himself a second brandy. This one he would drink in the parlor, his restlessness having abated. Thinking about Abby and what he would do to her was more than satisfying, even though it would come later, maybe weeks from now.

The loss of Juliana was more imminent and gave him something to celebrate tonight. Too bad he couldn't give her a little of what Abby had coming, but some things just couldn't be.

Chapter Ten

Early the next morning, after a restless night Juliana went out to find Mugg working on building a chicken coop at the side of the barn.

"You've got a job at the Lazy Q if you still want it," she said.

Hammer in hand, Mugg stood and nodded. "I figured I did."

"Has Matt already gone?"

She tried to sound casual, but last night's meal had been tense, as if there were issues between them she didn't entirely understand. Juliana didn't like undiscussed issues. She'd had too many of them with Harlan.

Something was wrong. Whether it had to do with herself or with Kane, she wasn't sure.

"Matt said to tell you he was going back to the pasture. As for that other one, he's not been around."

"I'm not surprised. Look, I think I'll take Pepper out for a ride. I don't know when I'll be back. I'll wrap up some biscuit and bacon. That'll do me until dinner."

Leaving Mugg to his carpentry, she saddled the mare and without stopping rode to the western limits of the Lazy Q. When she headed out, she hadn't realized her destination. Something strong had called her here, she thought, as she gazed out on the land that had once been her birthright, the former Sullivan ranch, now part of the Half-Moon.

Memories of the scene in the Lone Star Saloon came rushing back, stinging her cheeks with embarrassment. The longer she stared at the rolling hills stretched out before her, the more she hungered for them. She wasn't acquisitive by nature, and the Lord knew she had enough problems with the ranch she already owned. But her father had loved this land, and so too had her mother, before Edmund Montgomery came into her life.

Getting it back would be a tribute to both of her parents, an acknowledgment that those years they spent taming this part of Texas had meant everything to her.

Unfortunately, there was only one way to accomplish this particular goal. She had to face Jack Hunter again. So be it. She would do what she had to do.

She spent most of the day riding along the

boundary between the two properties, recalling the happy days she'd spent on the Sullivan ranch, and sometimes, when she couldn't help it, the less than ideal time in the early days of her marriage on the Lazy Q.

She'd been seventeen when Harlan took her as his bride. Some females were women at that age. Not Juliana. She'd been little more than a child. But when he proposed, the loving grandparents who had raised her were dead, and she could not tolerate the thought of living with her stepfather.

Harlan had been kind, for a while, but he had never been kind in bed, and she had grown up fast.

Bitter memories would do her little good now, she thought as she rode Pepper slowly home, not wanting to push the mare in case she was in foal. Another three to four months would have to pass before she knew for sure.

Back at the ranch house, she caught Kane skulking outside the barn as if he were up to something. She would have questioned him about why he wasn't working on the fences, but she had other matters on her mind. Not that any work he did was even passable. Whether or not he was a gunman—something she found hard to believe—Matt was right. She ought to get rid of him, right now. But she needed him for one more chore, something even he could handle.

"Please have the carriage ready early in the

morning," she said. "There's a trip I have to make."

"Yes, ma'am," Kane said with unusual politeness. "It'll be waiting for you whenever you want."

With a nod, she hurried inside to clean up after her long day in the saddle. Another tense meal followed, with only her and Matt at the table and Mugg hovering over them to make sure everything was all right. Then she went up to a night made far more peaceful because she had a mission the next day.

It wasn't anything she wanted to talk with Matt about. He would try to give her advice on the matter, except that his advice tended to come in the form of an order.

Before going to bed, she laid out her clothes, wanting to be presentable for the planned visit to the Half-Moon. One of her golden silk gowns, she decided, and her best black cloak with the matching feathered bonnet. More than ever, she needed to take care of business in the right manner, to demonstrate that she was respectable and responsible, and that her extravagant offer in the saloon had not been a whim.

Her most fervent hope was not only that Jack Hunter would be present when she called, but also reasonably sober. She figured that catching him early would help her chances of success.

And if possible she could also talk to Brent

Hunter and his wife about her mother's last days. Surely they knew something. Not everyone in the county could be ignorant about her mother's passing.

Early the next morning, when she emerged from the house she found the carriage ready and waiting, the top down, the gelding frisky in its traces. Kane was holding the reins.

Hurrying out the kitchen door, Mugg stepped around her. "I'll take those," he said to Kane, then turned to her. "Let me help you up, Mrs. Rains. You look fine today, if you don't mind my saying so."

Kane readily gave up the reins, then stepped away from the carriage, regarding her with unusual attention. Something in his eyes sent a shiver down her back. Today would definitely be his last day. She would take care of it when she returned. His firing had been postponed too long; thinking she had to have a reason other than not liking him had been a mistake.

The early morning was cool and overcast, and the horse trotted along quickly up to the main road that linked the scattered homesteads of the county. Not far ahead it forked into two branches, one headed south toward town, the other due west. It was west for her, without stopping until she reached the Half-Moon. The cool air stung her cheeks, but it was a good feeling, and she was glad Kane hadn't put the top up as he should have. Mostly she was glad to be doing something besides moping around, going over scribbled words she had long ago memorized.

In buying the land, she was proposing nothing that wouldn't be of benefit to both the Half-Moon and the Lazy Q. Which didn't mean the Hunter clan would see reason. Matt, for example—

The roar of a gunshot shattered the thought, and the horse took off at a run, throwing her back in the carriage seat. Vainly she pulled back on the reins, as panicked as the horse, but the pace only increased, bouncing the carriage over the uneven road surface and throwing her from right to left until she could barely remain upright.

Blood racing, she screamed out, but she could barely hear her voice over the pounding hooves and the creaks and groans of the carriage. Galloping at a killer speed, the gelding soared over the top of a rise, and the carriage landed hard on the down side of the hill, canting dangerously to the left. She was thrown against the side, bruising her arm, but she scarcely noticed. In the wake of the runaway horse, the tilted carriage skittered from side to side. All was a blur—the sky, the horse's flanks, the wobbling traces. Juliana's heart pounded; her breath faltered.

She was scarcely aware of a second horse riding close, keeping pace with the carriage, of strong hands reaching for the reins, of the gradually decreasing pace, of those same hands reaching for her, roughly tugging her out of the carriage, one arm cinched around her body as her rescuer held her close against him, her feet dangling inches above the fast-moving ground.

"Matt!" she cried and held on tighter as he brought his mount to a halt.

A crash and a wild, desperate neigh brought her head whipping around, and she watched in horror as the carriage turned sharply on its side at the edge of the road, carrying the gelding with it.

"Are you all right?" he asked.

She nodded, and he eased her to the ground, dismounted and ran to the overturned carriage. Moving quickly, he fought the traces and the thrashing horse. Hand at her throat, Juliana started to run toward him, but Matt was fast and suddenly the horse was free, staggering onto shaky legs. Then, with an unrestrained shake of the head, he loped across the field beside the road. Even from a distance, she could see the terror in the horse's round dark eyes as he halted and pranced nervously about in the tall grass.

Watching, still hearing echoes of the desperate neighs and piercing creaks of the tottering carriage, she felt everything crash in on her. No longer able to stand, she collapsed in the middle of the road, unmindful of the hard rocks beneath her, or of the dust swirled to choking thickness by the thundering wheels of the carriage.

And then Matt was kneeling in front of her, brushing her cheeks, and she realized she was crying. Foolish, foolish tears. No life had been lost, no limbs injured; the only things destroyed were her beautiful new carriage and her peace of mind.

But all the reasoning in the world could not stop the tears. Matt would take it as a sign of weakness. The truth was, with fear abating, she was growing angry. What had happened? And why? She had been so sure of her mission, so glad to be underway. And now . . .

He took her in his arms and held her close. How comforting were those arms and that broad chest, but the anger, the questions, would not stop tormenting her, and she pushed him away, no longer crying.

"There was a gunshot, Matt. It frightened the horse and he took off." She said it defiantly, as if he were laying blame on her for the near disaster, when in truth he hadn't said a word. "It was all so fast," she added, then put the tormenting question to him. "What happened?"

She could feel him stiffen. The look in his eyes would have been terrifying, had he directed it toward her.

"I don't know what happened, but I aim to find out."

He stood, pulling her up with him. His hands rested gently on her shoulders as he asked again, "Are you sure you're all right?"

"I'm fine. Really."

When he let her go, she swayed, but he was already heading for the overturned carriage, its left wheels still spinning slowly in the air. Kneeling in the road, he studied the undercarriage with what seemed to her alarming thoroughness.

Heart in her throat, she hurried to his side, but he stood, placing himself between her and the carriage, blocking her view.

"Anybody near the carriage before you headed out?"

"Kane put the horse in the traces for me. Why? This was an accident, wasn't it?"

Even as she asked the question, she knew the answer. She felt the blood drain from her face.

"You deserve the truth, Juliana. Someone cut through the axle—not all the way, just enough to weaken it. The same someone who fired the shot."

A chill took hold of her, and she pulled the cloak tight against her body.

"It was Kane, wasn't it? Why? I hardly know the man."

"He got off a couple of shots at me two days ago."

"At you?" She felt stupid, confused. Nothing was making sense. "You didn't tell me."

"I didn't want to worry you. I figured it was my problem, not yours." Cursing, he glanced back at the carriage. "Shows you how wrong I can be." Then to her, "Whatever's going on, you can be sure the bastard's not acting on his own."

Juliana felt hollow inside, as if someone had cut out vital parts of her, and she looked beyond Matt, at the stretch of pasture beside the road. Having ridden beyond the boundary of the Lazy Q, she was looking at land she wanted to reclaim. But did she really? Did she want to remain in a place where someone wanted her dead?

If not, where was she to go? Saratoga seemed so safe, so far away. But safety would come at a great cost. She thought of her mother. There were debts to be paid and vows to be kept, vows that could be satisfied nowhere else but Texas.

Besides, she couldn't let herself be run off. This was now her home.

Heartsick, Juliana felt a return of tears. "Edmund," she whispered. Just saying the name stiffened her resolve, and the tears dissolved. "He's behind this somehow."

"Are you any kind of danger to him?" Matt asked.

She stared down at her dust-covered cloak and shoes. Straightening her bonnet, brushing the loose hair from her face, she looked back at Matt. "Look at me. How could I be a danger to anyone?"

"You could be, Juliana. Believe me, you could be."

Matt stared at her as he spoke, locking his gaze with hers. What thoughts lay behind those piercing eyes? she wondered. What meaning behind his words?

Possibilities occurred, warm and tempting possibilities, shaking her more than ever, and her pulse quickened. Wanting to touch him, she kept her hands at her sides and concentrated on what he had asked.

"If hating a man can put him in danger, then Edmund had best beware. I hate him for what he did to my mother."

"And what was that?"

"Besides marrying her when she was most vulnerable and taking her from me? I don't know. But he did something." She sighed. "Dear God, I must sound pitiful, but there you have it. My mother's letters"—she caught her breath, but she could not stop—"through the years her letters were about nothing but good times and happiness. I thought all was well. Then suddenly, without warning, he wrote me bluntly of her death. No details, nothing to explain what happened."

She could not tell him of the final letter, the pitiful one his sister Abby had neglected to send until long after the writer's death. Each word was private, meant for only a neglectful daughter, each word full of pain.

"I wasn't here often enough to know how things were," Matt said. "Ask around. What about Doc Gibbs?"

"He's gone. Disappeared. I had hoped to talk to your brother, but . . ."

Her voice broke as she stared beyond him at the tangle of leather and wood and metal that had once been her beautiful carriage.

"I'd best get you home," Matt said.

He whistled for his horse, which was grazing at the side of the road. Mounting, he pulled Juliana into his arms, as easily as if she weighed no more than a feather, settling her across his thighs, his arms on either side of her as he gripped the reins. It was an intimate position, but she wouldn't have given it up at that moment for a new carriage.

"Cover your ears," he said, then whistled shrilly for the carriage horse. "I imagine he'll follow. Let's get going."

"I really am all right," she said, wondering if she shouldn't assert herself and sit up as straight as she could. But as she looked one last time at the carriage, thinking of what could have happened, what had been supposed to happen, anxiety overcame her, smothering the brief sense of strength. She found herself holding on to Matt, afraid to let go, afraid that if she did she would imagine herself plunging down the road once again, returned to that moment of sheer terror, tossed about like a fallen leaf, powerless, unable to do anything but scream.

Matt must have felt her tremble, for he grasped the reins in one hand and put his free arm around her, holding her against his chest. She cursed her weakness even as she leaned into him. She had not been coddled in years, not since her grandparents had died, and never like this. Harlan had seen to her material needs, but not once had he sought to comfort her.

Matt felt so good, so strong, and she could do nothing but lean into that strength. It was an indulgence, and she began to think unwelcome thoughts, about what it would be like to have a man like him make love to her. Could it be so different from her previous experience? It was a foolish question, since the answer was one she would never know.

By the time they rode into the backyard of the ranch house, she had worked herself into an acute state of embarrassment. He had kissed her once, thoroughly kissed her because she had practically dared him to. Today he had saved her life. More, in doing so he had risked his own. Not because of who she was; he would have done the same for anyone.

And here she was coming up with all sorts of inappropriate thoughts, indecent images of what it would be like to lie in bed beside him and let him take off her clothes. An antidote to terror?

Maybe. But giving herself to Matt Hunter held a terror all its own. She could not do so, then watch him walk away.

In the empty backyard, he eased her to the ground, then dropped beside her.

"Go inside, Juliana. There's something I need to do."

It was an order he didn't have to give. Hurrying around him, she fled into the house, then slowed, moving through the empty kitchen, through the dining room and into the parlor. In the middle of the heavily furnished room she began to tremble again, from so many emotions she couldn't sort them all out.

"Kane's gone," Matt said behind her. She started, not having heard him come in. "He had some tackle in the barn," he added, "but it's not there. Mugg said he rode out not long after you left."

Juliana rubbed her arms. "I was going to fire him when I got back."

"He saved you the trouble."

"I never had anyone try to kill me before."

"Few people have."

"He shot at you."

"Mostly trying to scare me away."

"But you don't scare easily."

"Whether you realize it or not, neither do you. After what happened today, most women would have been in hysterics."

"I was, inside."

"Yeah, well, so was I."

"I don't believe you."

He almost grinned. She could tell by the expression in his eyes.

"You got any whiskey in the house?" he asked.

She shook her head. "Not even cooking sherry."

He stepped closer to her. "You need something," he said, a thickness in his voice that hadn't been there before.

"Do I?" she asked, and then softly, "Does it have to be a drink?"

Another step, and they were almost touching. Unfastening the catch at her throat, he slipped the cloak from her shoulders, and as if he did so every day, he removed her bonnet and tossed it aside, pulled the pins from her hair and watched it tumble down in a thick, golden cascade.

"I kissed you once, Juliana. I'm going to do it again."

She stared at his lips. "That seems perfectly reasonable to me. Except Mugg—"

"—is busy building some kind of pen behind the barn."

"Good for him."

"Yeah, good for him."

He slanted his lips against hers. She had to grab his arms to keep from falling.

He broke the kiss.

"I'm weaker than I thought," she said, then without thinking wrapped her arms around his neck and kissed him hard, opening her mouth just a little so that she could feel the moistness of his lips better. She was going on instinct. She'd never done anything like this before.

He didn't stop her from what she was doing, even when she broke the kiss and studied his throat, trying to get control of herself.

"Look at me, Juliana."

"No."

He bent his head to touch his lips to her mouth. Her eyes darted upward.

"That's better. And if you're weak, Jules, let me know when you're strong so I can rest up for you."

"Jules?"

"I don't know what to call you. I'm not good with sweet talk."

"What are you good at?" Her breath was so ragged, she could barely get the question out.

"You tell me."

He kissed her again, this time using lips and tongue, taking a while to explore the inside of her mouth as thoroughly as he'd been getting to know the outside. Juliana's blood was racing, everything about her turning hot, frightening her with the intensity of the sensation, but not enough for her to stop him. Whatever was happening, it couldn't be bad, not after what she'd been through. Besides, everything he did felt so good—the touch of his mouth, the taste of his tongue, the way he was beginning to run a hand down her side, stopping tantalizingly close to her breast.

She arched her back.

"Juliana!"

The sound of her name echoed harshly through the parlor. Matt broke the kiss. "Easy," he whispered, then lifted his head, and they both looked toward the front door. She straightened and dropped her arms, but she did not move away from him. She didn't have the strength. Instead, she stared in horror at Edmund Montgomery standing inside the open door.

Edmund was bad enough, but he was not alone. Beside him stood a couple she vaguely recognized—the preacher of the small church in Diablo and his wife.

Chapter Eleven

Juliana stared at the intruders. A scream caught in her throat. She wanted to run from the room, let the tears flow, give way to the hysteria she'd been barely holding under control since the accident. This intrusion was too much, too cruel. She had managed to get through everything else, even near-death, but not this.

The preacher's wife ended the awkward silence.

"Please forgive us, Mrs. Rains, for coming in this way without being invited, but we were worried about you."

She walked across the room and held out her hand, cutting off access to the door, Juliana's wished-for exit. Juliana's second choice was crawling behind the sofa. She was far too painfully aware of what she must look like in her soiled dress, hair tumbled to her shoulders, face smudged, her lips surely reddened by Matt's kisses.

And there was the little matter of her cloak and bonnet on the floor beside her, hairpins scattered about the rug. And Matt, her accomplice, standing so close she could hear his breathing.

"I should have introduced myself," the woman went on, as if she'd done nothing worse than catch Juliana napping. "I don't know if you remember me, it's been so many years. I'm Mary Crawford and this is my husband, the Reverend James Crawford."

She gestured back toward the door. The reverend, tall and thin where his wife was short and round, acknowledged the introduction with a nod, but he held back, apparently not so inclined as his wife to act as if nothing untoward had been taking place in the parlor.

Juliana nodded in return. She ought to do something, say something, anything, but Mrs. Crawford saved her the effort.

"Matt Hunter," the woman continued. "It's been years since we've seen you as well."

Juliana looked sideways at Matt, but he was directing all his attention to Edmund. Looking at Matt came close to being a mistake. She had an almost uncontrollable urge to lean against him and rest her head on his shoulder.

But this scene was her embarrassment, not his, and she must handle it as best she could.

She looked back toward the door. Edmund, ever the dignified banker in his suit and tie, hat in hand, graying hair combed neatly away from his lean face, was staring at her. For a moment she saw hate in his eyes and then, worse, scorn as he glanced at the cloak and bonnet on the floor.

And then the scorn was gone, as easily shed as a reptile might slither from its skin.

"Juliana, my dear," he said, walking toward her, his voice filled with concern. "At last we have a chance to see one another."

Juliana crossed her arms. Her expression must have stopped him, because he came to a sudden halt. "I'm so glad to find that you're all right," he added.

Matt broke in. "She's fine. Any reason she shouldn't be?"

"We were on our way here to visit you and welcome you home," the reverend said, "when we came across your carriage. At least I believe it was yours. I saw it when it was delivered to the livery stable in Diablo, although it was hard to identify from its condition beside the road."

"Did you get a good look at it?" Matt asked.

"We could hardly do so," Edmund said, "what with the fire and all."

Juliana and Matt exchanged a hasty glance.

"It must have been quite a blaze," Mrs. Crawford said, "although it was dying out by the time we got there. Still lots of smoke, you understand. Dear me, what a mess it was, the metal twisted, the wood still smoldering, and the leather—oh, my, it does put out quite a smell when it burns, doesn't it?"

The reverend stepped up beside his wife. "Perhaps, my dear, we should avoid the details. We have yet to know if the carriage belongs to Mrs. Rains."

"It was mine," Juliana said. "I had an accident, a runaway horse. It was fortunate that Mr. Hunter was nearby to rescue me." She looked at Edmund, proud she could do so coolly. "Otherwise I might have been seriously injured."

"Or worse," Edmund said without a blink.

Juliana brushed a patch of dirt from her skirt and smoothed her hair. "But there was no fire when we left."

"That must have been terrible," Mrs. Crawford said.

"The good Lord must have been looking out for you to send Matt in your path," the reverend said.

Juliana wondered if Reverend Crawford was being sarcastic since he'd caught the two of them ready to disrobe.

"Please sit, my dear," his wife said. "You can't have been home long."

As kind as the woman was being—and there was a stiffness about her that said the kindness was an effort—Juliana really didn't want to sit. She wanted to be alone, crawl into bed, pull the covers over her head. Perhaps if she suggested she needed rest, needed solitude . . .

Mugg chose that moment to enter, his hulking frame filling the doorway to the dining room.

"Pardon me for interrupting, Miz Rains, but the carriage horse just came loping in. I thought you'd want to know."

"Thank you, Mugg, that is a relief." Juliana's Saratoga training as wife of the wealthy Harlan Rains came to the fore. "Could we possibly have tea? I'm sure my guests would appreciate it after their long ride from town."

"I've already put the water on," he said and backed out of the room.

With the Crawfords staring after the unusual housekeeper, Juliana took the opportunity to pick up her belongings from the floor and rest them on the arm of the sofa, sitting beside them with as much aplomb as she could manage. "Mrs. Crawford, please join me. Would anyone prefer coffee? Mugg would be happy to prepare it as well."

She looked at Matt, to let him know that despite the circumstances, she really was all right. He nodded briefly.

"I've got work to do," he said. "If you'll excuse me, Mrs. Rains." With a nod to the reverend and a last quick glance at Juliana, he was gone.

Juliana felt as if all air had left the room—a silly reaction. She was still light-headed, painfully aware of the judging eyes resting on her. He was right to leave. This little social scene was hers alone to deal with.

By the time Mugg returned with a tray, the reverend and Edmund were seated opposite the sofa, and Mrs. Crawford was chattering on beside Juliana about the changes in Diablo over the past few years.

No one spoke of Iona. No one offered a sympathetic word concerning her death. For Juliana it was an omission not to be borne. There was something about coming close to death, she found, that removed all sense of caution.

"Were you close to my mother?" she asked Mrs. Crawford, then shot a quick sideways glance at Edmund. Sipping his tea, he stared back at her over the rim of his cup.

"I feared it was such a painful subject," the woman said, "and after all you've been through today . . . well, I hesitated to say anything. To answer your question, sadly, no, I was not close to Mrs. Montgomery."

"But she went to church," Juliana said. "She wrote me that she did."

"Oh, yes," Reverend Crawford said. "She never missed a Sunday, right up until the end. Mr. Montgomery was always by her side." He spoke as if Edmund's presence had been a sacrifice, as if it conferred some kind of sainthood on the aggrieved husband.

"So what killed her?"

Both the reverend and his wife gasped. Edmund was not so easily shaken.

"Now, now, Juliana, isn't this a subject best discussed between the two of us?"

"Then you tell me, Edmund. Why did she die? I was led to believe there was nothing wrong with her, that she was ecstatically happy as your wife."

She threw the words out as a challenge, daring him to tell the truth.

He set his cup down on the table beside him. Even in his silence she felt his hatred. It came at her in waves, like heat. How could the Crawfords sit there and not perceive the struggle that was going on between stepfather and stepdaughter?

"She drank."

Edmund's words hung in the air. Juliana held very still, feeling as if the man were piercing her heart with the tip of a very sharp knife.

"Oh, dear," Mrs. Crawford said, a hand to her cheek.

"Since you want to know, Juliana, I feel you deserve the truth," Edmund added.

Juliana brushed a lock of hair behind her ear, then gripped her shaking hands in her lap. "You're saying my mother was addicted to alcohol."

"To sherry at first. Then brandy. Toward the

end I would occasionally find empty whiskey bottles under her bed."

Edmund gave each detail with a growing sadness in his voice. He played the oppressed, despairing husband very well.

"Why?" Juliana asked.

Mrs. Crawford patted her hand. "You're under enough stress, Mrs. Rains. Mr. Montgomery is right. This is a subject best discussed another day between the two of you."

"And I offer my services as well," the reverend said, "should you feel the need to talk. These family crises can be painful indeed."

Juliana looked at Edmund. If he had once wanted privacy for their talk, he didn't want it now. He was practically smiling at her, though the smile was small and meant only for her, a reptilian smile to match his reptilian eyes.

"What did you mean by 'why,' Juliana?" he asked. "I truly want to help you all I can."

"Why did she drink?"

"Oh, dear, I hadn't wanted you to know. Alcohol was a weakness with her. It showed up soon after our marriage. You couldn't have realized, of course, choosing to live with your grandparents as you did. I think it was in part grief because of your leaving."

More pricks of the knife. His words hinted that the choice had been all hers, as if he hadn't taken every opportunity to make an eight-year-old child, mourning for her father, feel unwelcome in his home.

"And then, of course," he added, "you married and moved so far away. I do believe that was when the heavy drinking began."

She'd thought herself prepared for whatever Edmund might tell her, but his harsh words stunned her, the knife plunging up to the hilt. He was good. She had to give him credit. He knew just what to say to hurt her the most.

"Her letters—" she began.

"Her letters were always cheerful, were they not? It was something she insisted upon. I wanted to write and let you know of her condition, but she would not have it."

Both Crawfords looked at Edmund with sympathy, but their eyes were dark with pity when they looked at Juliana. Her stepfather seemed so totally believable, so entirely compassionate, she, too, might have been trapped into believing his story and blaming herself for her mother's decline. And she was to blame. But not entirely.

Iona's last letter was seared into Juliana's mind. Edmund had helped her write the others, she was convinced, helped her with the lies. But the last rambling cry for help had been written by Iona alone. Edmund didn't know of its existence, or it would never have made its way into Abby Hunter's possession.

"Thank you for telling me," she said as she

stood. "Now, if you don't mind"—she smiled at the Crawfords—"I really do need to rest."

"Of course," Mary Crawford said. "We've been thoughtless, keeping you from rest for so long." She hesitated. "About Mugg—are you sure you want him as your housekeeper? A man . . . it's so . . . unorthodox."

Letting Matt practically make love to her in the parlor could also be considered unorthodox, was a thought Juliana kept to herself.

"Mugg will be fine," she said, not bothering to elaborate.

It was the reverend's turn to offer advice, repeating his offer to be available if she needed to talk to someone, but she wasn't listening. How could she when Edmund was watching her with almost lascivious intensity, standing behind the Crawfords so that only she could see him.

The look was too much, too brazen, too challenging. Juliana's insides roiled with anger and pain.

She waited until the Crawfords had made their goodbyes and were getting into the carriage before calling Edmund back onto the front porch.

"If I could talk to you a moment," she said, leaning against the door frame as if she did not have the strength to stand.

"Of course," he said, and she could see the uncertainty in his eyes.

"Edmund," she whispered, and he leaned close

to hear her. "You tried to kill me today," she said softly, repulsed by his presence, yet taking pleasure as his uncertainty turned to alarm. "Then you had Kane burn the carriage to hide the evidence. I'd hate for you to sleep easily tonight thinking you're going to get away with it. You're not. And do not come here again. If you step onto my property, I will shoot you on sight."

She closed the door on him and waited for the relief that her speech to him should bring. No such blessing came to her, no sense that she had somehow triumphed over her stepfather in any way. Instead, she felt weighed down by all the events of the day, and numbed by the accusations she had thrown at him, accusations that seemed much worse when she put them into words.

Drinking—why had she not known? Had it really been the cause of Iona's death? Had whiskey been the medicine her mother craved?

So many questions, and no possible answers that could do anything but hurt her further. Right now she couldn't think, couldn't even cry. Anger, hate, frustration and, yes, fear—she could not deny the sense of danger gnawing at her gut—robbed her of energy. She could barely walk up the stairs to her room.

Closing the door behind her, she moved by rote, unbuttoning her soiled gown, wiping her eyes, trying to do one thing at a time with full deliberation. Sunlight spilled crazily into the room, a surprise since it seemed to her the day had long ago been spent.

Somehow she must get through the next few hours, and then the next few days. She thought of Matt. She thought of his touch. For the first time in a long while, she did not want to go through whatever awaited her alone.

Matt was forking hay in the barn, working as if the devil himself was after him, when he heard the sound of a carriage moving down the road. He went outside in time to watch the Crawfords and Montgomery begin their journey back to town.

Slowly he walked back into the barn, cursing himself as he had been doing ever since he caught sight of Juliana's carriage teetering crazily behind the runaway horse. He had known to keep a watch on Kane, but there had been hours during the night when he hadn't been sure of the bastard's whereabouts. He knew them now. Kane must have sneaked into the barn to do his dirty work, setting up the accident that should have taken Juliana's life.

Hell, he hadn't even been around when she set out on the ride, not knowing she was leaving, thinking Mugg's presence was enough protection for a short while.

Grabbing the pitchfork, Matt attacked the hay, but he was seeing Juliana clinging to him, turning to him, losing herself in a kiss, and then handling the embarrassment of discovery as if she faced such moments every day.

What was she doing now? Throwing things? Crying? Plotting revenge? With a woman like her, there was no telling.

Except he knew no woman like her. The gunshot, the runaway carriage, the almost tragedy— they were enough to scare the hell out of any man, and terrify any woman. She must have been terrified, leaning into him the way she had on the ride home. But she hadn't lost control. Not until they'd gotten inside and he'd started what was supposed to be an offer of comfort.

Juliana had practically driven him out of his mind, kissing him like that, letting him do pretty much what he wanted, encouraging him to do things she might not understand. It didn't matter that she'd been married; the lovely widow was an innocent. And she had returned home to more trouble than he'd encountered during ten years on the trail. Returned to the not-so-loving bosom of her stepfather.

Nothing like families to do a person in. Especially when the sole member of that family was Edmund Montgomery.

Throwing the pitchfork down in disgust, he pulled off his gloves and headed for the house. The back door was open, but Mugg was not to be seen.

When he didn't find Juliana on the lower floor, he took the stairs two at a time. Hearing movement behind one of the doors, he knocked, then went in. After what they'd been through today, he couldn't see any need for standing on ceremony and waiting for her to respond.

She stood in the middle of the room staring at an open wardrobe, holding a wrapper close around her, golden hair in a tangle, her face still smudged. At her feet lay the discarded gold silk gown she had been wearing, along with lace-trimmed undergarments. When she slowly shifted her attention to him, she needed a minute to focus on him, to lose the emptiness in her eyes.

Anything he had planned to say to her, words of comfort, words praising her courage, fled. She was, he thought, the most beautiful woman he had ever seen, and he wanted nothing more than to take her in his arms.

She came to him, moving silently across the room, like a woman out of a dream. But she was no dream. She was flesh and blood, and his heart pounded in his chest.

"Make me forget, Matt," she said, her voice soft yet strong. "Make me feel that for a while everything is all right."

Chapter Twelve

Juliana rested a hand on Matt's warm and bristled cheek, letting him know she meant what she said. In truth, she had to touch him, to link the two of them together, to draw upon his strength.

"Juliana—"

"Words make me think, Matt. I don't want to think. I want to feel."

He grinned, and she put her thumb against the corner of his mouth, as if she could capture the perfection of that grin in her hand.

"Well, now, what kind of gentleman would I be if I didn't honor that request?" he said. "Besides, I'll bet I can come up with some words that would make you feel." He turned her hand to kiss her palm. "Of course I won't just be talking."

Shivers of pleasure rushed through her, all from the slight brushing of his lips against her hand.

The sensation was new, a simple act that brought on a powerful reaction. She felt as if another level of existence was opening up to her, that Matt was pulling her into an enticing darkness, a world where everything was good, where she would meet with no harm. Wrapping her arms around his neck, she gave herself to that world eagerly.

Matt's grin was replaced by a look of raw hunger as he thrust his fingers into her hair and kissed her, open-mouthed, tongue to tongue. She could think of nothing but how good he tasted, and how welcome was the heat he poured into her. The heat spread like warm honey throughout her entire being as she held herself as tightly as she could against him.

Breaking the kiss, he held her close. The break jarred and frightened her.

"Is something wrong?" she asked, whispering the words against the strong column of his neck, her heart pounding in her throat. Long ago she'd been trained to blame herself if the sex was not good, and she could only wonder what she had done wrong.

"I don't want to rush." His words came out thick and as enrapturing as his kiss.

She almost laughed at her foolishness. "Please rush. I'm starting to think."

He stroked her hair. "We can't have that, now, can we? You might change your mind."

But that she could not do. She was caught in something as compelling, as unavoidable, as the runaway carriage, only this was pure pleasure. She trembled as he ran his hands down her back, the thin layer of cloth separating the press of flesh to flesh; they were so close but not close enough. The wrapper was made of expensive silk, bought by another man, but it was this man who must rip it from her body.

As if he could read her thoughts, he opened the front of the wrapper and stared at her. Suddenly shy, remembering how that other man had derided her slender hips and small breasts, she slipped out of the garment and threw herself against Matt, feeling his rough shirt and trousers rubbing against her skin, thinking that if she moved quickly enough, if she aroused him as she was being aroused, he wouldn't consider her inadequacies.

Whatever she was doing must have been right, because he went as wild as she, covering her face with kisses, cupping her rear and holding her against his all-too-evident erection, nestling his hardness against her belly, making her own body cry out for him to ease that hardness lower and answer her pulsing demands.

With trembling fingers she worked at the buttons of his shirt.

"I'm too slow, too awkward," she said.

"Not awkward," he returned huskily. "Let me help."

In a few swift motions he turned what could have been an ungainly procedure into a smooth and efficient undressing. With equal smoothness he took her hand and led her to the bed, throwing back the covers and tumbling her beneath him against the soft down mattress, and she sank down into heaven.

As he covered her, he blocked out the world, giving her what she had asked for, drawing her into a universe of sensuality. He ran his hands along her body, as if he would feel everywhere at once. Arching her back, she thrilled to the touch of his tongue against her nipples, cried out, not in pain but in ecstasy, when he pulled gently at them with his teeth.

Everything was new, not only the gentle assault but her submersion in it, and yet it was all so completely right, so natural, she found herself smiling. Her hands moved instinctively to his shoulders, his muscled arms, his chest, his skin so hot she imagined the blood coursing through his veins. Such strange things were happening, their separate desires blending in a way completely foreign to her. When he ran his fingers through the nest of hair low on her abdomen, Juliana—always shy in the act of mating, always reluctant, always a little afraid—lifted her hips and eased her thighs apart, opening her body to him in complete abandon.

"You're wet," he said. "I wanted to go slow."

"Not slow," she moaned, shaking her head. Then, acting on instinct, she wrapped her legs around him and he entered her in one swift, smooth motion, thrusting in and out, driving her deeper into madness. When her body exploded, her whole world splintered into tiny crystals of pleasure and she could do nothing but hold on to him, feeling his own explosion, so violent it would have been frightening except that she knew it to be natural, she knew it to be right.

Juliana clung to him for an endless time, needing the precious moments of rapture to extend forever, knowing she asked the impossible but asking nevertheless. He made no move to shift away from her, and she wondered if he felt the same need, the same satisfaction with her that she had found with him.

But such questions involved thinking, and she had sworn not to think. When at last he brushed the sweat-dampened hair from her face, she eased from beneath him and rested her head against his chest, unable to look into his eyes, not wanting to find what she would read there. Not looking let her imagine lingering warmth in their depths, an expression of well-being, contentment.

Pressed against him, smelling his maleness and

the sharp scent of sex, she listened to his breathing and after a while gave in to exhaustion and slept.

When Juliana awoke, night had fallen and she was in the bed alone. Pulled from her dream of drifting in a void, she needed a long minute to place herself in time and space, to feel the bed beneath her, the tangled covers barely covering her naked body. Her naked body. That stopped her. She'd never slept without a nightgown.

In a rush, all that she had done came back to her, and with a startled cry she sat upright.

"I'm here, Juliana."

Matt's deep voice came to her through the dark, and she saw him standing by the window in a mist of moonlight, looking out at the world she had wanted to forget.

He was dressed in the work shirt and jeans he had taken off with such grace, his body lean and strong-looking and, as she knew very well, hard with muscled strength. The moonlight cast shadows on his finely hewn face, making him seem harsh, not at all the gentle man who had made love to her.

As close as he was, he seemed a mile away, and in her nakedness she felt vulnerable, soft and weak. Propping the pillow against the iron headboard, she leaned back and gripped the covers close to her throat.

"What time is it?" she asked, as if that mattered.

"Close to midnight."

"I slept for hours," she said in amazement.

"Peacefully at first, then fitfully. Anybody ever tell you that you talk in your sleep?"

He spoke as if a dozen men could have testified to that talk. Before Matt, there had been only one, and her husband had not been inclined to talk about her when he could talk about himself.

Her heart pounded. "Did I say anything interesting?"

"Nothing that made sense."

"I guess I'm glad."

He hesitated a minute. "Are you all right?"

She could have wept at the question. All right? She didn't know what that meant anymore. Nothing in her existence was as it should be, except, of course, for the time she'd spent in his arms. But he didn't want a lecture, a list of all her woes. Men did not like clinging women. It was one of the lessons she'd been taught.

"I'm fine," she said, then couldn't keep from adding, "Why wouldn't I be?"

"You don't always have to be tough, Jules."

"Was I tough when we were . . ."

Her voice trailed off. What was she thinking, asking such a thing?

"You were spectacular."

His answer pleased her enormously, but she

couldn't let him know it or he might think she really cared for him. She had needed him, that was all. She could not admit to anything else.

And yet when she looked at him, her heart swelled with a new feeling of warmth, of rightness because he was here with her, no matter how distant he was holding himself. Having taken what she offered, he could have gone away while she slept. But he had remained.

With tremendous effort, she kept her voice carefree. "You were pretty spectacular, too."

Spectacular did not begin to describe what he had brought to her. She had not known she had such wildness in her, that she could revel in what her husband had called the pleasures of the flesh.

She was surprised when he chuckled. "What's so funny?"

"I was remembering the two of us when we were young, you so prim and proper, and me an idiot running wild. Whoever would have thought this day would come to be?"

"It came at a great price."

"I'm sorry, I didn't mean to make light of what we just did. Or what happened earlier."

He sounded as if he wanted to come to her again, to hold her in his arms. But that would be wrong, and she asked hastily, "Why were you there?"

"You mean on the road this morning? When I saw the carriage was gone, I figured you were going to call on Jack. Not a good idea, Juliana; not a good idea at all."

"That's my business."

"You don't know him the way I do."

The words bore a knife-sharp edge, and she remembered that he had troubles, too; his mother had been killed by his father, and it mattered not whether the killing had been in a drunken rage. Worse, when Matt had tried to help that same father newly released from prison, his reward had been ejection from the land that should in part have been his.

Tears welled in her eyes, not brought by her own troubles but by his. It seemed the past reached out with rabid claws to shred any peace the present might offer.

She felt linked to him in more ways than just the sex, and her heart went out to him.

"Jack's been friends with Edmund for a long time, hasn't he?" she asked. The question came out of nowhere, yet the answer suddenly seemed very important for them both.

Staring into nothingness, she sensed Matt watching her across the dark, but when he answered, there was no hesitancy in his voice.

"Since they were young, back in New Orleans. My mother, too. We were always told they were best friends."

His voice was low, and she could only imagine

what he was thinking as she brought up what must be painful yesterdays.

"Why did they come to Texas?"

"Jack won title to the Half-Moon in a poker game. Brent was already born, and Quint was on the way. With a growing family, he needed the land. I don't know why Montgomery followed them. I never asked, and Jack never said."

Juliana tried to picture Edmund as young and adventurous, the years of so-called respectability ahead of him, but all she could see was the scornful, cruel man he had become.

"There's something you ought to know, Matt. I told Edmund I knew he tried to kill me. Don't worry, the Crawfords didn't hear. They were already in the carriage."

"I'm not sure that was smart."

She held the covers tighter. "I don't always do smart things."

"So what did he say?"

"I closed the door on him before he could respond. I also told him I'd shoot him if he came around again."

She could feel him assessing her as best he could in the darkened room, shaking his head. "What am I going to do with you?"

You've already done just about everything. Juliana swallowed the words.

"Would you really shoot him?" Matt asked.

"I don't know. I've never even held a gun.

Pretty bad for a Texas girl, wouldn't you say?"

"Do you have any idea why he's after you?"

"I don't think he wants me to find out why my mother died."

"You think he had a hand in it?"

"It's possible." She almost told him of her mother's final letter, but she couldn't, not until she knew more about what lay behind it.

"When you met with him at Sam Larkin's office—"

Juliana sat up in the bed. "When I what?"

"The day you went into the Lone Star. I saw you walk onto the sidewalk from Larkin's office, and a few minutes later out strolls Montgomery."

"This morning was the first time I've seen Edmund since I returned."

A chill washed over her, and a sickness of heart so strong she thought she would throw up. Tossing the covers aside, she grabbed the wrapper from the floor and tugged it on, tying the sash firmly at her waist.

"He was listening," she said as she began to pace, the thoughts coming at her like bullets. "There was a closed door, and I remember thinking it would be a good place for someone to hide and listen. No wonder Larkin was nervous when I got there."

"Think carefully, Juliana. What did you and Larkin talk about?"

"I asked him what he knew about my mother's

death. I asked about the doctor, but all I learned was that Gibbs had disappeared. Larkin kept telling me I should ask my stepfather what had happened." She laughed bitterly. "So why didn't he simply open the door and let me put the questions to him?"

She pictured the scene, her throwing out heartfelt questions, Larkin stalling, and only a few feet away Edmund listening in secret and smiling his reptilian smile.

She stopped and looked at Matt. It was almost a mistake, for it made her want to throw herself into his strong arms more than ever. It took all her own fast-dwindling resolve to hold back.

She twisted her hands at her waist. "Edmund told me today my mother was a drunk. The Crawfords confirmed it—not in anything they said, but they didn't contradict him either. In their eyes he's practically a saint. I could probably ask any of the townspeople, including my own lawyer, and they'd feel the same." She laughed harshly. "Poor man, they'd tell me, shouldering the burden of an alcoholic wife."

"I wish I could help you, but I haven't been around much over the past few years. When I have been, the talk's been about horses. And I was on my way to England when Iona died." He hesitated. "I gather the talk is that drinking killed her."

"Edmund as much as said it outright." She

shuddered. "For what that's worth. I find nothing about the man truthful or even tolerable."

"We got us a bond there, Jules. He's tried more than once to bring the Half-Moon to ruin."

This time she didn't flinch at the name he'd given her. "Hate's a strange bond."

"Yeah, well, you and I don't exactly lead ordinary lives. And it wasn't hate that put us in bed together."

Whatever he meant by the words, all she could think of was how he was standing by the window in his work clothes and she was in front of him, naked beneath a thin layer of silk. If only they could fall back under the covers, both stripped of their clothes, and he could hold her in his arms.

But she couldn't let herself go down that path, couldn't let him know how she felt—certainly not until she herself understood a great deal more about those feelings.

"I'd like to lead an ordinary life, if I knew what it was," she said.

"I'm not sure that's true. Otherwise you would have stayed back East."

"You know nothing about my life there." She shook her head. "I'm sorry, I didn't mean to sound so harsh. It's true that I was taken care of in Saratoga."

But I wasn't loved. Any more than she was loved now.

"It just wasn't home," she added. "I had hoped Texas could be that."

For a moment her thoughts threw her back to the morning and the runaway carriage, clinging to the useless reins, terrified for her life. She waited until the moment of panic passed before saying, "Now I'm not sure." She hated the tremor in her voice. "Look, Matt, we both know that what happened between us can't happen again. So much occurred today, I wasn't thinking straight."

"And now you are."

No! "Yes, as straight as I can."

Why did he have to keep looking at her like that? What could he see in the dim light? The seconds ticked away with excruciating slowness. He seemed to be waiting for her to say something, maybe that she wanted him back in her bed every chance she could get, that she felt safe and protected only when he was near. That he was the only man who had ever made her feel like a woman to be valued.

At last he moved out of the moonlight and toward the darkened door. "Go back to bed, Juliana, and get some more rest. I'll see you tomorrow. Don't worry about Kane. I imagine he's several counties away by now, if he didn't head south for Mexico. You did something terrible to him today, and to Edmund. You survived."

Then he was gone, leaving her with his scent on her body, with memories so jumbled, so extreme, she could barely sort out the good from the bad.

She stumbled back to the bed, knowing that any hope for rest was gone, managing to cling to one thought above all others, one small ray of hope. Matt was right. She had survived.

Chapter Thirteen

Matt felt the bunched muscles between his legs, the stored power that was the essence of Dark Champion. Settling into the saddle, he had only to say, "Let's go, DC," and the stallion exploded along the oval track Matt had laid out for him.

Leaning low over the long and splendid neck, he let the horse go all out—as if a tug on the reins could have stopped him. Days of relative inactivity gave the thoroughbred impetus to fly as Matt had never seen him fly before, hoofs pounding against the hard ground, the long, strong legs devouring the furlongs. Four times they flew around the quarter-mile path, one full-mile run at a record pace by Matt's estimate.

He could have ridden forever. Instead, he let the animal ease off slowly as they made the fifth and final circuit, then came to a complete halt in the middle of the field, man and horse alone beneath a clear blue sky.

It was a strange track for a horse with DC's noble ancestry, a narrow strip circling a cow pasture on a run-down ranch, no fancy cinders covering the surface, only wild grass and weeds.

The day following the carriage incident, during one of the few times he and Juliana had talked, she'd suggested he lay out the track on the perimeter of the land he had cleared of loco weed, and he'd been more than willing to comply. Mostly that had meant clearing rocks, driving stakes, checking the ground with meticulous care to ensure a smooth race.

He relished the work. It kept him from thinking about Juliana all the time—her troubles, the link with his own troubles, the way she'd been in bed. She'd gotten under his skin in a way no other woman ever had, and he saw no sign she was going away.

But she was sensible. She'd talked about nothing except clearing the track, and he'd accepted her offer. She seemed to have gotten over what had passed between them a hell of a lot quicker than he.

He concentrated on what he was doing now and on what he planned to do. Dark Champion was bred to run, and to win. Matt felt it in his gut, even more now than he had back in England when he'd bargained with the countess.

Dismounting, he stroked the stallion's sweat-streaked neck. "Great going, DC," he said. "You are a champion indeed."

The horse whinnied and shook his head.

Matt looked around the wide pasture bounded by forest and hills. He looked extra hard at the trees, where Kane had hidden to fire at him. But he wasn't expecting a repeat performance. He'd meant it when he assured Juliana the bastard was long gone, probably down in Mexico by now. If he didn't believe it, he would not have brought DC out for some overdue training.

"I hear there's a pickup race happening soon," he said to the horse, who was proving to be a good listener. "Nothing special, not like Newmarket, but still, there are some fine horses around here. What do you think, are you ready to take 'em?"

When DC turned his neck to look back at Matt, he almost expected the horse to nod.

He was debating whether to give DC more time on the track, or take him back to the barn for a good rubdown, when he caught sight of a horse and rider coming toward him. He recognized Juliana astride Pepper, riding slowly in case the mare was in foal.

She was wearing a split skirt and leather vest over a shirt the color of wild bluebonnets, and her golden hair was flowing free beneath a western hat. She looked glorious, and he felt a jolt of pleasure mixed with a measure of disgust. At this rate he'd never get her out of his mind.

Reining to a halt beside him, she slid to the ground, showing what an expert horsewoman she was. Cheeks flushed, her breast heaving with deep breaths, she took off the hat and shook out her hair. Matt absorbed every detail in one swift glance. He also remembered what she'd looked like wearing only a wrapper, and then wearing nothing at all. Did she know what the sight of her could do to a man?

"Something wrong?" he asked.

"Nothing, except I can't take a step without bumping into Mugg."

Matt smiled to himself. The day after the carriage accident, he and Mugg had had a long talk about protecting their boss from anything like that happening again.

"He's watching out for you."

"I know, but I'm not worried now that Kane is gone. And at least for a while Edmund is too cowardly to make another move."

"So what brought you out here?"

She started to say something, then changed her mind and studied DC.

"He's beautiful, Matt. Do you plan to race him soon?"

"There's a race a week from Saturday, outside of Bandera. He should be ready to do a little showing off."

She smoothed the hair away from her face, looked at the ground, then back at him, her fine, high cheeks still pink.

"You'll need money for a stake."

Matt held himself very still. "Yep, I will."

"I've got money."

"I'm not taking it."

"Consider it wages."

"For what?"

Her chin went up and her amber eyes flashed fire.

"Not for the rescue, or anything that happened afterwards."

"That's not what I meant, damn it." Matt took off his hat and slapped it against his thigh. "I haven't done anything on the ranch worth more than room and board—hell, not even that, and you know it. And besides, what makes you so all-fire sure I'm busted?"

As angry as they both were, the longer he looked at her, the more he wanted to kiss her, long and hard. He wanted to clear the air between them so they could get down to talking plain facts, the main one being there was no way in hell he could take money from her . . . even though he needed it, which was something he'd burn in fire and brimstone before letting her know.

Instead of kissing her, he turned and kicked a rock, which wasn't nearly as satisfying.

"You do what you have to do, Matt. If you change your mind about the money, let me know. If there's one thing I've found out in this life, it's that money is not the most important thing in the world."

"Because you've never been without it."

"But I've been without other things, and I know what matters."

She slapped her hat back in place and, without asking for his assistance, pulled herself back into the saddle. She studied the landscape, as if she had never seen it before.

"Mugg will put a plate out for you tonight. Since that's the way you've been taking your meals, I assume you want to continue." At last she looked at him. "I didn't mean to insult you about the money. Friends ought to help each other. Regardless of what's been going on between us, I consider you my friend."

Matt watched her ride off, spine stiff, her thick golden hair bouncing against her slender back.

A reasonable woman, he thought, as well as beautiful. And vulnerable. All of it totaled up to a deadly combination. When he looked at her, he felt like he was walking on quicksand. He couldn't run away no matter how hard he tried.

But he'd have to, eventually. The knowledge brought him little satisfaction.

In the meantime, there was the little matter of stake money, plus extra greenbacks to put down on a few side bets. If his luck held up, he knew just where to get what he would need.

He whistled for DC, who had sidled away to a thick patch of grass.

"Okay, Mr. Champion, or should I say Lord Champion since you were once owned by an earl? Never could keep all those titles straight. Guess it's a good thing the countess is far away in England and not here in Texas to point out my mistakes. She and Juliana could have some fine private talks on that subject alone."

Matt entered the Lone Star later that night, a few coins jingling in his pocket. Ken O'Malley waved to him from behind the bar, and he returned the wave. A whiskey would go down smooth, but he didn't want to spare the money. And he wanted to be cold sober when he sat down to a game of cards. He wouldn't be playing for fun.

Long ago he'd learned that one secret of success was giving the appearance that he didn't give a damn about winning or losing. Strange thing, over the years he'd developed a reputation for wanting nothing but a good time. Truth was that since the shooting, he hadn't done much of anything for fun.

Taking off his hat, he tucked his gloves at his waist and ran a hand through his hair, all the while studying the smoky room, sizing up who was playing, who was drinking, who was looking back at him.

His biggest relief came at not seeing Jack anywhere around. Tonight dear old Dad would only get in the way.

His eye fell on the man who'd insulted Juliana. What was his name? Oh, yeah, Ned. He would make a fine opponent across a poker table. Matt tossed his hat onto the end of the bar, then made his way slowly, deliberately, to the man's table, glancing casually at him and the two gamblers with him, at the pile of money in front of them, at the quick way Ned was dealing the cards.

"Mind if I sit in on the next hand?" Matt asked, pulling out a chair without waiting for an answer.

Ned looked at him with the same superior smile he'd given to Juliana when she foolishly invaded the Lone Star, only this smile was tinged with greed instead of lust.

"I got no problem with that. Do you boys agree? See, we're all fine. Nothing like taking a little Hunter money. If you've got enough to get into the game."

One of the men snickered, then sobered fast when he got a look at Matt's expression.

Matt sat back in the chair and watched the play of the hand, noticing the mannerisms of the men, the way they bet, the way they hesitated, figuring

Ned would be the one to pull in the money. He figured right.

Without warning, soft arms were wrapped around his neck, and he was acutely aware of heavy perfume and an underlying scent of unwashed body.

"Hey, sugar, don't see you much in here."

"Dammit, Madge," Ned drawled, "what're you wasting time with him for when you could have me?"

"I've had you, Ned," she drawled right back, getting a loud laugh from the other men. She leaned low and rubbed a rouged cheek against Matt's face. "I'm after fresh blood."

"I wouldn't be worth a damn tonight," Matt said, pulling her arms away from his neck.

Pouting, she backed off for a second, then came at him again, this time from the side, bending low to give him a good look at the pendulous breasts spilling over the top of her gown. Her faded hair was thick and wild, its few dark streaks as black as the kohl lining her eyes. Madge had been at the Lone Star for as long as Matt could remember. He would have been kinder to her, but he had other things on his mind.

Before she could speak, a hated voice rasped out over the crowd. "One woman ain't good enough for you?"

Slowly Madge backed off, giving Matt a good

view of his father standing inside the saloon door.

Matt kept his attention on the table. "Cut for deal," he said coolly, reaching for the cards, but inside he was boiling.

Jack was not done. Matt knew he wouldn't be.

"Edmund said he caught you and the Widow Rains as good as humping in her parlor."

That brought a rustling noise across the saloon. Every muscle in Matt's body pulled tight. He could take any ugliness his father threw at him, but Juliana was off limits. Jack had to know it. Even drunk, he wasn't a complete fool.

"Now, Jack," O'Malley said from behind the bar, "don't let the troubles between you two get to hurting anyone else."

"Ask the preacher," Jack snarled to no one in particular. "He was there. He knows what was going on."

Matt shoved his chair away from the table, fighting his rage. "Hold up on the dealing," he said to the smirking Ned. "I'll be right back."

As he made his way toward his father, he could hear chairs scraping, whispers, a few crude laughs, and from the corner of his eye he saw Madge beating a hasty retreat to the side of the saloon, getting out of what could be the line of fire.

Jack swayed but held his ground, his face heavily whiskered, his tight eyes bleary but watchful.

"You always like to put on a show in here, Jack?" Matt asked. "Let's take this outside."

"I ain't the one that's got something to hide."

There was a new harshness to his voice, a bitterness that Matt couldn't understand . . . unless his father knew everything about the day Elizabeth Hunter died. The ugly memories sliced through him. Damn it, Jack had been drunk, and he'd said nothing at the time. Jack was not a man to hold back when it came to criticizing his youngest son.

"We've all got things to hide," Matt said coldly. "I don't suppose Edmund told you everything about what was going on. About the accident that almost cost Mrs. Rains her life."

Jack rubbed his face. "Word spread about that, and whether you believe it or not, I was sorry to hear it."

"Did word include that when Edmund came in unannounced and uninvited, I was holding her while she was fighting back tears? The woman was terrified. Anyone would have done what I did."

He wasn't entirely lying. And he would have said anything to clear Juliana's good name.

"You're good at getting out of taking blame, aren't you, Matthew?"

The use of his full name stopped him for a moment. No one had ever called him Matthew but his mother, and she had always said it with love, even when he'd done something to disappoint her, which was just about every day of his life.

In that moment his hatred for his father was pure, and it ate like acid at his gut. He wanted nothing more than to smash his fist into his father's weathered face.

But his father was drunk and he was old and he, too, carried a lot of heavy weight from the past. Something stirred in Matt, an instinct buried so deep he hadn't known it existed, a sense of the natural bond between a father and his son, no matter how their lives had played out.

Matt swallowed his anger. Staring at his father, knowing they could never be close, he felt a sense of loss far more intense, more painful, than the hate. He was about to take Jack by the arm and do whatever was necessary to get him outside when Madge stepped between the two of them.

"Come on, Jack, we've known each other for a long time. I've got a room upstairs where you can sleep it off. Hell, I'll get us a bottle of whiskey. We'll have us a real toot first."

"Good idea," O'Malley said, coming around the bar waving a full bottle. "This one's on me."

Madge hooked the bottle with one hand and with an arm linked around Jack, guided him to the stairs at the back of the saloon. But not before she glanced at Matt and winked, as if to say *You had your chance.*

Matt watched, seeing his father for the first time as a weak man trapped in a life not entirely of his making, a life marked by failure and tragedy. In that moment Matt understood why his father drank.

"He'll be asleep before long," O'Malley said in a low voice that only Matt could hear. "Don't know what's got into him. He'd just about given up the drinking."

"That was before I got home."

The barkeep had no response. Matt waited until his father was upstairs and behind a closed door before returning to the gambling table. Somehow in the middle of the crowded saloon, he felt very much alone.

Ned continued to smirk up at him, whipping him back into the matter at hand.

"You want to tell us about the Widow Rains?" Ned asked.

Matt regarded the man with great care, clenching and unclenching his fists as he took his chair. "Are you given to gossip, Ned? I thought this was a card game, not a women's sewing circle." He leaned forward and cut the cards, turning up the ace of spades. "Guess it's my deal."

Shuffling the cards, he tried to recapture the

anticipated pleasure of taking every cent Ned had brought to the table. But the joy had gone out of the occasion. He was taking care of business, and nothing more.

Chapter Fourteen

Matt counted out the money at the outdoor registration table.

"...ninety-five, a hundred. That should be right, George," he said over the noise of the racing-day chaos around him.

"It is, Mr. Hunter." George Livingston, the officiating representative of the loose-bound Bandera Racing Club, smiled broadly as he handed Matt his receipt. "Glad to have you back racing again. It's been a long time." He glanced up at the dark clouds rolling in. "If we *have* a race, that is."

"We will."

"Wish I had your confidence," George said. "The word is you've got quite a horse running today." He glanced at Matt's registration form. "Yes, here it is, in the last race, the mile."

"That's right."

"Are you familiar with the course? The mile is cross-country, you know."

"DC and I looked it over yesterday."

"DC? Oh yes, Dark Champion, I see here on the form." He studied the paper. "Hmmm, that name sounds familiar."

"He hasn't raced around here."

With that, Matt tucked his receipt in his shirt pocket and headed out for the creek-side wooded area where he'd set up camp. Men and horses passed on both sides of him as he walked along the rough dirt road, wagons creaking, dogs barking, hawkers setting up food stalls. It was the usual circus that went with horse racing. He'd have no trouble finding someone to bet with on any of the races.

He also knew Livingston was continuing to think about DC, about where he'd heard the name before. He would either remember on his own or someone would tell him this was the horse Matt had brought back from England, and then someone else would remember the New-market racing form of so many months ago, the one that had labeled the thoroughbred a killer.

He probably should have written *killer* in the space beside DC's name. That way he could clear things up right away.

Thunder rumbled in the distance. He could sense the restlessness in the animals. DC wouldn't be any different, pulling at the tether, bobbing his head, dancing around impatiently.

When Matt finally got to the small secluded campsite, he stopped a few yards away and shook his head. DC didn't seem in the least edgy. On the contrary, the stallion was standing peacefully in the shade, as if listening to the nearby creek babbling over its rocky bed, instead of the oncoming storm.

DC might also have been enjoying the way Juliana was stroking the sensitive space between his eyes. Juliana, who should have been miles away at the Lazy Q, safe under the watchful eye of Mugg Snelling.

Two reactions hit Matt fast: the temptation to grin at her and make a fool of himself, and an equally strong temptation to give way to anger.

Anger was safer. Besides, he had no business being glad to see her. It wouldn't do either of them any good.

He ran a hand through his hair. "What are you doing here?" he snapped.

Juliana continued stroking the horse, but he thought the color drained from her face. "I came to watch this magnificent animal race."

"I guess you rode over here all by yourself without a thought of any danger. It's a long way. What did you do, leave in the middle of the night?"

She abandoned DC and turned to face Matt. She was wearing a gray cloak and a bonnet that framed her face, and it seemed to him that with her fine features and deep-set amber eyes she looked particularly fragile, like someone who needed to be held and protected.

But looks could be deceiving. She wasn't backing away from the thousand pounds of horseflesh that was nudging her for attention.

"I am in absolutely no danger," she said, chin tilted, a defiant light in her eyes.

A man could take only so much. "Oh, yes, you are." He walked toward her. "From me."

That got her backing away, edging toward a line of thick bushes that grew close to the creek bank.

"What are you doing? For goodness' sake, Matt, we're outside."

"I chose an isolated place to set up camp. How did you find me anyway?"

"Someone said he saw you headed down this way. I just kept walking until I found DC."

While she talked, she continued to back away, but Matt was gaining on her.

"I have to tell you, Jules, seeing you out here is doing some strange things to me. Like giving me an itch I need to scratch."

He could have told her more—that seeing her like this, having had no idea she was within twenty miles of him, hit him hard, shook him, made him lose his sense of loneliness. No one in all his life had been able to do that. No one until

Juliana. And that shook him all the more.

"What are you going to do?" she asked.

"I don't know. I'll think of something."

She stopped backing away. Unfastening the tie at her throat, she took off the bonnet and tossed it onto the bush at her back. Then she smoothed her hair and stared at him, the defiance in her eyes warming to something far more powerful. He wondered if she understood just how strong she really was.

"I meant it when I said I came here to watch the race," she said.

"I meant it when I said you ought to be home."

Neither spoke for a moment; they just stood there staring at one another, and all Matt could think of was how he wanted to hold her and forget the rest of the world.

"You scare me sometimes, Matt."

"You scare the hell out of me."

"Then why aren't we running away from each other?"

"Damned if I know."

And then suddenly they were in each other's arms and Matt was kissing her, thrusting his arms underneath her cloak to hold her close, tasting sweetness, thinking about how much he wanted to drag her behind the bush and show her exactly what she was doing to him.

He'd never had his fingers itch so much to touch a woman in all her intimate places, just touching, not even doing anything about it, just touching and rubbing and . . .

He was vaguely aware of someone coughing behind him. Juliana stiffened in his arms, and he had no choice but to break the kiss and turn around. He caught sight of Brent at the same time as DC whinnied.

"A little late there, buddy," Matt said to the horse, then looked at Brent and on to the pair behind him, Quince and a woman he took to be Quince's wife, Glory.

Juliana stayed within the circle of his arm, but the look on her face was almost as stark as when she'd faced Edmund and the preacher.

"Surprise, surprise," Matt said. He looked at Juliana. "Did you know they were here?"

"She rode with us," Brent said.

"Actually in the carriage with me," Glory Hunter said, walking forward, hand extended. "I'm Quince's wife, Matt. It's good to meet you at last."

With Juliana shifting away from him, Matt took the extended hand. Like Brent, Quince had married a beauty, a redhead with flashing dark eyes, mostly flashing amusement right now. He couldn't really blame her.

"I guess you know by now you married into an unusual family," Matt said.

She laughed. "I know." Nodding toward DC, she added, "That's a beautiful horse you've got there. Let us know when you put him out for stud."

Matt nodded. He should be long gone by then, but something was keeping him from saying it out loud. Or rather, someone. He'd told Juliana he wouldn't be at the Lazy Q for long, and he still meant to move on, but somehow his leaving had become a private matter between the two of them.

"Where's your wife, Brent?" he asked.

"We both figured it wasn't a smart thing for her to travel, what with the baby on the way. We've still got a couple of months to go."

"Abby's going to pitch a fit when she finds out we were here," Glory said. "She and Jonah should be back from New Orleans soon, but they'll be going to the fort."

That left only one Hunter unaccounted for. He looked at his brothers, and he could see they were thinking the same thing.

"Should I expect any more surprises?" Matt asked.

Brent shook his head. "Pa decided not to come with us."

"Meaning he said it would be a cold day in hell before he watched DC in a race."

"Something like that," Brent said.

A sudden wind sent leaves scattering, and thunder rumbled, still distant but closer than before.

"I hope you're not camping out," Matt said.

"We took rooms in Bandera," Quince said. "Join us if you can."

Matt thought of Juliana standing close enough for him to touch, thought about being with her in a hotel bedroom, in a hotel bed. But that would shoot to hell anything that was left of her reputation. He'd done her enough disservice already.

"I'll stay out here with DC, then head for home in the morning. It's getting close to the first race. I'd better get moving if I want to place some bets."

Without looking at Juliana, figuring she was better off with him out of sight, he walked around his unexpected visitors and headed back toward the field where the races would be held, nodding to Quince's wife as he passed. He hated to leave, yet at the same time, he had to force himself not to break into a run.

As he hurried along, a strange thought hit him, more a feeling than a thought, a sense that he was walking away from his life, and a mood settled on him as dark as the clouds overhead.

Still tasting Matt on her tongue, still shaken from the interruption of their kiss, Juliana watched as he walked away alone—his choice, his preferred way. She felt as if a gulf were opening between them, a chasm that could never be breached.

What was happening to her? Why did she feel she was tumbling down into a deep, dark hole where light could never reach?

But she couldn't let the feeling show. She had three pairs of eyes on her, sympathetic eyes. In some ways, dealing with Edmund Montgomery was easier than dealing with the Hunters. She didn't have to hide her hatred the way she hid her sense of loss.

Grabbing her bonnet from where she'd tossed it on top of a bush, she smiled and tugged it in place.

"Now then," she said, knowing her voice was too bright, too sprightly to be anything but fake, "I guess DC will be all right here by himself. I wouldn't mind putting some money down myself."

Brent offered his arm, and she took it, following in the path Matt had set, and they were soon in the midst of the confusion of race day. Juliana had been around racing long enough to know who was taking bets, even the informal kind at a pickup race like this one. Telling Brent she would be fine, she dropped his arm and headed for one of the busiest gamblers, a short, full-bellied man in a black suit and string tie who was pulling in money from a crowd around him, jotting notes on a small piece of paper after shoving the cash into a leather pouch suspended from his wrist.

It wasn't as fancy as the gambling system in Saratoga, but probably just as efficient.

For a moment the crowd around him thinned. She was about to move up to him when she saw a tall, rail-thin man talking to him. A chill ran down her spine. Her attorney, Sam Larkin, was peeling out bills as if he printed them himself. Lawyering in Diablo must be more lucrative than she'd thought.

Watching the man, she remembered sitting in his office, wondering why he was so nervous, ignorant of who listened on the other side of a closed door, hearing every confidential thing she said. The chill turned to hard, hot anger. With grim determination she walked up behind him, waiting quietly until he had finished his transactions with the gambler and turned.

When he saw her, he sucked in a gasp. "Mrs. Rains!" he said, his eyes wide and startled.

"Mr. Larkin—just the man I wanted to talk to."

She kept her voice low, casual, almost friendly, though the effort was eating her up inside.

"Since my carriage was wrecked last week, I haven't been able to get into town. Would you mind stepping aside so we can conduct our business here?"

"I . . . I don't see how we could do that," he said, stumbling over every other word. "It would be totally out of place."

"Still, let's do it, shall we?" She walked a half-dozen steps away from the gambler taking the bets, giving Larkin no choice but to follow.

"What I want is simple," she said. "I haven't forgotten the small legacy from my father. I'd like the money now, and of course the proceeds from however you invested it. I know," she said, ignoring his thunderstruck look, "I should have mentioned it the other day. You were probably going to bring it up yourself, but I kept going on about other matters. It won't amount to much, but I would like to have the cash."

Larkin cleared his throat. "That may take some time."

"I understand. A week? Two weeks? A month at the most. And of course I'll want to see all the documentation on the money invested and the returns. My late husband taught me about horse racing, and he also taught me about the handling of money."

She lied, at least where Harlan Rains was concerned. Everything she had learned had been on her own, but that didn't mean she hadn't learned a great deal. Including when a man was lying and when he was trying to cover something up.

Harlan had never been able to keep from her his visits to his whores. At the time she had been crushed, but strangely, the memory strengthened her now.

She looked over her shoulder and saw Brent

talking to a man she did not recognize, but he had one characteristic that made him enticing. He was wearing a badge.

"Excuse me a moment, Mr. Larkin, but I see a friend over there. If you have any questions about what I'm asking, please let me know."

With a polite nod, she left the open-mouthed lawyer and hurried to Brent's side, smiling up at the lawman as if she had known him all her life.

She looked at the badge. Texas Ranger. Perfect.

Brent made the introductions, and she found herself shaking hands with Ranger Grant Zachary. To Juliana's eye, he looked the way a Texas Ranger ought to look, tall and broad-shouldered, rugged more than handsome, with leathery skin, sandy hair, intelligent gray eyes.

"Could you pretend to be very friendly with me?" she said softly. "Lean down as if we're sharing a confidence?"

"It would be my pleasure, Mrs. Rains."

When he did as she asked, she glanced back at Larkin, but the lawyer had disappeared. She did see Matt, however, standing a good distance away, watching her with an expression she could not read.

Tall and lean, his features sharply hewn, Matt seemed at odds with all the activity around him, the families arriving, the children playing chase. They looked at one another for a moment, and

Juliana felt a fist tighten around her heart. Then he turned and walked away, leaving her with the same helpless feeling she'd experienced when he'd left her at the creek.

She took a deep breath and turned back to Zachary. "I'd better place my bet before the racing starts."

"I'll go with you," the ranger said. "If you don't mind."

"I'd be honored. There's not much chance I'll be cheated with you by my side."

But it was with a heavy step she walked beside the ranger. All she could think about was the way Matt had looked at her, and more, his leaving without coming over to join her.

A man apart, that was Matt Hunter. Even when he was with her, when they were kissing or holding one another, she knew he held something back from her. The realization brought tears to her eyes, but she blinked them away. She was being foolish; and if she expected some kind of commitment from him, even a hint of real affection, she was laying herself open for a world of hurt.

The first four races went quickly, Juliana winning more than she lost. Brent and Quince grinned at her ability to pick out a fast horse, and Glory gave her a big hug every time she won. She didn't see Matt again, but she figured that after he placed his bets he had returned to DC, which, she admitted, was his rightful place.

She also did not see any sign of Sam Larkin, but she hadn't expected to.

The first rumblings of disquiet came not from the darkening clouds but from the crowd outside the fence where the track had been laid, a track not much better than the one Matt had fashioned in a Lazy Q cow pasture.

"Killer horse," she heard more than once, and "Dark Champion is well named."

"I was afraid of this," Brent said.

"Afraid of what?" Juliana asked.

"That word would spread about the horse. Back in England, DC took an unkindly view of finishing his races. He injured one jockey, killed another, and those are the ones I know about. Could be others."

"Still, the stallion's a beauty," Quince said with a shake of his head. "Let's hope Matt didn't make a big mistake."

"There's nothing wrong with Dark Champion. I would ride him," Juliana said, drawing sharp looks from the men and an understanding nod from Glory.

Whatever response her remark might have drawn was lost in the roar of the crowd as the riders came in on the horses scheduled for the race. Juliana counted sixteen entrants—all fine, spirited animals—but no DC. She could hear the buzz around her, talk about the killer horse already causing trouble, about maybe being disqualified, and she could picture Matt, having been thrown by the stallion, lying at the side of a field somewhere, or back by his isolated campsite.

She felt physically ill just thinking about the possibilities, ready to run down to the creek and look for him, when Brent said, "There he is."

"Making an entrance," Quince said with a hint of pride in his voice.

And there Matt was indeed, riding in behind the other thoroughbreds, sitting tall in the saddle, his hat pulled low on his forehead. As always, he looked as one with the horse, man and animal seeming to have the same rhythms, the same rocking forward progress. And, too, the same pride.

There was no doubting Dark Champion's magnificence, his black coat sleek as polished ebony, his head held high as he pranced. Matt had a magnificence of his own, his back ramrod straight, dark hair bound at his nape with a leather thong, his sculpted features rigid as he stared straight ahead.

The crowd fell silent as Matt and DC passed, but then it was all noise and cheering as the horses spread out at the starting line. Much of the mile-long race couldn't be seen from where the crowd was standing, nothing but the start and the finish lines, the major part of the track having been laid out through woods and across a couple of water hazards.

Dark Champion was the last to take his place, restless, dancing around, giving Matt a hard time, although Juliana could not see any sign of stress in his face or in the way he sat in the saddle. One thing she did notice: He was the only rider not holding a whip.

DC had barely gotten in line when the starting gun fired. Instead of racing forward with the other thoroughbreds, he reared, nostrils flaring, then turned in a tight circle, fighting the bit in his mouth. Matt flattened himself along the horse's neck, his lips moving, and Juliana would have given the south pasture to know what magic words he was whispering.

Whatever Matt said worked, for suddenly DC was in fearless pursuit of the other racers, his strong legs rapidly regaining the distance he had lost. And then they were all out of sight, their departure marked by a clap of thunder so loud it seemed to split the heavens, sending down a torrent of rain.

"Let's get out of this," Brent said, and Quince put his arm around Glory.

"I'm not leaving," Juliana said. "I've been in rain before."

"But not lightning," Quince said.

"It's far away from here," she said, wondering

why she was doing this, standing in a storm, staring at a field without horses, waiting for a man who was in truth a stranger to her to cross the finish line.

Juliana did not try to analyze her reasoning. All she knew was that she could not leave. Neither did the Hunters. An eternity passed before she saw the horses come into view, a blur through the rain, no horse distinguishable from another until one broke from the pack, a black streak heading for the finish line, a thing of beauty until a jagged streak of lightning rent the sky, striking a tree in the woods on the far side of the field.

Sparks flew against a background of deafening thunder, and with the crowd scattering around her, Juliana watched in horror as Dark Champion reared and pawed the air, then came down hard, jarring his rider, who somehow managed to hold on until the stallion bolted across the finish line scant seconds ahead of the charging pack. Only then did the rider drop the reins and fall from the saddle onto the muddy ground, lying on his back as the rain pelted down on him.

Without thinking, barely hearing the shouted protests of Brent and Quince, the frantic call of Glory, Juliana slipped through the fence and ran to Matt, dodging horses and riders and officials who had crowded onto the field.

Kneeling beside him, she brushed the matted hair from his face.

"Matt, say something," she said frantically. "Please, please say something, anything."

His eyes fluttered open, then closed against the driving rain.

And then he smiled.

"We won, Juliana. And there's something better than that. Dark Champion finished the race."

Only the knowledge that the Hunter brothers were coming up behind her kept Juliana from giving Matt a congratulatory kiss.

"Good for DC," she said. "He deserves a warm stable and a pile of the best food, right? Which he can get if you come into town with us. There will be room at the hotel."

She stood and backed away before he could think of an argument. Pawing restlessly not three feet from his fallen rider, Dark Champion rolled his eyes at Juliana.

"Good job," she said to him, and she got the feeling he understood.

"How did you get Matt here?" Glory asked, looking around the crowded town hall.

Standing behind his newest sister-in-law, Matt answered before Juliana had a chance. "She lied."

"I didn't lie," Juliana said. "This is where we're having supper."

"You didn't tell me it was a full-blown social."

"Races like this one always have socials," Glory said.

Matt shrugged. After any race he'd ever been to, he was always riding on, counting his winnings, shrugging off the losses, planning on where he would settle next. He told himself it was the rain and DC's comfort that had drawn him here, but he was honest enough to admit that the woman beside him—the one with the pile of yellow hair on top of her head, with a few tendrils trailing down her slender neck, the one with the delicate features and the strength of ten men, the one in the blue silk dress that outlined her womanly curves—that woman might have had something to do with his decision.

Quince ambled over. "Glory, looks like they're about to clear the floor for some dancing. Are you up to it? We've had a long day, and I don't want to tire you."

"Let's just see who can outlast the other," Glory replied, taking his hand and leading him away.

"I don't dance," Matt said.

Juliana looked at him with a thoughtful expression in her eyes. "I'm sure you don't."

He couldn't tell if she was criticizing or simply stating a fact, or maybe saying something else he couldn't figure out. All he knew for certain was that with no more than a look she had him back to walking on quicksand.

Beyond her he saw Grant Zachary make his way through the crowd toward them. He'd met the ranger after the race and learned he was a special friend of Brent's. But Brent had ridden back to the Half-Moon, declaring he didn't like to leave Crystal alone too long.

"Would you like to dance, Mrs. Rains?" Zachary asked, with no more than a nod to Matt.

"I . . . why, yes, I would like that very much," she said after a second's pause, leaving Matt to watch as she took the ranger's hand, let him hold her at the waist, then twirl her around the dance floor to the music of the fiddle band at the far end of the hall.

Taking it all in, down to the smile on Juliana's face as she looked up at the ranger, Matt was fast losing the good feelings he'd gained from the race. His mood wasn't helped any when the music ended and Zachary led her to a group of people at the side of the floor. Matt recognized a few from Diablo, including Quince and his bride.

Juliana seemed to be giving her attention to one person in particular, a dark-haired, pretty woman Matt didn't know. They talked animatedly for a few minutes, and then the music started again. He could tell the ranger was asking her for another dance, but she shook her head and headed back toward him.

"You take care," Zachary said to her, then with a nod to Matt, "You'll see to her, right?"

"Of course," Matt answered, irritated. What did Zachary think he was going to do to her? He was honest enough to admit the lawman's question might not have been out of order. He and Juliana hadn't been alone together since the interrupted kiss by the creek. Matt never liked to leave anything half done.

"I'm going back to the hotel, Matt," she said, avoiding his eye. "I've developed a terrible headache."

He knew her well enough to know she wasn't telling him everything.

"Must have been the dancing."

"I guess that's it," she said, then lost herself in thoughts he could not begin to understand.

"Who was the woman you were talking to?"

"She's from Diablo. Melinda Barton's her name. I didn't know her, but I gathered from what she said she was a friend of Brent's."

"Brent was never big on women friends."

"I know only what she said. Look, Matt, you stay on here. The hotel's just across the street."

"Nope. I'll get your cloak and walk you over. Anyway, I need to look in on DC down at the stables."

He could see she was only half listening.

"Of course," he added, "you could come with me to the stables and we could strip down naked and roll in the hay."

"Um-hum."

Matt gave up. "I'll get your cloak."

Crossing the muddy street required some maneuvering, but she declined his offer to carry her. In the small hotel lobby, he watched as she hurried up the stairs, then went on to the stables, where he would be spending the night alongside DC, feeling restless, dissatisfied, and not knowing what he was supposed to do about it.

But he made sure he was up early the next morning, heading back to the hotel. He got there in time to see Quince and Glory getting ready to ride back to their ranch, and mingling with several others from Diablo.

"Where's Juliana?" Matt asked, pulling Quince aside.

"She took an early stagecoach," his brother replied.

"She couldn't have." The speaker was the woman Juliana had been talking to at the dance. "Hello," she said with a smile. "You don't know me, but I'm Melinda Barton. Your brother Brent and I used to be very good friends." She sighed. "But that's another story. Anyway, she couldn't have gone to Diablo. That coach doesn't leave for an hour."

The brothers looked at one another.

"On the other hand," Melinda went on, "she did seem very interested in Winding Creek. I was just there visiting my aunt, and I was telling her about it. Especially how curious it was to see Doc Gibbs there. You know, he used to live in Diablo, and then just disappeared one day. And there he

240

was in this little old town not much bigger than a puddle in the road. Would you believe he wouldn't talk to me? I swear, he acted like he'd never seen me before. I wrote Mama all about it—"

Matt quit listening and turned to Quince. "I need a favor."

"You're due. I don't think you've ever asked me for one in your life."

"I'm asking now. Can you hook DC to the back of your carriage? I don't want to take him with me."

Quince stared at him a moment. "Sure, Matt, whatever you need. But there's something going on here I don't understand."

"I wish I could tell you—hell, I wish I knew for sure myself."

"Women have a way of turning a man's life upside down."

"It's not that. Or maybe it is. I'm not sure anymore."

"I am," Glory said, but Matt was already hurrying out the door, figuring out how he would get to this Winding Creek, wondering where it might be and how much trouble Juliana could get into before he arrived.

Chapter Fifteen

By the time Juliana got off the stage in Winding Creek, night had fallen and the only lights to be seen were in the small stagecoach office set back from the road.

Chilled, she pulled her cloak tight and watched as the driver scrambled to the top of the coach for her small valise, then dropped to the ground beside her.

"Someone meeting you, miss?"

"This is a surprise visit," she said, taking the valise and putting on a brave face. "Do you know if there's a hotel or someplace I might stay?"

He scratched his scruffy beard. "I hardly ever bring anyone here. Unless there's someone waiting to catch the stage, I just drive on through." He nodded to the squat, dilapidated stone building that served as way station for the line. "Ben'll be in there. He'll help you."

He hesitated, looking up and down the deserted road. "San Antonio's not far away. That's where we'll be putting up for the night. I'll take you there if you like. Sure hate to leave you alone like this. Winding Creek ain't much of a town."

"Thank you, but this is where I need to be."

He spat a stream of tobacco juice into the dirt. "Suit yourself."

Climbing back to his perch, he picked up the reins, shouted, "Let's go, boys," in his gruff voice, and the stage was soon creaking and swaying down the road, stirring up dust in its wake.

Juliana listened for as long as the sound came to her. In the following silence she looked back down the road. Not a light in sight, nothing but closed-up buildings rising out of the ground like tombstones.

She shook off the thought.

"Doc Gibbs," she said, needing to hear a voice even if it was her own, "you'd better be waiting out there somewhere with answers. I've got lots of questions, and right now you're my last hope."

But of course there was no response, not even the sound of the wind. She stretched, twisting her back to get the kinks out after the day-long ride, then with a sigh picked up the valise and entered the office, stopping for a minute in the doorway to look around. Benches lined the rock walls on each side of the room, and the wooden floor was ingrained with dust that went back to the Republic days. Opposite the door, a counter ran the width of the office. Behind the counter sat a gray-haired man, looking older than the dust, his face propped in one hand, snoring loud enough to shake the birds' nest out of the rafters.

Beside him, a single lantern provided light.

"Ben?" she said, then repeated the name louder, walking to the counter and dropping her valise hard on the floor. She finally had to shake his arm to get his attention.

He snorted awake, rubbed his rheumy eyes, and blinked at her.

"Stage oughta be along any minute now," he said with a sniff.

"It's come and gone. Is there a place in town where I can stay? The driver said you could help me."

He cleared his throat. "That's a tough one," he said, scratching the bald spot on top of his head. "The hotel closed down last year, and we never got us one of those boardinghouses like some of the other towns in these parts."

Behind her the door opened and closed. "I'll take care of the lady."

The deep voice shot into the room, and Juliana's heart started racing. Closing her eyes for a minute, she felt a moment of joy, then tamped it down.

Turning, she stared at the tall, dusty figure standing in front of the door, lean face bristled, hat tugged low over steady, watchful eyes.

"What are you doing here, Matt?"

I'm here to help you in any way I can.

But that was only what she wanted him to say.

"Damned if I know," was what she heard.

Ben sat up straight. "See here, young fella, we don't abide no cussin' around here."

"I can see you haven't been around Mrs. Rains long," Matt said, speaking to Ben but looking at Juliana.

That just about killed any joy she'd felt when she'd heard his voice.

"Miz Rains," Ben said, "I take it that's you, little lady. Well, Miz Rains, you two seem to know one another. You got any objection to going with him? We got us a deputy if you do. Say the word and I'll fetch him for you. Tom Rollins don't put up with any foolery."

She hesitated, locking her gaze with Matt's. She felt tight inside, and needy, wanting him to do or say something rather than just stand there confusing her.

"There's no need to summon the deputy," she said at last. "Mr. Hunter and I are indeed acquainted."

"Suit yourself. I just remembered the Cochran place. Young couple with a baby—they packed and took off a month or so ago, left furniture and all. Ran up a few debts, they did. Their home ain't much, but it's a roof over your head in case we get some weather."

"It sounds wonderful," she said.

"Glad to oblige. You'll find the cabin behind the stables. Don't imagine it's locked. Most folks around here don't fool with such as that."

Juliana thanked him and with a deep breath hurried past Matt and out the door, but he was close on her heels, stopping long enough to grab the reins of the horse he had left outside.

She set a fast pace at the side of the road, headed toward the center of town.

"Don't try to stop me," she said, sounding braver than she felt, listening to the reassuring sounds of his solid steps behind her and the clop of the horse's hooves against the hard dirt.

"You're going the wrong way."

She whirled and crashed into him. For a moment she stared at the front of his shirt, breathing in his scent, holding on to the valise to keep from pressing her hands against his strength.

"I lied," he said. She stepped away and looked up at him as he added, "The stable's this way. But I wanted you to stop and talk."

Taking a deep breath, she stared into the surrounding darkness. "You heard Doc Gibbs is here, didn't you? Like me. I had to talk to him, to find out everything he can tell me about my mother and how she died. I didn't have any choice."

"You had one choice. You could have told me what you were planning."

Something in his voice caused her heart to quicken.

"This is my problem, not yours."

"That sounds good, Juliana, and maybe that's the way it ought to be. But it's not the way things are working out right now. For one thing, you wouldn't have found out about Gibbs, at least not so soon, if you hadn't been at the race."

"Something is wrong with that logic, Matt."

"There's not a lot in my life that *is* logical. So I just go on instinct. And instinct told me you were getting into something you couldn't handle."

"And you can."

"Damned if I know."

She looked up at the outline of his face, the familiar tilt of his hat, the line of his jaw. "You're hard to argue with."

"That's the first time you've said that. I got the feeling you liked to argue."

Juliana was grateful for the darkness, otherwise he might see the tears in her eyes. Didn't he know what he was doing to her, just being here? Didn't he understand how he was tearing her up inside, opening up all kinds of possibilities for hurt? Didn't he know that she had almost jumped for joy when she'd heard his voice?

Of course she hadn't let that joy show. And it wasn't unmixed. She shouldn't need him. She'd been telling herself how she could get along on her own.

And maybe she could, without any other man. But Matt was different.

And the middle of a strange town in the middle of the night was no place to be thinking about the secrets of her heart.

Turning from him, she set out once again. "You'll let me know if I make another mistake, I'm sure."

"It's become my lot in life."

If only that were true.

Without further talk, they soon found the stable, and behind it the Cochran house, a small, boxlike clapboard structure sitting at the far end of a weedy patch of ground. The moon came from behind a cloud to light their way, lending an eerie, otherworldly glow to the scene. Juliana's step slowed, and, handing her the reins of his horse, Matt walked ahead of her. When he stepped onto the porch, the floorboards creaked, as did the door when he opened it. Wrapping the reins around a porch rail, Juliana walked in after him.

In the dim light drifting in through a window, she saw that Ben hadn't lied. It wasn't much more than a musty single room. There was a dusty hearth, cobwebs in the rafters, and the scurrying of mice.

"If you'll be all right, I'll see if we can't get a lamp from the stable," Matt said. "I need to take care of the horse anyway."

Then he was gone, leaving her in the doorway watching him lead the horse away, looking more than ever like the loner he was. Though he had come after her, he still kept himself apart.

I love him.

Juliana could deny her feelings no longer, and she whispered them out loud. "I love you, Matt Hunter."

She wouldn't ever tell him, but saying the words somehow gave her comfort, made sense of everything she had done with him, even the arguing. And look at her, a dusty mess, her bonnet askew, no doubt dark circles under her eyes, pale, gaunt, not anyone a man who looked like Matt could be interested in.

What kind of woman would he want? He wanted her in a physical way, but that was because she had thrown herself at him, had made herself available. In her bedroom she had practically ordered him to disrobe. She would have blushed at the memory except that she knew she would do it all over again if she got the chance.

But it wasn't just the lovemaking that meant so much to her. She liked being with him. No matter his mood, or hers, she felt better when he was near, as if the day—or the night—might not be so bad since he was near.

Moving by rote, questioning her sanity at the same time as she kept smiling to herself, she hung her bonnet on a hook by the door and was about to take off her cloak when she saw Matt coming back across the field at a fast pace, an unlit lantern swinging in his hand.

He stopped outside the door, putting the lantern on the porch. "You want to see Gibbs tonight? Maybe catch him unaware?"

"Could we?"

"Why not? I found out where he lives. Apparently, he's pretty much kept to himself since he showed up here a few months ago. He's taken few patients, the stable boy said. Seems to me it's time to make a house call on the doctor."

Juliana's heart was in her throat as she and Matt retraced their steps to the street, then hurried down the road to the far edge of town, turning toward a shack sitting out by itself in the moonlight against a stand of trees. Even though it was occupied, it looked no better or worse than the abandoned Cochran house.

No light came from within the shack, and Juliana grabbed Matt's hand. "He may not talk to me."

"We'll have to convince him where his best interests lie."

Juliana hesitated, staring at the darkened shack, and a chill shot through her.

"I don't know why I'm suddenly afraid."

"You don't have to do this. I'll go in alone. Unless you don't want to know what Gibbs has to say."

"That's not it. It's just that something feels wrong." She sighed. "I'm being foolish. Of course I want to know about my mother. I have to know."

"Then that's all you should think of. I'll go on ahead—"

"No. I'll go with you. I don't know what got into me. I'm not given to premonitions. He's probably in there snoring away, and when he's faced with having to tell the truth, he will. We'll give him no choice."

For all her brave words, she walked cautiously toward the dark cabin and, taking a deep breath, thinking of her mother, she stepped onto the porch and knocked at the door. She got no response.

"Dr. Gibbs, I need to talk to you," she said loudly through a crack in the door. "I'm Juliana Rains, Iona's daughter."

Still no response. Matt took her place and knocked, then turned the knob and stepped inside ahead of her. He came to a quick halt.

"Don't look, Juliana. Get out of here."

But he spoke too late. Peering around him, she

saw the body of a man in the middle of the room, his feet dangling above the floor. In horror she looked up at the rope bound around his neck, and on up to the rafter from which he hung.

She gasped and covered her mouth with her hands, holding back a scream.

Matt moved fast, setting upright the over-turned chair beneath the suspended body, then stood on the chair. "He's still warm. This must have just happened."

Pulling a knife from a back pocket, he sawed at the rope, at last lowering the body onto the floor and feeling for a pulse at the man's wrist and throat. Juliana knelt beside him, wanting to help, too stunned to know what to do.

After a moment, Matt sat back on his heels. "He's gone."

"But he can't be," she whispered, knowing as she said the words how futile they were. She glanced briefly at the doctor's crimson face, at the open lips and protruding tongue, at the open, staring eyes.

It was the sightless eyes she could not take, and she looked away with a shiver, head bowed, her fists clutched to her stomach.

"You need to get out of here," Matt said, taking her arm.

"I'm not going to be sick, I promise." But she did not look at the body again.

A sense of hopelessness settled over her. "He

killed himself," she said, disbelieving her own words. "We were so close to talking to him." She looked at Matt in wonder. "Why would anyone do such a thing?"

Matt brushed the hair from her face and touched her cheek.

"I don't think he did."

"What do you mean? We saw him hanging there, the chair where he must have stood . . . I don't understand."

"Look at the table overturned by the fireplace. Looks like there was a fight. And there are burns around his wrists. Gibbs was bound before that rope ever went around his neck."

Juliana stared at Matt, unable for a moment to comprehend what he was saying.

"That's—" she began, but Matt signaled for her to be quiet and nodded toward the door, gesturing for her to move away to the far side of the room. Suddenly shots boomed out, coming from the porch, splintering the door. Moving fast, Matt tossed the chair through the lone window at the side of the room, shattering the glass, then dove outside. Juliana screamed. She couldn't stop screaming. Without a thought for her safety, she threw open the front door in time to see a shadowy figure run into the dark stand of trees with Matt in swift pursuit.

Frantic, her heart in her throat, she looked around for a weapon of any sort, asking herself where she would put a gun if she wanted it close by. There was no place, only the bed. Hurriedly she tossed back the thin mattress and with a sob of gratitude grabbed the pistol she found hidden there. Holding it to her bosom, she ran outside and, screaming for help, followed the path she thought Matt had taken, running hard, ignoring the pain in her side.

The sound of yelling slowed her for a minute. She couldn't be sure it was Matt. Nothing must happen to him; nothing mattered but him. Following the dirt path, she let the thrashing noise of a fight guide her forward. And then suddenly there was silence. She halted, and in that moment understood true terror.

Gripping the shaking gun in both hands, she pointed it straight ahead and forced herself to move forward, knowing the answer to Matt's question about whether she was capable of shooting anyone. Tonight she could.

She came upon the clearing slowly, barely able to make out the figure of a man lying on the ground, another standing over him.

"Don't move," she said, her voice as shaky as the gun. "I'm holding a pistol and I'll shoot if I have to."

"I sincerely hope you don't have to."

"Matt!"

She flung the gun aside and threw herself at him. He caught her and held her close, and she listened to his ragged breathing. With her heart still in her throat, she eased away from him and forced herself to look at the man lying face down in the dirt. Matt used the tip of his boot to turn the body over. The first thing she saw was the knife protruding from the man's chest, then the blood spreading dark and wide on the front of his shirt. Last she looked at his face.

Even in the dim light she recognized him.

"Kane," she whispered, then turned her face against Matt's shoulder, but the image of the dead man refused to leave her mind.

"I didn't mean to kill him," Matt said, "but after I knocked his gun away, he came at me."

"I heard you fighting. I was afraid I wouldn't get here in time."

"It wasn't much of a fight. He—"

The sound of approaching voices stopped him, and a half-dozen men broke into the clearing. At the front of the pack was a large bearded man wearing a badge, his gun drawn and pointing at Juliana and Matt.

"I'm Deputy Tom Rollins," he said, speaking slowly, looking from the body to Matt and Juliana, his dark eyes settling on Matt. "I'd be mighty obliged if you'd tell me just what is going on here."

Juliana tried to speak, but the world began to spin, turning dark as pitch as she passed out in Matt's arms.

Chapter Sixteen

Juliana awoke to the sound of a crackling fire, her senses at once alert. With a soft cry, she sat upright in bed. In the dim light she could make out a fireplace, flames, a hearth and the man standing beside it.

"Matt," she said. "What's going on? Where am I?"

"You fainted."

"Fainted?" She looked down at herself, at the nightgown she was wearing, floral cotton, a gown she'd never seen before, so large it hung off one shoulder. Looking back at Matt, she covered herself with the blanket. "I've never fainted in my life."

"You've never come across two bodies in one day either."

"Oh." She stared into the fire, and all the events of the evening came back to her in a rush.

"Gibbs is dead," she said.

Matt nodded, his gaze warming her more than the blanket. "I'm sorry," he said.

"He's gone. I can't talk to him." She closed her eyes and remembered the dash through the trees, the terror she'd felt, and then the clearing. . . .

Her eyes flew open. "Kane. He's dead, too, isn't he? I remember him lying there. Oh, Matt, are you all right?"

"He wasn't tough when it came to fighting, at least not fighting someone who could fight back. Empty carriages and weak men were more his targets."

"So he killed Doc Gibbs."

"The deputy agrees he did, and then hung around when he saw us coming. He was probably wanting to search the house, see if Gibbs left anything behind—money, maybe letters, notes. But there was nothing but a pouch of coins hidden behind a stone in the fireplace. Rollins and I looked while you were resting."

A feeling of helplessness settled on her. "I'll never get Edmund now. I'll never prove he did something to my mother. And I was so close."

"Edmund's going to a hell of a lot of trouble to keep you from getting answers to your questions. Melinda Barton said she wrote her mother about Gibbs being here. Edmund probably got wind of it and sent Kane to do his dirty work.

But he's made a mistake somewhere, I feel it. The trick will be to find it."

She shuddered and hugged herself, letting the blanket fall. "It's my problem, not yours, Matt. I've involved you enough already."

He started walking toward her slowly, his boots barely making a sound against the bare wooden floor. Now was the time to tell him how she felt, and in a perfect world he would confess he felt the same. But she saw nothing of love in his eyes, though they held all the heat she could ever want.

"We'll talk about it tomorrow, Jules," he said. "Right now you need to get through the night."

Juliana's heart skipped a beat. Unable to watch him, she looked around at the small room. "This is the Cochran place, isn't it? I see my bonnet by the door. It seems I put it there in another life."

While she spoke, she kept throwing quick side glances at him. With each look, she knew more and more that her feelings for him had reached the deepest level of which she was capable. She loved him—deeply, wildly, completely—and she would do anything he wanted, anything he asked.

But that didn't mean she didn't also feel a bittersweet regret that her love was not returned, and a yearning for a life she could never have.

"The deputy's wife was good enough to give us covers for the bed." He spoke calmly, taking off his boots one by one and tossing them aside, then pulling his shirt free of his pants.

With the toss of the first boot, Juliana forgot about the room. She forgot, too, about wanting anything from him he wasn't able to give.

"What are you doing?" she asked, knowing full well the answer.

"I plan to test the mattress."

"It's fine."

"From a woman's perspective."

"You don't want my perspective?"

He unbuttoned his shirt. "Sure, but it's not all I want."

Warm tingles ran along the surface of her skin, and her stomach tightened. "The bed's awfully narrow."

"We'll lie down in layers."

He was standing over her now, and she could do nothing but stare at his open shirt, at the exposed skin and muscle, and the dusting of dark chest hairs.

"Matt—"

"I'll go to the stables if you prefer. I've slept on hay before." He hesitated. "Nope, forget the offer. Not after what we've both been through."

Hurriedly he finished undressing and slipped under the blanket beside her. He lay on his side and pulled her against him. His hand felt warm and comforting against her back . . . until she looked up at the way he was looking down at her.

"Who undressed me and put me in this gown?" she asked, barely able to speak above a whisper.

He kissed the corner of her mouth. "Again the deputy's kindly wife. She wouldn't let me within twenty yards of you until you were tucked in. She knew a lady when she saw one, and I could spend the night in jail if I didn't treat you right. She as much as said so."

"You're risking arrest."

"But it's worth it."

With that, he covered her mouth with his, and she quit thinking altogether, her hands hungry to touch him, to feel his hard body, to show him with her explorations what she could not tell him in words. With a little maneuvering he had the gown off her, and they were skin to skin. This time she knew what to expect—not the quick, painful coupling she'd known before Matt, but heat and moisture and pleasure she could not begin to explain. But, oh, she could anticipate it. Already her body was pulsing, and she felt the dampness between her legs.

Looking up at him, she brushed the hair from his forehead, loving everything about him, but especially the way the firelight cast shadows across his face.

For just a moment she thought of the danger he'd faced tonight, running after an armed killer because of her. Worst of all, he had killed a man.

She could never make that up to him.

But she could try.

Running her hand down his chest, stroking his abdomen, watching the fire in his eyes, she took hold of his sex. His sudden intake of breath was all she could have wished for.

"Show me what you want me to do," she said.

He covered her hand with his and guided her in a firm, stroking motion, and she could feel his hardness, the coursing blood.

Suddenly he pulled her hand away. "I can't take it," he said with a rough laugh. "You are driving me out of my mind."

And then he was kissing her open-mouthed, using his tongue, letting his hands stroke her, cup her breasts, run wildly over her skin, and at last he slipped his fingers between her legs and brought her close to madness. The room was spinning, the world was spinning, and she felt tight and hot. The moment was beautiful because it was a time of pure sensuality without any thought except that she wanted more; she wanted the time to last forever.

When he settled on top of her and eased the hard, full length of his sex inside her, instinctively she wrapped her legs around him and pressed her hands against his buttocks, her fingers sensitive to the play of his muscles as he began to thrust deeper and deeper. The thrusts grew rapid, and when the world exploded, she could do nothing but hold on to him as tightly as she could, losing herself completely in his arms.

Her cry of joy mingled with his, and they clung to one another in a kind of sweet desperation, holding on to rapture, to comfort and completion, and, for Juliana, holding on to love. Even as the rapture died and he nestled close beside her, holding her near, she could feel nothing but contentment. She knew it wouldn't last. Eventually she would have to consider her problems, and he would consider his.

But for this moment they had had their fill of the real world. She would leave the bitter truths for tomorrow. Tonight she would steal a moment's peace in his arms.

Over the next few hours, while the fire slowly died, she remained in his arms, slipping in and out of sleep, listening to his breathing, feeling his flesh against hers. In that way, feeling no regrets, she made it through the night.

Early the next morning they went to the stagecoach office, where Juliana was able to book passage on the morning stage to Diablo.

Waiting near the road, with Matt close beside her, she watched Deputy Tom Rollins come hurrying toward them from town.

"Glad I caught you," he said. "I've been thinking over what happened last night. Ma'am, Mr.

Hunter here said Doc Gibbs tended your ma when she was dying and you wanted to talk to him about her."

"That's right," she said, not looking at Matt.

"He also said this Kane fellow worked for you for a spell."

"Not very long," she said, feeling Matt's eyes on her, wishing she knew exactly what had passed between him and the deputy. "He just left one day without telling me."

"Seems to me the two of 'em, Gibbs and Kane, had some sort of trouble between 'em. Bad trouble. Either of you have any idea what that might be?"

Matt spoke up. "We'll be trying to find out exactly that when we get back to Diablo. This has been quite a shock for Mrs. Rains, as you can understand, and she's just now able to think about what happened."

Rollins took off his hat and scratched a thumb across his forehead. "I appreciate that, ma'am."

"Please thank your wife for taking care of me last night," Juliana said. "I don't know what made me faint like that."

Rollins chuckled. "I do. Several of the men with me got a little queasy themselves." He looked beyond her. "Here comes the stage now. I'll be sending a report on to your sheriff. If either of you find out anything, I'd appreciate it if you'd tell him. I hate to bury two bodies without knowing what was behind their deaths."

She was about to turn from him when he said, "One more thing. A few folks heard the doctor mumbling something about respectability not being all it seemed. You have any idea what that could have been about?"

"No, I don't," she said, but she had an idea that Gibbs had been talking about not his own respectability, but that of Edmund Montgomery. She wanted all the more to weep for her lost last chance to find out for sure everything he'd known about Iona.

She also wanted to throw out the name of her stepfather, but a warning look from Matt kept her silent. He was right. Deacon of the church, respected banker, Edmund would probably convince any lawman who questioned him that his poor distraught stepdaughter was not right in the head.

As the stagecoach rolled to a halt in front of her, she watched the deputy back away, then turn for the short walk back to the center of town, leaving her with an empty feeling, a sense that she should have done more than she had, that the trip to Winding Creek had been nothing but another tragedy, for Gibbs most of all, but for her, too.

Except for the time with Matt. And even that had not come without pain.

Within a short while she was settled in the small conveyance as it rumbled along the road, wishing Matt could have traveled inside with her instead of leading the way on horseback, but already four other passengers were crowded on the narrow seats. She contented herself with an occasional glimpse of him out the window.

The journey back to Diablo took most of the day, with only two stops, and dusk was falling by the time the coach lumbered into town. Too tired to return to the Lazy Q that night, she let Matt walk her to the Diablo Hotel.

The minute she stepped into the normally quiet lobby, she knew something had happened. A half-dozen people were scurrying back and forth, the clerk behind the desk barked out orders for food and a seamstress, and there was enough bustling about for President Hayes to be a guest.

A woman's shrill laugh halted the bustle. Everyone stopped in place, Juliana and Matt included, and stared at the winding staircase. The first thing Juliana saw on the top step was a fine leather slipper peeking out from beneath a red silk gown, the hem scalloped to reveal rows of delicate lace, as far from homespun as a gown could get. Then came the second slipper, and finally the woman in all her glory descended from the upper floor, with rounded hips, a narrow waist, and a pair of full breasts spilling out of a sinfully low-cut bodice.

"My God," Matt said.

"No, darling," the woman trilled out, "it's just your countess."

Juliana glanced at Matt, then at the woman. She was beautiful, no question, her black hair piled elaborately on top of her head, with lots of tendrils allowed to fall about her face. She had full red lips, long lashes and dark eyes flashing more than just a casual interest in Matt's direction.

"Oh," the woman purred as she looked at Juliana, "you have a companion. How sweet." She hurried down the steps and held out her hand, whether to her or Matt, Juliana wasn't sure, but neither of them took it.

"I'm Lady Charlotte Kingbridge," she said to Juliana, dropping the hand, and then to Matt she added, "I just had to come to Texas to make sure you were taking care of my wonderful Dark Champion. Oh, I've got business in the state, you understand, but I wouldn't forgive myself, and neither would you forgive me, if I didn't visit this charming town."

Charming town? Juliana thought. *Does she mean Diablo?*

She looked at Matt for answers to a dozen unformed questions, but he was staring in bemusement at the countess. And not in total surprise.

The two did indeed know one another. How well? They must have been close for her to travel to this out-of-the-way town in Texas solely to renew their acquaintance.

A sinking feeling took hold of Juliana. From the moment she'd entered the stagecoach, she had felt a separation from him. In the lobby of the Diablo Hotel she felt it all the more.

Worse, she felt dirty and dowdy and very close to screaming, which would contribute little to the genteel picture she wished to present to Matt's titled visitor.

Gripping the handle of her valise, she looked at him. "The hotel looks far too busy. I'm sure I can get a room at the boardinghouse for tonight. It's only a short walk away, and I know you and the countess have much to talk over."

"Don't be ridiculous," he said.

Juliana bristled, knowing the countess was watching the exchange.

"You know how I am," she said with a false laugh. To the countess, she said, "Lady Charlotte, if you'll pardon me, I've been on a stagecoach all day and would be poor company for anyone. Perhaps you can visit my ranch while you're here."

"That sounds delightful," the countess said. She glanced at Matt for a second. "I'm sure we can find much to talk about. There must be several things we have in common."

With a nod, Juliana hurried from the hotel, knowing Matt was following, but she did not look at him or speak or do anything but concentrate on getting across the street and down the block to the boardinghouse as quickly as possible, ignoring the bank as she passed it and Sam Larkin's office next door.

Anne Pals, owner of the boardinghouse, met her at the door and welcomed her inside. Putting herself in the woman's hands, Juliana not only admitted her cowardice, she reveled in it. She had one more chore, but that could wait until morning. Somehow she needed to get out to the Lazy Q without seeing Matt or the countess.

She certainly didn't want to hear him tell her he and the beautiful woman were no more than friends.

Chapter Seventeen

Matt watched the boardinghouse door close, shutting him out, shutting Juliana in. She seemed a million miles away and as unreachable as a star.

He stared a long time at the boardinghouse, looking to the second floor when he saw a light appear in a window. He ought to feel good about getting her back to Diablo unharmed. She'd stirred up some serious trouble with her questions about her mother. Two dead that Matt knew of, and near-death for herself.

But she really wasn't safe, not from Montgomery and not from him. Too well he remembered how she felt in his arms. And he was left wondering if she would ever be there again. In her own best interests, the answer ought to be no.

He glanced at the Lone Star, directly across the street from the boardinghouse, and thought about tossing back some whiskey. He'd killed a man. He hadn't let himself dwell on the fact, but he was thinking about it now. The hanging body, the fight, Kane's vicious turn on him, as much as throwing himself against the knife he hadn't seen—the images would stay in Matt's mind for a long time.

A drink would be welcome, all right, but the way his luck had turned on him right after the race, Jack would already be in there a few shots ahead of him.

The best thing for him was to keep walking to the stable, get a fresh horse and ride out to the Lazy Q. In the morning he could send Mugg into town with the wagon to bring Juliana home.

And that would include avoiding the hotel and its newest resident. What was going on with the countess? He'd hardly said more than a few dozen words to her back in England, and he knew for sure she hadn't come all this way because of him.

Not that Juliana would be inclined to believe him.

He was on his way to the stable when he made out the figure of Edmund Montgomery crossing the street in front of the bank, heading for the hotel. The banker was slicked out in frock coat and tie. Word of the countess's arrival had obviously spread.

"Montgomery," Matt called out.

Montgomery turned to see who called, then

waved him off. "Is that you, Matt? I can't talk now. I'm busy."

"The countess will wait. I thought you might want to know about what happened in Winding Creek. Before I talk to the sheriff, that is."

Montgomery halted. "I don't know what you're talking about."

"Not entirely, you don't. If you're expecting a report from Kane, you'll be waiting a long time."

"Kane? I don't know anybody by that name."

Montgomery sounded innocent enough, and truly puzzled, but he did not continue into the hotel. Standing in a spill of light from the hotel's open door, he watched Matt approach.

Drawing near, Matt shook his head. "That's strange. I could have sworn he said . . . Never mind. He was dying, and a dying man's liable to say anything."

Montgomery seemed to think that one over for a minute, not knowing for sure whether Matt was lying or not, then returned to his old bombastic self.

"See here, Matt Hunter, if you're implying that some man's death has anything to do with me—"

"Two deaths. And yes, you might say I'm implying you're involved."

"You always were irresponsible, a hothead, and everyone knows it," Montgomery said with a sneer. "Throwing baseless accusations around can get you horsewhipped."

"Don't you want to know the name of the second man who died? An old friend of yours, Doc Gibbs. But of course you knew he was in Winding Creek. Melinda Barton's mother told everyone in Diablo her daughter had seen the doctor there."

Matt was guessing, but the look on Montgomery's face told him he was guessing right.

Montgomery closed the short distance between them, his dignity marred by an ugly sneer as he brought his face close to Matt's. "You'd be wise not to spread such ugly talk. I am not without resources, and I will not tolerate such rumors, especially from a Hunter. Do not forget I still hold the mortgage on the Half-Moon. If you value your life and the well-being of your family, you will leave me alone."

He backed away, then added one last jab. "And, of course, there's always my troublesome stepdaughter. So many potential victims, one hardly knows which one to choose."

Matt watched as the banker strode toward the hotel, stopping at the door to smooth his hair and paste a smile on his face before entering. After only a moment, the countess's shrill laughter echoed from the hotel.

The clatter of an oncoming wagon drove Matt to the side of the street. Standing in the shadow of the bank, he continued to watch the hotel, considering everything Montgomery had said.

He did not take the man's threats lightly, but now that Kane was dead, whom would he get to do his dirty work? Matt had threatened Montgomery with reporting what he knew to the sheriff, but without proof of the banker's role in Juliana's near-death crash in the carriage and the murder of Doc Gibbs, talk was all he could offer.

Talk wasn't good enough. Whether Juliana wanted him around or not, she'd have to put up with him for a while longer. With thoughts of her lingering in his mind, he made his way to the stables at the far end of town. He'd get a fresh horse and make the long ride out to the Lazy Q. He did his best thinking when he was riding alone.

Juliana had been home only a few hours, going over her mother's letters in the parlor, looking for anything she could use against Edmund, when she heard a carriage pull up in front of her house. Hastily she shoved the letters into a cabinet drawer and went to answer the knock.

She opened the door to see Glory Hunter, accompanied by an obviously pregnant woman she took to be Brent's wife, Crystal.

"We should have come calling earlier," Glory said. "I've been worried about you ever since you left Bandera."

"And it's long past time for us to meet," Crystal said after being introduced. "Brent doesn't know I'm here, by the way, but I'm going crazy sitting around all day. Being crazy is not going to do our baby any good."

"Please come in," Juliana said. She had to shake off the mood that reading the letters had brought. Company would be good. It would help her forget the past few days. She might even quit wondering where Matt had gone. She hadn't seen him since she'd walked into the boarding-house the previous night, but she knew he had sent Mugg into town with the wagon to bring her to the Lazy Q.

The visitors had barely walked into the parlor when Mugg appeared. "Would you ladies like tea?" he asked.

Glory looked at Mugg's apron, then at his bearded face. "Yes, thank you," she said, and when he had returned to the kitchen, she added to Juliana, "Your housekeeper?"

"I'm lucky to have him," Juliana said.

"So how is Doc Gibbs?" Crystal asked when they were settled into the parlor chairs. "I'd find it comforting to have a doctor near when the baby comes."

Juliana couldn't answer right away.

"What's wrong?" Glory asked, moving to sit beside her on the sofa.

"Dr. Gibbs is dead." Juliana knew of no other way to say it, and no way to soften the circumstances except to describe them. Neither woman spoke until she had finished. She described everything—the dark town, the doctor's isolated cabin, the tragic manner of his death, and even the inglorious end of his killer. The only thing she left out was how she and Matt had spent the night.

"Poor Matt," Crystal said with a shudder. "He actually had to . . . to take a life."

"He was very brave," Juliana said, aware of the thoughtful way Glory was watching her. "I hoped to talk to Gibbs about my mother, to find out exactly why she died. Edmund said she drank." She looked from woman to woman. "Is that true?"

"You need to talk to Abby," Crystal said. "She knew her best."

"But Abby isn't here. I need you to tell me."

Crystal looked at Glory for a moment, then back at Juliana. "Then the answer is yes. You deserve to know the truth. I never saw her take a drink, but she wasn't herself at times and . . ."

"It's okay," Juliana said. "Tell me everything. I should have been here to see for myself, but since I wasn't, I need to hear it from those who were."

Crystal gave her a warm look of sympathy. "I could tell by the way she behaved. I've seen the effects liquor can have on people, and I know. But, Juliana, it never made her mean or ugly, the way drink can do to some people. It just seemed to sap the strength from her."

"And Edmund?"

Glory and Crystal shared a look; it was Glory who answered.

"I wasn't part of the family until after Iona died, but from the talk, I gathered he gave the *appearance* of taking care of her more than he gave actual care."

Juliana could sit still no longer. Standing, she paced behind the sofa, watching as Mugg brought in the tea tray.

"I baked a cake while Miz Rains was gone. Won't hurt my feelings if you pass it up." He settled a thoughtful look on Juliana. "It'll do you good to get a little food down. The chickens eat more'n you do."

The women watched as he left the room, then shared a smile.

"Is he as good as he seems?" Crystal asked.

"Better. While I was gone, he took the stove apart to clean it."

Taking a deep breath, she returned to the sofa to serve the tea, keeping her hands busy, even sampling the cake, but, good as it was, the single bite caught in her throat.

Setting aside her cup, she rested her hands in her lap. "I don't know what to do. I can only guess why Kane went to Winding Creek and why he . . . did what he did there. You must understand that I put nothing past my stepfather, but as for outright accusing him of hiring a killer, I have no proof."

"What does Matt say?" Glory asked.

"He agrees. But we haven't talked about what we'll do now."

"You should have seen the look on his face in that Bandera hotel when he found out you were gone."

"Angry, I imagine."

"The Hunter men do like to be in control," Glory said. "But I'd say he was more worried than anything else."

Crystal spoke up. "Trust him, Juliana. If there's one thing I've learned since meeting Brent, it's that these brothers are special."

"Amen," Glory said.

"Matt's not like your husbands," Juliana said. "You didn't know him before his mother died. He was wild, and I don't think that's ever left him. Look at the way he went to England to buy Dark Champion. He's a good man, better than he realizes, but he's also a wanderer. He's told me so himself."

"Then change his mind," Glory said.

"You're assuming I want to."

"Do you know how you say his name?" Crystal asked. "Your voice softens, even when you're describing something ugly."

"Am I that obvious?" Juliana asked.

"Probably not to him," Glory said. "The Hunter men can also be a little . . . how shall I say it? . . . not insensitive really, more like unaware of subtleties."

"Right now Matt is probably being unaware with a countess."

"A countess?" Glory asked.

"Lady Charlotte Kingbridge sold him Dark Champion. She's staying at the Diablo Hotel. Apparently, she arrived yesterday. Matt must have made quite an impression on her."

"A dowager sort?" Crystal asked.

"Not anywhere near. She's a beauty. I think the best word to describe her would be voluptuous."

"Good word," Glory said, then added, "No, a bad word."

"No man could be unaware enough to overlook her charms," Juliana said. "Please, let's talk about something else. Crystal, when is your baby due?"

Crystal straightened in her chair and placed a hand against the small of her back. "The midwife says in a couple of months, but I don't think I can make it past a few weeks."

Juliana looked at Crystal's swollen belly and thought of the child growing inside. For the first time in her life she truly envied another woman.

"I wish I knitted," she said.

"I've taken it up. And stitching. Brent won't

let me do anything that looks the least bit like work. The poor child will have to wear six layers of clothes to get use out of everything waiting for him. Or her."

Juliana listened while the two women went on to talk about possible names for the newest addition to the Hunter clan, no one bringing up the baby's grandfather. If they had, Juliana could have contributed nothing other than to describe how she'd approached him in the saloon. Bringing up the confrontation seemed pointless. Matt had told her his father wouldn't change his mind about selling the land.

When it was time for the women to leave, Juliana walked them to their carriage, promised to make a return visit, and watched the trail of dust stirred up by their departure. Then she went around the house to the corral. What she needed was a good talk with someone to whom she could open her heart.

When she slipped inside the gate, Pepper came to her at a trot and nuzzled her neck.

"Sorry I've been neglecting you," Juliana said, rubbing behind the mare's ears. "I've had visitors. Two very nice women who mean well. But they don't know Matt the way I do. He's not like his brothers."

Pepper bobbed her head in agreement.

"I wish you could answer something for me. Why am I even considering linking myself to a strong-willed man? I've been down that road, and I'd be a fool to go down it again." In a softer voice she added, "No matter how much I love him."

When Matt did not return on the second day, Juliana knew what she had to do. Asking Mugg to hook the horse to the wagon, firmly declining his offer to take her where she wanted to go, she went into town, left horse and wagon at the stables after ordering another carriage, and strode down the street and into the Diablo State Bank.

A young clerk sitting behind the counter closest to the door sprang to his feet.

"How can I help you, miss?"

"I'm looking for Mr. Montgomery."

An older man behind him walked over. "Mr. Montgomery is elsewhere today. But any business you have with him—"

"Thank you, but it's personal."

The two men looked at one another, but Juliana didn't bother to explain.

Leaving the bank, she considered dropping in on Sam Larkin to remind him about her money, then decided on another course. Rounding the corner, she walked up the hill toward the house where her mother had lived most of her married life.

As grand as it appeared, overlooking all of

Diablo, it also seemed sterile, coldly perfect without any human touch.

Halfway up the hill, she saw a woman walking toward her, a tall and sturdy woman of middle age with an empty straw basket in her hand. She stopped in front of Juliana and frowned.

"There's no one home, if it's Mr. Montgomery's house you're going to."

"Are you the housekeeper? Hilda—isn't that your name?"

The woman squinted at her, and her broad lips flattened. "You'd be Mrs. Rains, the stepdaughter."

"Yes. I wanted to talk to you about my mother."

"Not much to say."

"Were you there the night she died?"

"Not in the room. Bad heart, they said. Why are you just now coming around to ask questions?"

"I should have been here months ago. I didn't know she was ill." Juliana looked beyond the woman to the house. "Has he changed her room?"

She saw no need to identify the *he.*

"He never goes in there. I gathered up most of her belongings and passed them on to the Hunter girl. It's Mr. Montgomery you ought to be talking to. He's not been around much the past few days. Now I'd better get to my shopping. There's supper to fix, whether he bothers to eat it or not."

Juliana watched as the housekeeper continued down the hill. She stood still until the woman was out of sight, then turned back toward the house. Somehow she could hear her mother calling her. Real or imagined, the whisper of her name caused her heart to pound. Without knowing exactly what she was doing or why, she continued her upward trek.

The steps leading to the narrow veranda appeared recently swept, as was the veranda itself. Indeed, it looked as if no one ever stood out here and gazed around at the wonderful view. There should have been a rocking chair. Even when she was a little girl at their ranch house, Juliana could remember sitting at her mother's knee as Iona spun out tales that began with the magic words *Once upon a time.*

She tried the door, but it was locked. Leaving the veranda, as if Iona herself were directing her steps, she walked around the house and up the back stoop. The knob to the door turned easily in her hand. Hilda either had forgotten to lock it or wasn't in the habit of doing so.

Heart in her throat, she slipped inside, hurried through the pantry and the kitchen, not looking to right or left, then down a long hallway, looking for bedrooms, ignoring the parlor and dining room toward the front. Later, perhaps, she would study the details of the other rooms, but right now they seemed no part of her mother.

The large bedroom behind the first door she came to clearly belonged to Edmund. Massive dark furniture took up almost every square foot of space. A smaller room down the hall was different, sparsely furnished, with a ruffled cover on the four-poster bed, an oak wardrobe and matching desk, lace curtains at the window, a stand with a washbasin and pitcher. The wallpaper was a print of small pink flowers, but there were no pictures hanging on the walls, just one wood-framed mirror over the washstand.

Juliana breathed deeply, but she could detect no scent of her mother. There was nothing personal she could hold against her heart.

Taking a deep breath, she went through the wardrobe, but found only a pale blue wrapper and a pair of worn bed slippers. Then she turned to the desk. Was this where her mother had written her letters? Edmund would have stood over her for all but one.

A sheet of unused foolscap and a quill pen were in the single drawer, as if waiting for one more letter to be written, one last communication between mother and daughter.

Juliana sat on the side of the bed for a moment, almost giving in to tears, then stirred herself. Hilda would be coming back soon. Hurrying out, she dared a quick look in one more room—Edmund's study. Like his bedroom, it was darkly furnished with overstuffed chairs and a massive mahogany desk. She threw herself into going through the desk drawers, looking for something that might connect her stepfather to Kane, a scribbled note, a letter, a receipt, anything . . . she really didn't know what she was looking for.

So engrossed was she in her search, she didn't hear the front door open, didn't know that anyone else was in the house until she became terrifiedly aware of footsteps in the entryway and the opening of the study door.

Edmund, looking coldly triumphant, stepped inside. "There she is, Sheriff Dawson," he said. "Just as I feared when I summoned you. I want this woman arrested for illegal entry."

Behind him loomed the sheriff. She had a dim impression of formidable size and a frowning face, but the only thing Juliana could concentrate on was his badge.

Chapter Eighteen

Matt hadn't been in the Diablo jail for ten years, but nothing had changed much, with pegs for keys on one side next to the gun rack, and on the other the same cluttered desk with the same straight-backed chair.

The only real change was the sheriff sitting in the chair. Years ago, Rafe Dawson had replaced Sheriff Miller, who on many an occasion had taken pleasure in throwing Matt's sorry carcass in a cell.

Even seated, Dawson appeared tall, strong, with only a slight paunch showing his middle age. Everyone said Dawson was an honorable man, but at the moment Matt didn't give a horse's behind.

Thumbing his hat to the back of his head, Matt stared down at the sheriff. "Where have you thrown the desperado?"

"Matt Hunter, as I live and breathe," Dawson said with a nod. "I heard about you from my predecessor."

"Mrs. Rains," Matt said, not bothering to hide his impatience. "Where is she?"

"In the back cell."

"Is she all right?"

"Under the circumstances, I'd say she's fine."

"Giving you much trouble?"

"Other than insisting she's innocent and saying stuff like I arrested the wrong person, no, not much trouble."

Matt stared at the closed door leading to the cell area and tried to picture Juliana behind bars, but the image wouldn't come. Holding back his temper, he returned to the sheriff.

"What are the exact charges?"

"Illegal entry, attempted theft. Montgomery claims he had jewelry he'd bought for his late wife and that Mrs. Rains was out to appropriate it for herself. That was the banker's word—appropriate."

"Did you see the jewelry?"

"No, but he claimed he would bring it along when it came time for the trial."

Matt shook his head in disgust. "That's absurd, and you know it. In the first place, she might have a legal claim to the jewelry since it belonged to her mother. And in the second place, she wouldn't want it to begin with."

"That's pretty much what she said. But I did catch her going through Montgomery's desk. And Montgomery told me she'd already asked about anything that might have belonged to her mother."

Something seemed wrong about what Dawson was telling him, but Matt let it go.

"Why were you with Montgomery?" Matt asked.

"He happened to see her from his office window when she was going around the side of the house. He hurried out, being naturally curious, and saw his housekeeper walking up the street, so he figured the prisoner was up to no good."

"And instead of going up to talk to her, he got you."

"I'd say that turned out to be a smart move on his part."

"Smart or crafty. What about bail?"

"The circuit judge isn't due here for another two weeks. I'd get the justice of the peace, but he had to leave a few days ago to bury his dad out in Sweetwater."

"Has Mrs. Rains had any visitors?"

"Anne Pals from the boardinghouse brought some food over last night, but Mrs. Rains said she wasn't hungry. Haven't heard from anybody this morning."

"I don't suppose her lawyer's been down to check on her."

Dawson shook his head. "Sam also represents Montgomery, which makes things kinda touchy, seeing as how Montgomery brought the charges against her."

"We need another lawyer in this town."

"And a doctor." Dawson waved to the papers on his desk. "I got a telegram from the deputy at Winding Creek about Doc Gibbs and a man named Kane. You were mentioned, along with the prisoner. Mrs. Rains didn't seem inclined to talk about what happened, kept saying I should ask her stepfather. You got anything to add?"

"Not yet. I need to talk to my client first."

"Your client?"

"Mrs. Rains. I've decided to represent her."

"I don't know about that. You got a law degree? Has the state of Texas seen fit to put your name on a license?"

"I don't need either one," Matt said. He hadn't any idea whether what he was saying was true or not, but it sounded good. "Right now I want to see her." He held out his arms. "Search me if you want. I'm not armed."

"Neither was the prisoner."

"You searched her?"

"She gave me her word she didn't have a gun, a knife or a saw." Dawson pushed his chair away from the desk and grabbed a key from one of the pegs. "Come on back. You've got a right to see your . . . client. She's the only prisoner right now. Getting lonely, I expect."

He opened the door, passing the first of the Diablo jail's two cells, stopping at the second, a small corner area no more than five feet square, its lone furniture a narrow cot. Juliana stood by the high barred window, looking up at the sky. She turned and stared at Matt. A yellow silk gown hung on her body, as if she'd lost weight overnight, and her hair was pinned carelessly at her nape. Her eyes looked bruised, but a spark flared in their depths—a spark Matt took to be fury.

Despite the flare, she looked lost and very much alone. Matt felt as if he'd been kicked in the gut. "I got here as soon as I could," he said.

"We've both been busy," she said.

Her voice sounded tight, as if she had to force the words out.

They looked at one another a minute; then he turned to the sheriff. "I'd like to talk to my client in private."

"You got the right," Dawson said, unlocking the cell, then closing it firmly after Matt walked inside. The clanging of metal against metal echoed in the cell.

Matt kept his silence until the sheriff had closed the office door, leaving him and Juliana alone.

"Your client?" Juliana asked, remaining by the window, her back rigid.

"I figured you would prefer me to Larkin."

"I don't need a lawyer. I didn't do anything wrong."

Matt took off his hat and tossed it onto the cot. "You were caught in Montgomery's house without his knowledge or permission."

"The back door was unlocked. I didn't break in."

"Did you find anything?"

"Nothing." Only then did the tears begin to well in her eyes. In an instant he was taking her into his arms and holding her close as she collapsed against him.

"This is ridiculous," she said against his shirt. "I'm so embarrassed."

"Because you were caught? Trust me, Juliana, you'll get over being in jail."

"I don't like this place. It's horrible, but that's not why I'm embarrassed. I didn't find anything. Edmund outsmarted me. And now he's claiming I was after some jewelry I didn't know about and don't believe even exists. There's no way in hell he bought my mother jewelry." She sighed. "And listen to me, I'm talking like you."

He stroked her hair and almost smiled. There was no one in all the world like Juliana Rains, man, woman or child.

She drew away, taking him by surprise, and

looked up at him with eyes that were definitely sparking.

"And what am I doing cuddling up to you? I can practically smell the countess on you," she said.

"Close—you're smelling horse. I haven't seen Lady Charlotte since the night we both saw her at the hotel. When you went to the boarding-house, I rode on out to the ranch. After making sure Mugg was coming into town after you, I went to Quince's place to take care of DC and bring him to the Lazy Q. I didn't get back until last night. That's when Mugg told me you hadn't returned from town and he was getting worried."

"And you rode in to find out I was a jailbird. That is what a prisoner's called, isn't it?"

Matt figured it wouldn't be smart to tell her *jailbird* was only one of the names being tossed around Diablo. Everyone in town was talking about her arrest, and he hadn't heard a word in her defense. He'd picked up all the negative talk he ever wanted to hear in the few minutes it took to get from the stable to the jail.

"The idea now is to get you out of here. Although I have to confess having you confined this way relieves a man of worrying about what you're up to."

"I'm not your concern, Matt. I admit I've made a mess of everything, but that's my problem."

Matt stared down at her, at the tilt of her chin,

the determination in her gaze, but mostly he saw the half circles under her eyes. Her hair was a mess, her gown wrinkled, her face gaunt. She had never looked more beautiful.

"Would you have any objection to being kissed?"

The defiance softened, and she said in a small voice, "I was wondering whether you would."

With his hands resting lightly on her shoulders, he tried to keep the kiss gentle, just a brush of his lips against hers, but suddenly he was holding her tight and she was clinging to him, her mouth open. Their tongues were put to work in a kiss as passionate as any they had ever shared, as if both of them had exploded and they were caught together in the resulting flames.

She broke the kiss and backed away.

"This is insane," she said, her breath coming in small gasps.

"You'll get no argument from me. But what were you thinking of while we were kissing?"

She looked away, then back to him. "That's a ridiculous question."

"It wasn't about where we are, was it? It was about you and me and how the kissing felt good."

"All I'll say is it didn't feel bad," she said.

"You're the one sounding like a lawyer."

When she looked past him to the bars of the cell, the light that had been in her eyes died. She rubbed her arms. "How did you stand it?"

"You mean when I was thrown in here? I was a kid and didn't know I was supposed to be afraid. And I was usually drunk."

"Drunk? There's an idea."

"I should have brought liquor. Instead, all you've got is me."

She looked at his mouth. "Then maybe you need to kiss me again."

"And if I don't stop at kissing?"

"We have a habit of getting interrupted."

Matt stepped close and twisted a lock of hair behind her ear. "What's the sheriff going to do, throw us in jail for indecency?"

"I don't think it's indecent." She spoke softly, her eyes downcast.

He lifted her face and kissed her. "Let me make you feel better, Jules."

Her answer was to return the kiss.

"Hold on," he whispered into her ear. "That's all I ask, hold on to me."

Easing around to stand between her and the office door, he fondled her breasts, kissed her neck, her throat, then licked the pebbled nipples pressing against her bodice.

She shivered and clung to him. "We shouldn't do this."

"Wrong. This is exactly what we should do."

He didn't let her think, didn't give her the chance to push him away. Backing her against the side wall, he pulled up her skirt and petticoat, bunching them at her waist, then let his fingers work their way to the opening in her under-clothes and to her damp sex. He could feel the tightening of her muscles as he stroked her.

"Oh, Matt," she whispered, using both hands to cling to his arms and burying her head against the curve of his shoulder as he continued the strokes.

"Keep holding on," he said.

Suddenly she stiffened against him and buried her head deeper to muffle her cry. He could feel the tremors rippling through her, and he pressed his fingers hard against her sex until she slowly, very slowly relaxed. But she did not let go of him and he did not let go of her. When her breathing grew more regular, he removed his hand and smoothed her clothing into place, then backed away.

At first she didn't look at him, her head bowed almost in shame, her arms wrapped around her middle.

"I can't believe that happened. It was so fast," she said.

"Fast isn't necessarily a bad thing."

When she looked up, she had a worried look in her eye. "You're still . . . you know," she said.

"It'll take a while for the little rascal to settle down."

"The little rascal?" For the first time since he'd entered the cell, she came close to smiling.

"He keeps acting up when he's around you. The name seems to fit."

"Somehow I feel guilty."

"Guilty is not a word you want to use when you're in jail."

"Matt, you're not taking me seriously."

"If I get much more serious, someone will have to lock *me* away."

Again she almost smiled, and the tightness around her eyes began to ease.

She tried to smooth her hair. "I must look awful."

"You're beautiful. I don't think I've ever told you that. I guess I figured you knew it."

"No one's told me that since my mother." Her shoulders fell, and she sat heavily on the cot next to his hat. "Oh, Matt, what am I going to do?"

"Are you asking as my client?"

"You can't be my attorney."

"Who's going to stop me? Not Larkin. I have a feeling he'll stay away from you as much as possible."

"Okay, let's say you're my attorney. What are you going to do now?"

"Get you out of here. If I'm going to earn my pay, I'd better get to work."

He no sooner called out the sheriff's name than Dawson was striding through the door. While he was unlocking the cell, Matt leaned close to Juliana.

"Remember, you owe me."

That brought a glint to her eye, which was all he could do for her at the moment.

Grabbing up his hat, he left fast, not looking back, not slowing down until he was on the street, asking himself what he was supposed to do next. Frustration welled in him. A couple of wagons rolled by, and a few horsemen headed out of town, and on the opposite sidewalk most of the dozen pedestrians cast him a curious glance. Why not give them something else to talk about besides Juliana? Why not do something he'd been wanting to do for a long, long time?

Swiftly he walked down the short block between the jail and the bank, went inside and, without a glance at the two clerks behind the long counter, slammed through the door bearing Montgomery's name in fancy gold scroll.

He caught the banker seated behind a broad desk, a look of surprise and fear in his eyes. Throwing down his pen, Montgomery shot to his feet. "What do you think you're doing?"

Planting his hands firmly on the desk, Matt leaned close, his face almost touching Montgomery's.

"I'm going to get you, Edmund, one way or another. You've got blood on your hands and I know it. Just how much is the only question. Somewhere, somehow, you've made a mistake, and when I find it, you'll be the one behind bars."

Montgomery paled, but he stepped back and straightened his coat. "You're a ruffian, Matt Hunter, just like your father. Get out."

"Oh, I'm getting out, all right. But you ought to know a couple of things. Unlike my father, I'm cold sober and plan on staying that way. And I know you for the bastard you are."

Matt turned on his heel and retraced his steps out to the walkway, drawing a deep breath of air when he was away from the bank. What he'd done was probably foolish, alerting Montgomery to the danger he faced, but it felt good to say the words, to watch the fear in his eyes. For once, the banker's suave manner had been shaken.

But that didn't get Juliana out of jail. Or make her any less lonely while she was locked away. She needed to know she had the support of people other than him.

Crossing the street, he passed the hotel and went on down the side street another block in the direction of the church. The door to the sanctuary was locked, and he went around to the back where the Reverend Crawford and his wife lived. He caught the couple as they were coming out the front door.

"Good morning," he said. "Glad I caught you."

The reverend nodded and his wife smiled, but neither looked overjoyed to see him.

"Good morning to you," Mrs. Crawford said.

"What brings you to my door?" Crawford

asked. "I've not seen you here before."

"You've heard about Mrs. Rains."

"A terrible thing," the reverend said. "Poor woman, she's obviously distraught, losing her husband and then her mother, coming to live out in the country all by herself. Not once have we seen her in town except when she's been here on business, and then only seldom. Usually she sends that man she calls her housekeeper."

"I don't hear much sympathy in your voice."

Mrs. Crawford spoke up. "Oh, Mr. Hunter, we feel sorry for the woman."

The reverend patted his wife's arm. "But we can't condone her breaking the law. Mr. Montgomery was most distressed when he had to bring charges. He sought our counsel on the matter, and we told him he should do as his conscience directed."

Matt swallowed bile. Asking the reverend to visit Juliana in her cell, to bring her comfort and company, probably would not be a good idea. What she would get was a lecture on the error of her ways.

"Now if you will excuse us," Crawford said, "we were on our way to the hotel. Lady Charlotte is holding a soiree in her suite and we've been invited."

"I wouldn't want to hold you up," Matt said, stepping aside.

He watched the Crawfords hurry in the direction of the hotel and decided to follow them. He was curious to know what might have inspired Lady Charlotte to hold a soiree in Diablo.

When he got to Main Street, he saw a familiar figure at the door of the hotel. Texas Ranger Grant Zachary nodded to him.

"Have you got any influence with the sheriff?" Matt asked without preamble.

"Depends on what you need."

"He's arrested Juliana Rains. I want her freed."

"Let's go," Zachary said, and the two men turned back toward the jail.

"You don't want to know why she was arrested?" Matt asked.

"I assume it's not for shooting up the town."

"Edmund Montgomery is accusing her of attempted theft."

"Any enemy of Edmund Montgomery is a friend of mine."

Inside the jail, the ranger got right to the point.

"I'll take responsibility for Mrs. Rains. You have my personal guarantee, Sheriff, that should this matter come to trial, she'll be standing before the judge whenever and wherever you want her."

"Grant," the sheriff said, "this is most unusual."

"I'll tell you what; if Mr. Montgomery has any questions about the situation, you tell him to talk to me."

"Good idea," Dawson said, grabbing the cell key. The two lawmen disappeared through the door, and in a minute Juliana was preceding them back into the office, a smile on her face.

"You do good work, Counselor," she said to Matt.

Before he could respond, the door to the street opened and Anne Pals walked in carrying a tray of food.

"It's getting crowded in here," Sheriff Dawson said. "You're suddenly mighty popular, Mrs. Rains."

Juliana sighed. "I don't mean to sound ungrateful, but what I really want more than anything is a hot bath and clean clothes." She eyed the tray. "And food. Thank you, Anne. Suddenly I'm ravenous."

"I'll tell you what," the boardinghouse proprietor said. "You come with me and I'll get you just what you need. I've got some clothes that ought to fit just fine. Now, you men do what you have to do, and I'll take care of Mrs. Rains."

Juliana looked at Matt. "I haven't forgotten what I owe you," she said, then without explanation followed Anne Pals onto the street.

Matt stepped outside and watched as the two women hurried down the walkway, drawing the attention of everyone they passed but getting not so much as a nod.

Settling his hat low on his forehead, he crossed

the street, headed for the hotel with the ranger at his side. But first he watched as Juliana walked into the boardinghouse two blocks away. In going to the soiree, he had the purest of intentions, but she had a way of interpreting things as she saw fit.

Chapter Nineteen

Lady Charlotte Kingbridge had taken over the second floor of the Diablo Hotel, with all of the doors thrown open to the hall to accommodate the crowd. Her laugh brought Matt to the largest of the rooms, where she was holding court from a small Victorian sofa at the end of the room.

She and her lavish golden gown took up most of the sofa, but that didn't stop her worshipers from gathering around her like horses at a water trough. The biggest horse of all, Edmund Montgomery, was hovering the closest.

No more than a half hour had passed since Matt had accosted him in his bank office, leaving him red-faced and sputtering. Montgomery had made a remarkable recovery. He was looking downright suave, every gray-streaked hair in place as he raised the countess's hand to his lips.

She was regarding him with something less

than amusement when she caught sight of Matt.

"Matt the Wanderer has returned," she said. Though she didn't speak loudly, Lady Charlotte had a voice that carried across a busy room. Everyone fell silent and looked at him.

"Lady Charlotte," he said, taking off his hat and tossing it on a table, disencumbering himself for his assault as he made his way to the sofa.

Montgomery straightened. "Matt, have you just come from the jail?" With a sniff, the banker looked down at the countess. "Matt is friends with the woman I was telling you about, the thief who broke into my home. We can thank our sheriff for seeing she was promptly put behind bars. Though I hate to see a lady treated in such a matter, I fear Mrs. Rains is no lady."

The countess's dark eyes narrowed. "Is this true, Matt?"

"Partly. She's not a thief, she didn't break into his house, and she's not in jail."

Matt sensed the stirring around him and the sudden attention he had commanded. For him, there was only one other person in the room—the beautiful, watchful woman sitting before him.

"But she *is* your friend," the countess said. "That part's right, is it not?"

"I'd like to think I'm her friend."

One of the women in the crowd bustled close, and Matt recognized Melinda Barton, the woman who had seen Doc Gibbs in Winding Creek.

"Pardon me for interrupting, Your Highness"—Matt caught the countess's wince—"but all I can say is, Juliana Rains can never hold her head up in Diablo again." Melinda shook her head in disgust.

"The woman's a disgrace. She might as well work in the saloon."

"As bad as that?" Matt said coolly. Brent's wife, Crystal, had once been a singer at the Lone Star, and everyone in the room knew it, except the countess. Everyone also knew that Melinda had once had her eye on Brent—not that it had done her much good.

Matt himself wouldn't have known any of this if Glory hadn't filled him in when he went to get DC.

Melinda seemed not to notice the knowing smiles of the women around her.

"I feel sorry for her," Montgomery said. "She's had so much happen to her. Losing her mother while she was across the country must have been terrible. I know dear Iona missed her only child terribly and wanted her by her side at the end. Indeed, she missed her throughout the long years of their separation. I feel sure Mrs. Rains senses that and is filled with regret."

The banker sounded so reasonable, so caring, so sympathetic. This must have been the way he'd spoken of his wife while she was drinking herself into her grave.

General talk sprang up, and Matt picked up "poor Juliana" and "the scandal of it all" and "who would have thought she was that kind of woman."

He watched the countess, watched the darting eyes, the thoughtfully pursed lips and at last the speculative glance she gave him. Motioning him to her side, she shifted her skirt to make a place for him to sit.

"Edmund, darling," she said, smiling broadly at the banker, "do see if you can get me a glass of cool water. I find the room quite stifling."

Montgomery stared daggers at Matt, but, having been given his orders, he nodded and backed away.

"All right, Matt," she said, bestowing upon him the full force of her gaze, "you're up to something."

"No more than you."

Her lips twitched into a smile. "You doubt I came all this way to see that abominable horse?"

"I figured you had to get out of England."

Lady Charlotte looked around the room, nodding occasionally at her guests. "Let's just say I chose to investigate some of my late husband's investments with an eye toward perhaps selling them."

"And while you were in the area, you decided to drop by Diablo."

She leaned close, giving him a good view of

her ample breasts spilling over the top of her gown. "I wondered if you had learned what to do with a woman. I gather you have." She touched his hand. "Please don't bother to deny or admit it. I have never liked gentlemen who kiss and tell. Besides, I already know the answer. You have that look about you."

"I don't think I'll ask what look."

She laughed. "What a relief to talk to someone with subtlety. This Montgomery chap is really quite a bore."

"He's worse than that."

Her eyebrows arched. "Are you going to explain?"

"No. You'll have to trust me."

She sighed. "An honorable man. You do vex me, you know. Now, about this Mrs. Rains. I'm not egotistical enough to think you came here today simply because you couldn't stay away from me any longer. Therefore you have another purpose. I suspect it's this woman. *Cherchez la femme*, as the French say."

"After all this settles down about her arrest, she's got to live in the community."

"Which might prove uncomfortable. Oh, dear, she cares what people think."

"I don't believe she does, not right now, but the longer she lives here, the more likely her attitude will change."

He started to think of Juliana's life after he

moved on, but found any image he conjured up too painful to hold for long.

"Matt, you're smitten."

"I'm after justice," he retorted quickly. "And I never could abide small-minded people."

Lady Charlotte continued to study the crowded room. " 'Your Highness.' Good God. Americans do like a title, don't they?"

"And the English don't?"

"You're far too clever and not nearly enough of a sycophant. I do like toadies."

"Then you ought to like Edmund Montgomery."

"Not all toadies." She thought a minute. "Obviously, you've come to me for help. That's charming, you know—to want my help without wanting my money or my prestige. Whatever's left of either of them." She paused again, and a light sparked in her dark eyes. "We need a dance, something grander than this little gathering. Is there a ballroom available?"

"The town hall. I doubt it's ever been described as a ballroom. But dances are held there."

"Good. I'll get to work on this. Tomorrow night ought to be soon enough. All you have to do, Matthew, is get your Mrs. Rains to this hall, I'd say by ten o'clock, well after the festivities have begun. I'll take care of the rest."

He started to speak, but she waved him to silence.

"Now run along. Edmund is returning with the water, and I have work to do. I should imagine so do you."

The next evening at ten past ten, Juliana stood in the middle of the road outside the town hall and stared at the bright lights inside. Then she looked at Matt. He'd dressed up. She'd never seen him in a suit and white shirt. No tie, of course, the shirt remaining open at the throat, but for him a tie would have been overdressing.

He'd put on the suit for nothing.

"I am not going in there," she told him.

"Didn't Mugg bring the right clothes?" Matt asked. "I sent word to gather up what he thought you would need, him having been married and all."

Juliana fingered the lace-trimmed blue silk gown, one of her favorites.

"He did exactly right if I were going to a ball. Which I am not. Anne was the one who got me dressed and fancied my hair like this"—she waved at the tower of yellow curls piled atop her head—"but I realize now how ridiculous it all is. No one wants me in there. Least of all me."

"I do. The countess does. She sent you a special invitation."

"Yes, she did. Why?"

"It was her idea. You'll have to ask her yourself."

"I want to go home."

Juliana knew she was sounding petulant, but she'd had her fill of Diablo. She should never have agreed to stay in town one more night, but even using no more than words, Matt could be very persuasive.

"You will go home. I've hired a carriage and will take you there within the hour. That's a promise." His eyes gleamed in the semidark. "I have a debt I need to collect."

"I acknowledged the debt under duress. If you recall, I was behind bars at the time."

"Have you changed your mind about owing me?"

Juliana rested a hand against her burning cheek. "I just don't want to be reminded of the jail. I'm so embarrassed. I deserve whatever kind of reputation I have."

If only Matt would quit staring at her, she could regain her equilibrium. She felt freakish enough, gussied up in a way she hadn't been since before Harlan died. And then Matt had brought up what had happened in the jail. If she didn't love him beyond all measure, she wouldn't like him very much.

"If you walk away now, Edmund wins," Matt said.

"That's fighting dirty."

"Yep. He's the one who's been talking about the scandal of your arrest. Unfortunately, he sets the tone for this town. Once he's gone, everyone will be better off."

"So now you're putting the well-being of Diablo on my shoulders."

"Right now those lovely shoulders of yours are where the town's well-being belongs."

Self-consciously she touched her bare shoulders, wishing Mugg hadn't picked out a gown with quite such a low bodice. She doubted the selection had been an accident.

Matt leaned close. "Edmund is going to hate seeing you walk in."

"I certainly hope so. That's the only benefit I expect to get out of the evening."

Lifting the hem of her gown, she crossed the street and entered the town hall, pausing in the doorway to look around, not so much seeing as she was being seen, blue silk, fancy hair and all. Harlan had taught her how to enter a room. At least he had tried. She hadn't put the lesson to good use until now.

To her surprise, the technique of stillness worked. All the people who were gathering on the dance floor waiting for another piece of music to begin gradually turned toward her, singly, then in groups. She kept her place, even with Matt's hand against her back giving her a slight shove. She opened the fan dangling at her wrist— another of Anne's touches. Waving the white lace fan, she whispered, "Stop it, Matt. Trust me to know what to do."

Suddenly a voice trilled out. "Mrs. Rains, I'm so delighted you could make it."

Juliana turned toward the rustling sound of taffeta as Lady Charlotte strode toward her, hand extended. She was dressed in black, with diamonds glittering at her throat and dangling from her ears, her black hair arranged in an even more elaborate style than Juliana's.

Touching the countess's hand, Juliana smiled. "It was kind of you to invite me."

"Of course I invited you. You're one of the most prominent ranchers in the county, are you not?"

Not, Juliana thought, since the Lazy Q had yet to acquire either horses or cows. But soon, she promised herself, very soon she would start acquiring stock.

Lady Charlotte looked beyond her to Matt. "Do come in, Matt. The musicians are about to play a waltz. I'm certain you'll want to lead your lady onto the dance floor."

Juliana remembered far too well the Bandera social that had followed Matt's triumphant horse race. On that night he had stated he did not dance.

"I'm afraid, Lady Charlotte—" Juliana began.

"I'd be glad to," Matt said.

Before she could protest, he was guiding her

onto the floor, taking her hand, holding her firmly at the waist, and as the music began, he twirled her around the room.

"You said you didn't dance," she said.

"I didn't. This afternoon, while you were getting ready, Mugg taught me."

Juliana stumbled, then caught herself and once again found the rhythm. "Mugg?"

"His wife insisted he learn, even though all they did was dance around the parlor."

"Is there no end to what she taught him?"

"If there is, I haven't found it. Now if you don't mind, I need to concentrate."

She found herself smiling up at him, wanting to wipe the beads of perspiration off his brow. He had saved her from a horrible carriage accident, had ridden hours to protect her from a killer, had supported her in her hour of shame, but it seemed to her that he was making his greatest sacrifice at this moment.

She looked away from him, so filled with love she thought she might explode.

"Matt, can I make one request? Actually two."

"I'm counting one-two-three, but go ahead."

"About that debt I owe you."

"The one you wanted to forget."

"I've changed my mind. I've been thinking about the little rascal and decided there is only one honorable thing to do, and that's to follow through on my original promise."

312

"You'll do it because it's honorable."

"Yes."

He thought a minute. "I could probably let you do the honorable thing. And the second request?"

"If Mugg teaches you to polka, let me watch."

Under a full moon and bright stars, the rented carriage flew along the road to the Lazy Q.

"Everybody knew why we were leaving," Juliana said halfway through the ride.

"No, they didn't."

"The countess did."

"I'll give you that."

"Edmund knew, too."

Matt muttered under his breath.

"What did you say?" Juliana asked.

"You don't want to know."

Nodding, Juliana settled back in the carriage as best she could, occasionally holding on to the seat or the side to keep her balance. She tried not to grab hold of Matt, even though that was what she wanted to do more than anything in the world, but thought it wouldn't be smart to let him know it.

Not that he didn't already, but she liked to tell herself she could play a little bit at being standoffish.

When they arrived at the ranch house, she tried to descend from the carriage with a modicum of dignity, but Matt hopped out and swirled her into his arms, holding her close and kissing her with a thoroughness that drove her out of her mind.

"I've got to take care of the horse," he said between smaller kisses.

"I know."

"Maybe he won't get a thorough rubdown," he said.

"Save that for me."

"Hey, tonight's my turn, remember? You rub me."

"Are you really going to keep your hands off me?"

He kissed her throat, then worked his way back to her lips. "Forgive me if I touch you here and there."

Juliana found herself smiling against his kisses. "The *here* is okay but I'm not so sure about the *there*."

"Spoilsport."

She forced herself to push him away. "Get to the horse, then get to my room."

Without looking back, she hurried through the kitchen, but her steps slowed as she reached the stairs. Deep in thought, she walked up to her room and closed the door behind her. What was she really doing? She knew it wasn't just love that moved her to act in a manner so far removed from everything she had always thought about herself.

It was facing death and loss and accepting guilt; it was having her worst fears realized, public humiliation, the threat of another woman with Matt, the knowledge that he wasn't really hers no matter how much she loved him. She had done many things in her life for which she had regrets, but loving Matt and showing him in the only way she could would never be one of them.

Hurriedly she undressed, her fingers fumbling with the myriad buttons, kicking off the petticoats, ripping off the hose, and after she had slipped into the prettiest nightgown she owned, she worked maddeningly at the hundred pins Anne Pals had thrust into her fancy hair.

Last, she threw back the covers and lay on the bed, the pillows plumped behind her head, the lightweight top sheet pulled to her waist. With the lamp turned low on the bedside table, she took three deep breaths and was breathing almost normally when Matt strolled into the room.

He came to a quick halt inside the door. He'd shed his coat, and his shirt was half unbuttoned, his black hair mussed, his sleeves rolled back to reveal his bronzed and muscular forearms. He gave her a lot of places where she could look, and she looked at them all.

She tried to think of something clever to say, something light to let him know that what they were about to do was for sheer pleasure and nothing else. She made no claims on him. She wasn't a fool.

All the smart words stuck in her throat. For reasons she couldn't begin to explain, she wanted very much to cry, not for what they were about to do but because he wouldn't understand what she was really giving him.

Without saying a word, he walked toward her, shedding clothing with each step. Pulling back the sheet, he lay beside her and put his hand on her breast. She purred like a kitten and let pure feeling take hold of her, helping when he slipped her gown over her head, arching her back to let him touch and kiss her breasts, rubbing her palms against his taut arms.

His hands were wonderful on this night, working pure magic as he ran his fingers across her skin. She kissed him a hundred times, slanting her lips against his one way and then another, using her tongue to taste him, to absorb everything about him so that later she could recall exactly what it was like to be made love to by Matt.

When she took his erection into her hand, she knew what to do this time, to hold him firmly and to stroke, to feel the slick tightness, to press the fullness of him against her belly as she licked the side of his neck and kissed his ear.

The lovemaking was slow and thorough, the coils within her unwinding in a delicious promise of coming rapture. And then he was inside her and she stopped thinking about what she did, losing herself in a dark and purely sensuous world that began and ended with the man in her arms.

They climaxed together, held tight to one another; then, still with no words, as if all the talking they'd done earlier had exhausted whatever they could say, she lay in his arms, her last thought before falling to sleep a remembrance of how he had waltzed her around the room.

When Juliana awoke late the next morning, she was in the bed alone. Brushing aside a foolish feeling of abandonment, she hurriedly dressed, bound her hair in a tight knot at her nape and hurried downstairs to find Mugg rolling out biscuits in the kitchen.

"I'll have these ready shortly. Good to have you back," he said.

"It's good to be back." Opening the door, she took a quick look outside, but the only signs of life she could find were Pepper, DC and the carriage horse munching grass in the corral.

"Is Matt out working somewhere?"

"He's gone."

"Gone?"

"His brother Brent came and got him. He said there was trouble with his dad and Matt needed to come with him."

Juliana felt a jolt of disappointment. Before he left why hadn't he let her know he had troubles? Why didn't he share even a part of his private life with her?

"Did he say where they were going?"

"The Half-Moon, I imagine, but I don't know for sure." Mugg looked at her thoughtfully. "You want eggs this morning?"

The question was perfectly ordinary, and she had no idea why it filled her with such despair. Unless it was that even when one's heart was breaking, life went on.

"No eggs, just coffee and biscuits. I've got to start planning on getting some stock for this place. My late husband's records are here somewhere, probably in the parlor desk. They'll give me an idea about what kind of herd the land will support."

She knew she was rambling on, but she needed the sound of talking to fill the air, even if the sound was her own voice.

Pouring a cup of coffee, she started to leave the kitchen, then paused in the doorway.

"You give good dance lessons, Mugg. Your pupil performed splendidly last night."

Chapter Twenty

"I can't talk to him. Neither can Quince. He's just not listening. We thought you could give it a try."

Brent looked down at the field where his father was putting his thoroughbred Fancy Dancer through his paces.

"He's as fine a chestnut as I've ever seen," Brent added, "but he won't be for long if Pa keeps this up. He's acting like a madman."

Matt watched his father ride the lathered stallion the length of the field, turn him sharply, then race across the grass again. The brothers were sitting astride their mounts on a hill overlooking the pasture and hadn't yet been spied.

"What makes you think I can find out what's eating him? I'm the one he kicked off the Half-Moon, remember?"

"He's been muttering your name ever since

Edmund Montgomery was here this morning."

That stopped Matt.

"When you came to get me, you only said that Jack was in trouble."

Exactly why that should have taken him away from Juliana, Matt didn't know. But he was here, watching his father about to ruin a fine horse, and now he was hearing about the bastard banker.

"Have you heard about the race at that fancy new track they've got north of Fort Worth?" Brent asked. "It's a week away. Pa thinks this is the way to get ready."

"I heard about the race when I was in Bandera, but I hadn't decided whether to enter DC. Other matters got in the way."

Brent looked at him a minute. "I know about Doc Gibbs. He was a strange one, keeping to himself, but I never heard anyone complain about his doctoring."

"Not even in connection with Iona Montgomery?"

"He seemed worried about her, but then, he seemed worried about most everything."

Matt needed to tell him about Kane, about how Sam Larkin had sent him out to work at the Lazy Q, about Juliana's suspicious carriage accident. All anybody knew was that Kane had apparently had a grudge against the doctor and killed him before being killed himself.

That Matt had done the killing was something not generally known. He didn't plan on keeping it a secret, but other matters needed to be settled first.

"Go on back to the ranch house, Brent," Matt said. "I'll do what I can and meet you there."

Slapping his reins, Matt rode at a trot down the hill, eyes on his father all the while. Jack, hunched over the galloping stallion, whip flailing, didn't see him until he was almost in the chestnut's path.

"Whoa," Jack said, pulling back on the reins. Taking off his hat, he ran a shirt sleeve across his sweaty face. He had a hard, desperate cast to his eyes as he looked at Matt. "What the devil are you doing here?"

Matt looked from his father to the obviously spent horse, then back to his father. "What's going on?"

"I asked you . . ." Jack growled, then shook his head in disgust. "You never minded me in all your life. I had hopes for you at one time. Did you know that? I did. And so did your mother. We both paid a heavy price for being wrong."

Every word hit Matt like the jab of a knife. A hundred retorts burned inside him, and questions, too, like what was eating Jack, and what kind of heavy price had he paid?

But he knew his father well enough not to hit

him with a direct assault. Instead, he concentrated on Fancy Dancer.

"You planning on entering that horse in the race?"

Jack's eyes narrowed and took on a wily look. "The one up by Fort Worth? Why should it make any difference to you?"

"I'm just sizing up the competition."

"I was hoping you'd say something like that. I'd like to think I'd be taking your money, but I don't imagine that'd amount to much."

"You keep riding your horse the way you are and you won't be taking anybody's money."

Jack's face reddened. "It'll be a cold July in Diablo the day I take horse advice from you."

"Something's bothering you, Jack. For a change, I don't believe it's just me. What's your good buddy Edmund up to? Foreclosing on the ranch?"

Matt had thrown out the taunt as pure speculation, but the way Jack stared back at him, as if he'd been struck with a whip, gave all the proof Matt needed that he was right.

"Nothing's gonna happen to the Half-Moon," Jack rasped. He patted his stallion's neck. "Fancy Dancer and I will see to that."

Jack was trying to sound sure of himself, and confident he owned a winner, but Matt could hear the desperation in his voice behind the bravado. He ought to ride away, let his father handle his own problems. Brent was a good enough horseman to start again somewhere besides the Half-Moon, even with a baby on the way. But watching his father rein the stallion away from him and set out at a lonely trot across the field, Matt felt a world of past hurts and guilt crash in on him.

In all his life Matt had done no more than a few good things. Saving his money to buy Dark Champion was one of them, and doing what he could to protect Juliana was another. But he'd also done her wrong, leading her into thinking he would be staying around, even though he'd declared a long time ago he wouldn't.

She hadn't said a word about his staying, about her caring for him. She didn't need to. Too well he remembered the incidents in Winding Creek. He'd seen the look of joy on her face when she ran after him and Kane and discovered Kane was the one who had died. And he'd felt the way she clung to him every time they made love, giving him everything she had to give, being gentle and passionate and loving without asking for anything in return.

She was the best thing that had ever happened to him, but he was far from being the best thing that had happened to her. She deserved better.

Riding away from his father, he knew what he had to do. First he'd report to Brent, then ride on to Quince's ranch for the horse trailer his brother was building for him. He had one last chore to take care of as far as the Half-Moon was concerned—racing and winning—but when that was done, he would face the hardest challenge of all: telling Juliana goodbye.

The day of the race dawned overcast, but as time for the afternoon race grew closer, the skies cleared. Gamblers and racing aficionados packed the viewing area outside the fenced oval track, but Matt was too busy pacing up and down in front of DC's stall to notice.

"Where's Timothy Randall?" he asked for the tenth time since the young jockey's absence had been noted a half hour earlier.

"Brent and Quince are looking for him," Juliana said.

"That's what you told me before."

"It's still true."

Matt slapped his thigh and stared in the direction of the track. "The other horses are already out there."

"DC may have to be scratched."

That wouldn't happen, Matt told himself. He'd hired the young Randall himself, spent the past few days training him to DC's peculiarities, letting the horse likewise get to know the jockey. Tim had to be here. Otherwise . . .

"I can see what you're thinking, Matt," Juliana said, "but forget it. I know horse races. You're too heavy. In a field as good as this one, Dark Champion can't win carrying your weight."

She didn't understand, Matt thought as he looked at her, wishing that was all he had to do, look at the most beautiful woman at the track. And the most knowledgeable. She knew horse races, but she didn't know the importance of this particular race. Out there in the crowd were most of the people he knew, including Montgomery and the countess. Jack had already got himself one of the best jockeys around, and he'd pulled back on the rough training of his thoroughbred. But Matt remembered too well how Fancy Dancer had backed down from DC out in the pasture. Dancer was a great horse, but he couldn't be depended upon to win. He lacked the killer instinct.

And someone from the Half-Moon had to win. Matt didn't want to think about what would happen otherwise.

So where in the devil was this jockey he'd hired? He'd seen Randall's work at the Bandera race and knew what he could do. DC had even taken to him, something the persnickety stallion didn't do often. Matt had told Randall about Dark Champion's record, but the jockey had sworn he was not afraid.

Matt was staring inside the stall at the already saddled and waiting horse when he heard Juliana say, "Here he comes now," and a second later, "Oh, no."

Matt looked down the path leading past the other already empty stalls and saw his skillful jockey staggering toward him, a bottle in his hand. An empty bottle, from the way he was waving it around.

He came to a swaying halt in front of Matt. "In the nick of time," he slurred.

"You didn't tell me you had a drinking problem."

"I don't," Randall said, clearly trying to focus his eyes. "The man suggested I needed a snort or two because of DC's history and all, said it might give me a little push, and accepting seemed the gentlemanly thing to do."

"What man?"

Randall hiccuped. "Didn't give his name. Tall, way taller'n me, rich-looking chap. He paid for the bottle. Real friendly of him."

"Edmund," Juliana said, and Matt nodded.

Tossing the bottle aside, Randall staggered into the stall, patted DC on the nose and promptly passed out on a pile of hay. By the time he hit the ground, Matt was taking off his belt and throwing his hat aside.

"You're going to do this, aren't you?" Juliana asked.

"I don't have a choice."

Their eyes met. Neither spoke, but when she

looked at him the way she was doing, there was only one way he could respond. He took her in his arms and kissed her. Putting her arms around him, she kissed him back.

He shouldn't have touched her. He hadn't since the night he'd spent in her bed, the night following Lady Charlotte's ball. Touching her only a little made him want to do nothing but touch her more.

He backed away. "That was for luck."

"You once told me you were lucky with horses, far more than with women. Women are unpredictable, you said."

And so she was. He could never have predicted she would become more important to him than life itself.

He wanted to tell her his true good luck hadn't begun until he met her. But that would be doing her no favor. He'd leave their parting with a kiss.

Leading DC out of the stall, he pulled himself into the saddle. "You've got a horse race to watch, Jules, and it looks like I've got a little ride ahead of me."

He could hear the buzz of surprise as he rode onto the track and headed for the field of nine horses already lining up for the starting shot. He talked to DC all the way, mostly about what a beautiful day it was and what a romp they were going to have. He felt peace settle over him, the same peace he'd felt when he talked to the stallion for the first time all the way back in New-market.

With the track judges waving at him frantically, he took his time, knowing that to rush DC would be to lose him. Passing the competition, he spared a quick glance at Fancy Dancer, biting at the bit, then slowly turned DC to the outside slot waiting for him. He hadn't quite got up to the starting line when the gun sounded and the horses were off.

All except DC, who took a few precious seconds to dance around in place, but once he got his ears up and spied nothing but the haunches and flying tails of the other racers pounding down the track, Matt knew the race was won.

Like the champion he was, the black stallion settled down to business and flew over the hard dirt track. Matt kept him to the outside, avoiding the jostling and clustering and blocking that went on at the inside of the track. DC gave no sign he minded the longer path. In truth he seemed to relish the openness of the way in front of him, and his magnificent legs took the turns as rapidly as the straightaways. Matt could do nothing but give him his head and enjoy the ride.

It took the stallion only a few seconds to pass the field, leaving all nine horses in his wake. Matt had no idea of the horse's speed, but he sensed DC was running the mile-long race at less than a minute and three-quarters, setting an incredible pace, considering he had a full-sized man riding him and not one of the lightweight jockeys.

The back stretch flew by, the curves, and then it was an all-out dash for home. When they crossed the finish line, DC led the pack by ten lengths, and Matt gave him a victory lap at a far slower pace to start his cooling down. Matt grinned to himself. He wasn't giving the horse anything; DC was taking it for himself. Matt had the definite feeling his English killer horse could have run all day.

Eventually it was time to lead him to the winner's circle. The track owners made a big show of congratulating Matt and handing him the winning purse, a heavy sack of gold coins. When he looked around the crowd, he picked out his brothers and Juliana, but Jack was nowhere in sight.

It shouldn't have bothered him. He knew there was no way his father was going to congratulate him, but Jack should have been ready with a tongue-lashing, at least. He should have been there to damn him to hell. More than that, Matt needed to tell his father the money was going to pay off the mortgage on the Half-Moon—both the purse and his gambling winnings. He never would have run the race with any other thought in mind.

But Jack wasn't around. As always, he had gone off thinking the worst of his son, leaving Matt to accept praise for what had turned out to be a curiously hollow victory.

Chapter Twenty-one

Juliana stood apart from the crowd, watching Matt accept congratulations. She had never seen a horse run as swiftly and surely as Dark Champion, justifying everything Matt had ever believed about him. Holding the pouch of gold, he should have been celebrating.

He wasn't, though she doubted that anyone other than she realized it. Too well she saw the way his gaze darted about the crowd, seeking something, someone he did not find. He wasn't looking for her. He was looking for his father. A profound regret took hold of her. She and Matt were both caught in the tragedies of the past, and it colored everything about their lives.

Looking at him was painful, and she turned away in time to see the figure of a man in the shadows at the far end of the horse stalls. Jack Hunter, watching his son, kept his distance as he must always have done. She told herself to remain separate from whatever trouble existed between the two, but her heart wasn't listening. Without considering the wisdom of what she was doing, she started toward the man.

He moved away from her, hurrying from the stables and down a narrowing path away from the crowd. She kept after him, called his name, but he kept on going, even when the path took him into a stand of trees and brush.

She found him catching his breath in a small clearing much too reminiscent of a similar spot where Matt had chased down Kane. Jack looked bent and frail, his face heavily lined, his coat and trousers hanging on him, everything about him speaking of a man far older that his fifty-odd years. He managed to straighten, and she saw a terrible desperation in his watery gaze.

"Get away from me," he hissed.

Unexpected tears burned Juliana's eyes. "I can't talk to my mother, Jack, so I have to talk to you."

"What's Iona got to do with anything?"

"Nothing. And everything. Don't shut yourself away from Matt. And for God's sake, don't let him go away without talking to him. Without listening to him." Her voice almost broke. "Without making your peace."

"You don't know what you're asking."

"But I do. I—"

"No!" Jack cried out the single word as if it came from the depths of a broken soul. "He's my blood, my own blood, but he killed my beautiful Beth. This man you sleep with didn't tell you that, did he?"

"What are you talking about?" she cried.

"I'm talking about murder. I'm talking about lies and deception from the lips of my own son." He shuddered, then seemed to get control of himself. "She told me, when I found her, lying there with the last of her life's breath leaking out slow." He looked away from Juliana and stared into nothingness, his mind wandering back to that terrible time, and she could do nothing but stand in horror and listen.

"I held her in my arms, trying to give her comfort, knowing I was losing her. *Who did this?* I asked, and she whispered, *Matthew.*" Jack ran a shaky hand through his hair. "I was drunk, God knows I was, but there wasn't any mistaking the name. She said it twice. And then she just seemed to fold in on herself, and I knew she was gone."

Juliana closed her eyes for a minute, but the terrible words still hung in the air.

"You told Brent you did it."

Caught in reliving the past, Jack didn't hear her. "I picked up the gun and I looked at the blood on my hand. Beth's blood, shed by the son she loved. I knew he was bad, he'd always been bad, and I blamed myself for not seeing what was coming. She was hard on him. But she loved him, more than the other boys."

Juliana stood in the fading light, taking in everything, unable to accept the damning verdict against Matt, yet knowing Jack spoke the truth. The truth as he saw it, she told herself, and only as he interpreted the whispered name.

The tears finally spilled, dampening her cheeks, but Juliana was hardly aware of them. "You confessed to protect him."

Jack blinked and looked at her, pulling himself back to the present, and all the bitterness of the past burned in his eyes.

"Shows you what a fool a man can be. What did it get me? Ten years in hell."

"You loved him, too. You wouldn't have done it otherwise."

Jack shook his head. "Like I said, I was a fool."

Juliana's skin prickled, and she was suddenly aware of someone behind her. She turned in time to see Matt step from the shadows onto the path, the look on his face stark and cold, as if he had cast away all feeling. How long had he been listening? Too long, yet not long enough.

He glanced at her briefly, dismissing her because she accepted what his father had said. Or so he thought. How easily he dismissed her, how quickly he believed the worst of her, and her heart shattered.

His words were for his father. "I killed her, Jack, but I didn't pull the trigger."

"What'd she do, shoot herself?" Jack snorted in disgust. "I shoulda known you'd try to lie your way out of it. It's your own ma you're talking about."

"You think I don't know that? She was waiting for me that evening, trying one more time to re-form her rotten son. We'd had a terrible row ear-lier. *Meet me at the house*, she said. *We'll talk it over.* I knew I was in for another lecture, so when I rode up, I decided not to go inside. Instead, I went looking for my drinking buddies. They were always easy to find."

Matt closed his eyes for a moment, and Juliana felt his anguish. She did the hardest thing she'd ever had to do. She gave him the distance he wanted.

"If I'd met her," he added, his voice wooden as he said words he must have repeated to him-self a thousand times, "if I'd done what I prom-ised, she wouldn't have died." He looked at the trees, at the darkening sky, and last at his father. "You say you lived ten years in hell. So did I."

"Matt." Juliana swallowed the lump in her throat and repeated, "Matt, think. You and Jack both." She looked from father to son, then back to the son. "If neither of you killed Elizabeth Hunter, I mean actually pulled the trigger, who did?"

Matt turned to her, absorbing her words. "Someone who's gotten away with murder for ten years," he said, and she could see the dark begin to lift from his eyes.

"I know you're thinking it was Edmund," Jack growled. "You'd blame a plague of locusts on him if you could. He was my friend and Beth's friend way back in New Orleans, when we were no more'n young-uns."

"Such a good friend that he's kept a knife to your throat for as long as I can remember."

Jack waved a hand in disgust. "Are you talking about the mortgage again? Hell, I borrowed the money of my own free will. He didn't force me to sign a thing. He's trying to collect now because he's got expenses."

"He's already collected. I gave the winning purse to Brent. He's probably paying him off as we speak."

"No, he's not," Juliana said. "At the end of the race, Edmund and the countess took off in a buggy for Fort Worth. I saw them myself. He didn't look happy. And neither did she."

"You happen to know where in Fort Worth?" Matt asked.

"I heard mention of a hotel. Lady Charlotte wanted the fanciest one in town."

He looked beyond her to his father. "Let's go, Jack. I want you there when I put a few questions to him."

"I already know the truth."

"You don't know anything near the truth, but you're clinging to it because hatred for me has kept you going all these years. If I have to hogtie you, you're coming with me."

"So am I," Juliana said, wiping the tears from her cheeks. "I have a few questions to put to him myself."

She hurried passed them, cutting off any arguments Matt might give her. Later, she would tell him her own private, personal truth. She'd tell him she loved him and always would. And not for even the briefest of times had she believed he'd killed his beloved mother, Beth.

The carriage ride into Fort Worth took little more than an hour, but twilight had already descended on the busy cowtown by the time they arrived. The clerk at the hotel showed little inclination to divulge Edmund Montgomery's room number or even his presence as a guest until Matt leaned across the desk, grabbed the lapel of his coat and looked deep into his eyes.

"You are protecting a lying, thieving son of a bitch," he said in a low voice that only the clerk could hear, "and continuing to hide him just might get you thrown in jail." Letting the man go, he stood back. "That's my legal opinion, of course, and I could be wrong. We'd have to ask the sheriff about it. Or my Texas Ranger friend."

The clerk's eyes widened at the mention of the ranger. "Room 35, up on the third floor," he said hurriedly. "The countess is in the corner room next door." He cleared his throat. "Should I be sending for the sheriff now?"

"We'll let you know." Matt turned to Juliana. "I guess it wouldn't do any good to tell you to wait here."

"None."

He glanced at his father. Halfway into town Jack had quit defending his longtime friend, and Matt could see he was thinking long and hard, maybe adding things up and finding out Montgomery was coming out a little short of what he claimed.

As for himself, Matt tried concentrating on what lay ahead, telling himself to forget how Juliana had listened to his father condemn his youngest son, and forget, too, how she'd done little more than nod. Jack had sounded convincing. Hell, even he would have believed his father if he hadn't been involved.

But mostly he thought about how his name had been the last thing on his mother's lips. That was something Jack had never told anyone. Matt would be thinking about it for the rest of his life.

By the time he got to Edmund Montgomery's room, he had worked himself into a rage. He pounded on the door, then threw it open, not waiting for a response.

Halfway across the large room Edmund stood in front of the mirror combing his hair. He was in his shirtsleeves, his coat draped over the back of a chair. He stopped the combing and stared at Matt. "What the hell are you doing here? You're a madman." Then he saw Juliana, and last, Jack, his old friend, and the color drained from his face.

"What is this, a lynching?"

"A lynching could be arranged," Matt said. "After you tell us why you killed Beth."

Edmund's mouth dropped open; then he threw back his head and laughed. "You're all deranged. Get out of here or I'll summon the law."

Matt closed the door. "Go ahead. We can wait till the sheriff gets here."

"And while you're talking about Beth Hunter," Juliana said, stepping up beside Matt, "you might also tell me exactly what killed my mother. It wasn't just alcohol. Otherwise you wouldn't have sent Kane to kill her doctor."

For an instant, true terror flashed in the banker's pale eyes. "If Gibbs was killed, he got what was coming to him. Before he left his home in the East, he was an abortionist—did you know that? And not a good one. He botched several surgeries and the women bled to death. That's why he came to Texas, to keep from being thrown in jail. He confessed it all to me. The fool. And the laudanum was originally his idea."

Juliana stared at her stepfather as if seeing him for the first time. "You gave her laudanum. I should have known."

"It's not against the law. But that fool Gibbs became afraid she was taking too much. I had to get my own supply. And what did he do? He threatened to tell everyone about her problems. Hell, it was my problem more than hers." He shook his head in disgust. "When Iona finally died, the coward ran. The way he had run before." An ugly grin split the banker's face. "Too bad you have no proof of this."

"Oh, but I do." Juliana's voice was calm, but Matt saw that her hands were shaking. "Iona wrote me a letter confessing everything, all about the so-called medicine you gave her, the misery you put her through."

"You're lying. I supervised every letter she ever wrote."

"Not this one. She hid it, and when Abby got hold of it, she sent it to me. It's why I returned to Texas. In her misery, she cried out to me in the only way she could." Juliana's voice broke. "But the cry came too late," she whispered as if to herself. "I didn't hear it until after she was gone."

"Juliana," Matt said softly, wanting to take her in his arms.

Her eyes were round and warm when she looked at him. "I couldn't tell you. The letter hurt too much. We've got to stop him, Matt. No matter what it takes."

She was talking as if the bastard weren't standing only a few feet away, staring at her in mingled fear and contempt.

"Good God," Edmund said with a harsh laugh, "I am surrounded by weaklings and idiots. Iona was a fool. I only married her to make Beth jealous, and then I got stuck with her for years. I should have known when Doc Gibbs first prescribed the opium that she would get addicted. She got addicted to everything, including whining and clinging."

He made her pitiful condition sound like a crime.

"And as for you," he continued, gesturing toward Jack, "I've put up with your complaining for over thirty years. I'm sick of it. Beth should have married me when I asked her. Her life would have been so much better. She would still have a life."

He looked at Matt with madness in his eyes. "God, how I hate all of you Hunters. You cannot take care of what you have." He began to pace, slinging his arms to mark his words. "Beth sent for me, begging me for money. Did you know that, Jack? Everyone in town knew you were drinking. They knew you were sinking deeper into debt and you were fighting with your wife."

He stopped and glared at Jack. "I told her what

the loan would cost. I told her to give me what she'd been giving you all those years, but she wasn't willing. Imagine. I was supposed to keep on giving while getting nothing in return. She had to know which of us was the real man. I had to show her. But she fought, the fool. She wouldn't give in."

With a low, animal growl Jack went for him, but Matt grabbed his sleeve and pulled him back. Edmund reached for his coat on the chair, then faced them once again, a gun in his hand.

"This is a little trick I learned from precious Beth. She was at her desk, turning from me, pretending to be in pain, then suddenly she had a gun. She tried to kill me. But in the end she was weak. I turned the gun on her. She gave me no choice." He looked at Juliana. "I've never been without a weapon since that afternoon. I think the first person I shoot will be you, Stepdaughter, for all the years of misery I suffered with your mother."

"She loved you," Juliana said, showing no fear of the gun. "She didn't lie about that."

A knock on the door sounded like the blast of a cannon in the room, and the countess's voice drifted inside. "Edmund, it's time for dinner."

She was opening the door when Matt threw himself in front of Juliana. Jack, too, was in motion, leaping for the gun, and when it exploded, he took the shot straight on. He fell forward against Edmund, then slumped to the floor, leaving the front of Edmund's shirt streaked with his blood.

"Matt! Take this!"

Matt turned, but it was Juliana who caught the small pistol thrown by the countess. She whirled to face Edmund, the gun held high in both her hands. He stood looking at her, a sneer on his face.

"You're no stronger than your mother. You haven't the stomach to do what has to be done."

He lifted his own gun, but Juliana was already pulling the trigger. Her shot caught him in the heart.

For a moment, no one moved. Edmund stared down in disbelief at the sight of his own blood spreading down his already blood-stained shirt. He swayed once, eyes rolling back in his head, then slumped to the floor beside Jack.

Matt took Juliana in his arms, while the countess knelt on the floor beside his father.

"He's still breathing," Lady Charlotte said. "We need a doctor." She looked up at Matt, very much a noblewoman even kneeling on the floor. "Do you think we might find one in this godforsaken town?"

Juliana sat at the side of her hotel bed and smiled up at Matt. "He'll live," she said. "I still can't believe Jack will make it."

Matt knelt in front of her and took her hands. "You heard what I told him, didn't you? I said dying was the easy way out. He has a lot to make up for. Lying at his trial, for one thing."

"And the countess. She tore the ruffle off her petticoat to make a tourniquet."

"We've got a lot of good memories, Jules. We need to hold on to them."

She could hold her smile no longer. "I killed someone."

"So did I. But neither of us had a choice. Would our dying have been better?"

"If Kane had killed you, Matt, I wouldn't have wanted to live."

"You think I didn't die a thousand times while Edmund was pointing that gun at you?"

"He was mad and mean, and all because he loved your mother."

"He didn't love Beth. He wanted her. It's not the same thing."

"No, it's not." She looked at Matt for a moment without speaking. "But sometimes wanting and loving come together. That's how I feel about you, Matthew Hunter. I don't know what you want to do about the loving, but you're good at satisfying the wanting."

Matt kissed her hands. "I think I could be good with loving, too, if you gave me the chance."

She didn't answer for a moment. "You have to say it better than that."

He looked up at her. "I love you. How is that?"

"Good."

"I've never loved anyone but you. I didn't know there was such a thing as a love like ours."

"Better."

He tumbled her back on the bed and stretched out on top of her, stroking her face. "I love you and I want you for my wife, Juliana. You are brave and good and all those virtuous things, but it's not your virtue I'm interested in right now. I want to get inside your underwear."

"That's the best of all," she said, laughing.

On that night, Matt got everything he wanted, including her promise to marry him. But, as Juliana told him in the early hours of the morning, after hours of making love, she got everything she wanted, too.

Epilogue

A month after the death of Edmund Montgomery, Crystal Hunter brought a new life into the world, Elizabeth Abigail, born crying lustily as the morning sun rose a beautiful pink in the eastern sky.

A midwife aided in the delivery, but it was the proud new aunt Abby Tremain who carried the blanket-wrapped infant into the parlor where the rest of the family awaited.

"Has Brent seen her?" Glory asked.

Abby laughed. "He was there in the room during the delivery. We couldn't keep him out. He's up there right now cuddling and cooing with the new mother, who I can report is in fine health. Tired for sure, but happy."

Juliana stood apart from the others, wanting to take the baby in her arms but feeling that as the newest member of the Hunter clan, she ought to keep her distance. She looked around the room at the smiling faces—Glory and Quince, Jack, Abby's husband Jonah, looking resplendent in his uniform. Buck Taggart, foreman of the Half-Moon, was beaming at the baby as much as anyone.

Juliana settled last on Matt. While everyone else was looking at the baby, he was looking at her.

She knew what he was thinking. *We'll have our own before long.* She nodded, thinking the way they were going at the baby-making process, especially since their marriage a week ago, their own little Hunter would be making an appearance within the year.

Their baby wouldn't be the only addition to the Lazy Q. Though it was too early to know for sure, Juliana was convinced Pepper was in foal, proving that Dark Champion was well named both on the racetrack and off. That little bit of news she was keeping from Matt until an appropriate time, when he wasn't likely to bring up talk about her owing him a stud fee.

He loved her and he'd married her, but he didn't kowtow to her every wish. Most of them, but not all. He refused to accept payment for his wedding gift to her—title to the Sullivan ranch. Jack had given him the deed in exchange for the winning purse from the horse race.

Jack's laugh brought her back to little Elizabeth Abigail. He hadn't had a drink since the terrible evening in Fort Worth—"With a new baby on the way," he'd said in his Hunter way, "it wouldn't do a'tall to have a whiskey-smelling old man hanging around"—and he was still weak from the gunshot wound to his shoulder, but he was already getting his color back and in general looking more like the man who had sired three strapping sons and a beautiful daughter.

Settling himself in the parlor rocking chair, he held out his arms. "She's not official until Grandpa has held her."

"Papa," Abby said with a shake of her head, "whatever you say, but she looks pretty official to me."

With great care she rested the bundle in her father's waiting arms. While he was smiling down at the infant, she was letting out a Hunter-sized cry, high-pitched but full of gusto.

"I forgot to tell you she's wet," Abby said with an impish grin. "You know how your children are. We've always got to get in our comments about everything, and I guess the next generation is no exception."

Abby went from Jack directly to where Juliana was standing by the door. She gave her a big hug. "I've said it before and I'll say it again. Thanks for taming this wild brother of mine."

"He might argue with the taming part, but you're most welcome. I can never do enough to repay the kindness you showed my mother. And to think I ever believed you were negligent or uncaring when you sent her letter to me. I should have known you passed it on as soon as you got it."

The two were talking low when Matt eased close to Juliana and put an arm around her waist.

"I've got something to tell you, Jules, and I might as well do it now. While I was in town yesterday, a telegram came in from that ranger Zachary. It seems he caught up with your no-good lawyer halfway to El Paso. Sam Larkin is now in a West Texas jail charged with theft. Yours wasn't the only account he played fast and loose with."

"Jail?" Juliana said.

"If you think the Diablo facility was bad, you ought to get a look at the one in San Angelo."

Jack's gruff voice interrupted the conversation.

"I give up," he said. "I'll love little Libby at the crying end, but I don't quite know what to do with the other."

"I'd better go rescue him," Abby said and hurried to give assistance to her papa.

"Let's go outside," Matt said. "I've got something else to show you. With all the excitement last night about the baby being on the way, I tucked it away and forgot."

Juliana slipped out the front door with him,

and he led her to the herb garden next to the house. Pulling out a thick envelope, he placed it in her hands.

Opening it, she glanced through the papers hurriedly, then looked up at Matt. "A judge down in San Antonio has ruled I'm Edmund's official and only heir. These papers are about what that inheritance includes—not as much as you'd think, since he seems to have traded so many of his assets to the countess."

"No wonder she was giving us a big smile when she whisked off in that fancy carriage Edmund had rented."

Juliana laughed. Lady Charlotte had left the Fort Worth hotel the day after Edmund's death, expressing appropriate sorrow but smiling nevertheless. She had come to Edmund's room because she'd heard the commotion. Like Edmund, she always carried a little pistol, only on that evening hers had been put to a better use.

"There's one page here that's interesting," she said. "It's a deed to the land she traded to Edmund. It's probably not worth much, some bottom land around the Trinity River in Dallas. Now it's mine. Maybe I ought to see what I can get for it."

"I don't know," Matt said with a shake of his head. "Dallas isn't much of a town right now, not like Fort Worth or San Antonio, but you never know how it might grow. Let's put that deed away for our children."

"Our children?"

"Yep. I am a totally domesticated man."

"Ha!"

"Well, I'm working on it. And having a baby with you is about the second best thing that could happen to me."

"What's the best?"

"Our getting married. Are you sure you didn't mind a small wedding with just the family looking on?"

"I told you I didn't. I promise, Matt, I'll always tell you the truth. We've both lived with enough lies to last a lifetime."

Right there between the rosemary and the parsley, he gave her a big kiss.

From the corral came a loud neigh, and they both looked over to see Dark Champion frisking about the enclosure.

"He's going to be a papa, too," Juliana said, unable to hold in the news a minute longer.

"Good news all around, then."

Arm in arm, they headed back toward the house. Juliana knew it wouldn't be long before Matt was making excuses about leaving, and getting her back to the Lazy Q, which he had suggested they rename the Full Moon. She was thinking it over. All she knew for sure was that finally she was leading a full life. Being a part of the Hunter family, with all its distinct and strong-willed members, was the best thing that had ever happened to her.

"Let's go home, Matt," she suggested before he could say it himself. "That baby and her mother need rest."

"Home. I never knew what a fine word that was until I met you." He looked beyond her to the outbuildings and the surrounding land that were part of the Half-Moon. "It's people that make a place a real home. No matter where we are, Juliana, as long as I'm with you, I'll always be where I belong."

Half Moon Ranch

Somewhere in the lush grasslands of the Texas hill country is a place where the sun once shone on love and prosperity, while the night hid murder and mistrust. There, three brothers and a sister fight to hold their family together, struggle to keep their ranch solvent, while they await the return of the one person who can shed light on the secrets of the past.

From the bestselling authors
who brought you the *Secret Fires* series comes . . .

THE GHOST OF Carnal Cove
EVELYN ROGERS

"I am a man without conscience," claims the dark stranger who accosts her amid the pounding surf and tearing winds of Carnal Cove. Taunting her with legends of the place, Captain Saintjohn accuses her of being a seductress herself. Little does he know that Makenna Lindsay has come to the isolated Isle of Wight to escape just such temptations. But her troubled mind seems to conjure equally disturbing hallucinations at every turn: the piteous crying of an abandoned child, the silvery figure of a ghostly woman in white. But is her enemy her own imagination or the all-too-tempting promise of passion with a lover as wild and remorseless as the sea itself?

He rides out of the Yorkshire mist, a dark figure on a dark horse. Is he a living man or a nightmare vision, conjured up by her fearful imagination and her uncertain future? Voices swirl in her head:

> They say he's more than human.
>
> A man's life is in danger when he's around . . .
>
> And a woman's virtue.

Repelled yet fascinated, Lucinda finds herself swept into a whirlwind courtship. Yet even as his lips set fire to her heart, she cannot forget his words of warning on the night they met:

> Tread softly. Heed little that you see and hear.
>
> Then leave.
>
> For God's sake, leave.

Whether he is the lover of her dreams or the embodiment of all she fears, she senses he will always be her . . . devil in the dark.

___52407-4 $5.99 US/$6.99 CAN

Dorchester Publishing Co., Inc.
P.O. Box 6640
Wayne, PA 19087-8640

Please add $2.50 for shipping and handling for the first book and $.75 for each book thereafter. NY, NYC, and PA residents, please add appropriate sales tax. No cash, stamps, or C.O.D.s. All orders shipped within 6 weeks via postal service book rate. Canadian orders require $2.50 extra postage and must be paid in U.S. dollars through a U.S. banking facility.

Name_____
Address_____
City_____ State_____ Zip_____
I have enclosed $ _____ in payment for the checked book(s).
Payment <u>must</u> accompany all orders. ☐ Please send a free catalog.
     CHECK OUT OUR WEBSITE! www.dorchesterpub.com

In the midst of the vast, windswept Texas plains stands a ranch wrested from the wilderness with blood, sweat and tears. It is the shining legacy of Thomas McBride to his five living heirs. But along with the fertile acres and herds of cattle, each will inherit a history of scandal, lies and hidden lust that threatens to burn out of control.

Chase knows he has no legitimate claim to the Circle M. After all, his father made it painfully clear he wants nothing to do with his bastard son or the Comanche girl he once took to his bed. But Chase has his own reasons for answering Tom McBride's deathbed summons. He has a job to do as a Texas Ranger, and a woman to protect—a woman whose sweet innocence gives him new faith that love born in the darkest night can face the dawn of all his tomorrows.

___4853-1 $5.99 US/$6.99 CAN

SECRET FIRES

The Agreement

Constance O'Banyon

In the midst of the vast, windswept Texas plains stands a ranch wrested from the wilderness with blood, sweat and tears. It is the shining legacy of Thomas McBride to his five living heirs. But along with the fertile acres and herds of cattle, each will inherit a history of scandal, lies and hidden lust that threatens to burn out of control.

Lauren McBride left the Circle M as a confused, lonely girl of fifteen. She returns a woman—beautiful, confident, certain of her own mind. And the last thing she will tolerate is a marriage of convenience, arranged by her pa to right past wrongs. Garret Lassiter broke her heart once before. Now only a declaration of everlasting love will convince her to become his bride.

___4878-7 $5.99 US/$6.99 CAN